'This is a heartrending story tu[...] the-seat historical thriller. The [...] storytelling emotional and grippin[...] oil painting of its time.'

      – Susanna Beard, author of *Dare to Remember*

'The writing is beautiful and the story was just so intricate and enticingly, sympathetically weaved. This is next level.'

      – Anna Mansell, author of *The Man I Loved Before*

PRAISE FOR

'Cesca Major is so skilled at taking real historical events and weaving them into stories that are as fascinating as they are disturbing. They'll make the hairs on the back of your neck stand up.'
– Kate Riordan, author of *The Heatwave*

'I loved this historical thriller. Tense, compulsive, atmospheric and emotional, with two wonderful lead characters and an original plot that had me hooked from beginning to end.'
– Claire Douglas, author of *Then She Vanishes*

'It's chilling, tense, and atmospheric, with an irresistible premise.'
– Roz Watkins, author of the DI Meg Dalton series

'Breathtaking, pacy, and utterly compelling, it had me gripped until the very last word.'
– Cathy Bramley, author of *A Patchwork Family*

'C D Major is a truly gifted storyteller. I adore everything she writes.'
– Amanda Jennings, author of *The Cliff House*

'Atmospheric, chilling, and absolutely compelling – I loved it.'
– Rachael Lucas, author of *The Telephone Box Library*

The
Thin
Place

ALSO BY C D MAJOR

The Other Girl

The Silent Hours

The Last Night

Writing as Rosie Blake:

The Hygge Holiday

How To Find Your (First) Husband

How to Stuff Up Christmas

How To Get A (Love) Life

The Gin O'Clock Club

The Thin Place

C D MAJOR

 THOMAS & MERCER

Text copyright © 2021 by C D Major
All rights reserved.

Published by Thomas & Mercer, Seattle

www.apub.com

Amazon, the Amazon logo, and Thomas & Mercer are trademarks of Amazon.com, Inc., or its affiliates.

ISBN-13: 9781542023016
ISBN-10: 1542023017

Cover design by The Brewster Project

Printed in the United States of America

To Kirsty and Izzy – my wonderful friends and talented writers.

'Heaven and earth are only three feet apart, but in thin places that distance is even shorter.'

Celtic proverb

Prologue

She stands on the bridge. I stare from the window of the house.

I can see her top half over the thick stone. I can see what's in her arms.

It has begun to rain, the glass of the window that divides us spattered with tiny flecks. I can't drag my eyes away. My chest is squeezed tight as I hold my breath.

The wind lifts her hair as she looks out over the gorge. I imagine the drop: the water, the rocks below.

She takes a step forward and my breath comes in a rush, fogging the glass. I rub at it frantically. She stays standing there. Perfectly still.

Don't. Please. Please, don't.

My nose is practically touching the pane as I plead with her.

She knows I am watching.

One more step and she is right next to the wall, the stone separating her from the depths below. Her arms are enclosed tightly around the bundle.

Don't. I'll do anything. Please, please . . .

She looks back at me. Then she raises the bundle.

No. Please. I'm sorry. Please don't.

The movement is sudden; one minute the bundle is safe and the next she has thrown it over the wall. For a second I imagine it suspended, before it plunges out of sight into the gorge.

I scream and scream and scream.

Chapter 1

AVA, PRESENT DAY

'Sorry I'm late!' Fraser jogged towards her, shirt collar sticking up, tanned cheeks flushed.

'You're not late,' Ava soothed. 'The appointment isn't until 4 p.m.' She felt immediately better that he was here with her.

He took her hand. There was a faint sheen of sweat on his top lip and his five o'clock shadow was emerging. The end of the school year was always hectic, but he was also doing a handover with the old head of sixth form, whose paperwork was a mess. Fraser, a technophile and lover of spreadsheets, had been horrified at the endless scrawled notes and lack of any decent system.

'Shall we head inside?' Fraser squeezed her hand. 'Are you nervous?'

Ava bit her lip and nodded.

'It'll be OK.'

He stepped towards the electronic double doors of the hospital, which slid back to reveal a large foyer with signs pointing every which way and an endless labyrinth of corridors in salmon pink. Their footsteps echoed from the hard floor. Posters lined the walls;

signs overhead directed them to departments Ava had never heard of before.

Their destination was on the second floor and, as Fraser jabbed the button in the steel-grey lift, Ava felt her stomach roll. Gripping the chrome handrail, she steadied herself before stepping out.

Mint-green bucket chairs were bolted to the floor alongside a long reception desk staffed by a curly-haired woman with only the top of her head visible. She looked up from the file she had been studying and gave them a small smile, taking their details and directing them to take a seat. Someone would be along shortly.

There were a few other patients waiting, hurried glances as they passed, no conversations in the hushed atmosphere. Fraser nudged Ava as they sat, pointing past her to a sign that read 'Family Planning Advice: Rear Entrance'. Ava suppressed a giggle, grateful for his efforts to make her less edgy.

They watched a woman disappear into a side room and Ava clutched her hands tightly, her neatly clipped nails digging into the flesh. A name was called. She reached into her handbag for a hairband and tied back her shoulder-length hair. Another name was called until finally, 'Ava Brent!'

Ava looked up sharply and a large woman in a white coat and multi-coloured trousers glanced in her direction. 'Here,' she said, stumbling as she stood, feeling like a schoolgirl at registration.

Fraser joined her, taking her hand again as they moved across to the woman, who was summoning them to follow her with Ava's file pressed to her chest. Ava concentrated on his firm grip, his calm expression. It was going to be alright. They had been waiting for this appointment for weeks. She had barely thought about anything else. A seasoned news reporter, she had just about managed to hold it together on camera, act the professional.

Stepping into a dark room with pale grey walls, Ava stared around at the single seat in the corner, a reclining bed in the middle of the room next to a machine with an enormous range of knobs and buttons, a monitor and another, smaller, screen on a metal arm that could be moved at an angle.

'Pop yourself up on the bed, there,' the sonographer instructed in a rich, low voice after introducing herself.

Ava swallowed and stepped forward, struggling to get onto the bed gracefully in her lined pencil skirt. Fraser loosened his tie then sat in the only chair, scraping its legs as he inched it closer to the bed. Ava didn't dare look at his face, at his expression. This was it.

The sonographer had moved to sit on a low stool next to the bed, holding a tube of something in her hand. 'I'm going to need you to roll down the top of your skirt so I can put this gel on your stomach.'

Ava did as she was told, fumbling with the zip, feeling exposed as she rested back – the pale skin of her stomach, the fine white line from where she'd had her appendix out.

'This is your first baby?'

Ava nodded quickly as Fraser gave a quiet 'yes' next to her. The sonographer barely glanced his way.

'And you haven't had any problems?' she asked, her tone conversational.

Ava shook her head, brushing her fringe out of her eyes. She thought then of the booking appointment a few weeks before, of some of the answers she hadn't been able to give the midwife. Anxiety gripped her again. 'There are a couple of gaps in my family history.'

'Well, let's take a look. You lie back and we can see what's going on.'

The chair next to her scraped again but Ava didn't turn her head. She was frozen as she rested back stiffly, shocked by the sudden coolness of the gel. The sonographer lifted a white piece of plastic that looked like a microphone on a plastic spiral and rested it on Ava's stomach.

Immediately, the small dark room was filled with sounds. For a second it reminded Ava of a scene she had watched in a nature documentary about whales, a strange sort of underwater noise with alien hiccups and beats. It was loud, and peculiar, and Ava found her eyes drawn to the screen to her right, white lines and shapes moving on the black.

The sonographer was silent, the plastic wand prodding Ava's stomach as she roamed the surface of her belly. She paused, pressed a little harder and with her other hand pointed at the screen.

'That's the heart.'

There was a noise to her left from Fraser, an involuntary exhalation as his hand shot out to grab hers that rested at her side.

There was a heart.

There was a heart and it was beating.

Ava felt a whoosh of relief, as if her shoulders had been tense for weeks and now they could sink back down. Their longed-for baby was alive.

The voice of the sonographer returned as she pointed out the head, the buds that would be arms . . . legs . . . Ava couldn't drag her eyes from the screen. The sonographer started a series of clicks with a mouse, making marks on the frozen image.

'I'd estimate you are almost bang on twelve weeks.'

Twelve weeks.

She blurted out questions. Did the baby seem alright? Could she tell if there might be a problem? When should they return to the hospital? They spilled out of her and the sonographer tried to reassure her. Fraser sat back looking stunned. His eyes hadn't moved from the screen.

'Congratulations,' the sonographer said warmly. She handed Ava a roll of paper to wipe the gel off her stomach.

Ava took it all in, dazed. She really was pregnant.

She really was going to be a mother.

Chapter 2

MARION, 1929

What a marvellous treat! A tea dance in the day – the Savoy no less, and Mother has always been so against them. But it was my birthday and, truly, I pleaded with her for weeks and she relented. It was everything I imagined: the high gilt ceilings; winking chandeliers; the waiters in their fancy clothes; the dresses in every colour imaginable; fashionable hair styles – oh, how I wished Mother would have let me have a bob! The music from the band. Tunes that would stay in my head forever, I was sure of it.

Oh, it was just thrilling.

I gazed around at the other people, craving a friend like the ones chatting in a corner, heads thrown back, trilling laughs, light touches on the arm. Mother sat as my chaperone, a lemony expression on her face, managing to look like the only dull thing in the room. It made me frown and I didn't want to frown today, to be glum on my birthday; I wanted to pretend for a moment that I belonged among this vitality, these beautiful chattering animals.

He walked in with a rakish smile, looking like a Brontë hero: full red lips, an abundance of Byronic curls and heavy-lidded eyes. I thought I might swoon when he caught my eye. Hurriedly looking away – I didn't want him to think me loose – I felt my heart almost burst out of my chest as he made his way over. Mother watched my every move, hawklike, but how was I ever meant to find a husband if I was never allowed outside our house?

He held out a gloved hand and asked if I would join him in a foxtrot. So many girls there and he had picked me! I accepted with a ridiculous squeak, my movements clumsy despite knowing the steps. When I took his hand it felt as if someone had pressed a button on my flesh, a spark like the one in our new electric light, the hairs standing on the back of my neck. There was a yellow stain on the thumb and forefinger of his glove that I could have got rid of at home.

He drew me close and I forgot Mother completely, over-whelmed by the scent of wood, spice and summer, his breath warm from the lamb casserole he told me he'd had for lunch.

'I can make lamb casserole,' I said. I wish I could talk to men but nobody teaches you these things and I was too frightened to say much else, desperate not to trip or tread on his toes, desperate for the dance to go on and on.

We moved around the floor and I tried terribly hard to keep in time, not to mess it all up. I've always had unfortunately large feet and dancing with him was rather different from practising on my own in my bedroom. His name was Hamish and he was four years older than me – twenty-eight, which was perfect. He had a rich voice, the hint of a Scottish accent. His family are from there.

'I've never been,' I said.

He left me after that dance and I waited on the seat next to Mother, tapping my feet on the floor in time to the music, desperate for him to return. Why hadn't I been more scintillating? Why hadn't I worn something less dreary? I looked so plain in this grand setting in my brown dress, my dark blonde hair not as shiny as the other girls'. Why couldn't someone else appear and make him ragingly jealous? But, alas, Mother was soon glancing at her pocket watch like a Victorian governess and staring at the door. I thought I might weep there and then. Back to Barnes and our semi-detached house on Adams Street. Father sitting in our front room with the curtains closed. Mother would bring him food on a tray and tell me not to distress him.

I was waiting to fetch my coat and Mother had disappeared to the powder room when Hamish emerged through the double doors, looking all about as if he'd lost something. Then his eyes lit on me and I felt another leap inside, crumpling the ticket I was about to hand over.

He was disappointed to hear we didn't have a telephone and I cursed my luck. Father always said there was no point to them, infernal inventions that merely disrupted. Any sudden noises now made him tremble. He didn't even want a wireless in the house, even though he complained I'd played our old gramophone records half to death and he was sick to the back teeth of them.

Hamish wrote our address down in a small notebook he produced from an inside pocket. He had such an elegant hand, the writing so neat I could read it quite clearly upside down. He did seem very accomplished. He told me he would write as I saw Mother reappearing, her mouth still in its thin line, the grey roots of her hair combed flat.

'I would like that,' I said, and the smile he gave me in return was filled with such sweet promise I thought I might dissolve right there in the foyer.

My days then seemed useless, chores taken up with fancies – that he might sweep up to our gate and take me out of there.

The carriage clock was loud as I took Father his tea on a tray. He didn't meet my eye; he'd had the shakes again. The dark room, musty with the smell of old books and urine, depressed me further. I couldn't sleep for thinking about him: Hamish West. I dreamed of escape, lay with my feet up on the wall, head dangling over the edge of my bedspread, and tapped on it as if doing the Charleston and he was right there opposite me, curls framing his beautiful face, his full, red lips smiling over at me.

Chapter 3

AVA

'Ava!' Her mother answered the door in a floury apron, a wooden spoon in one hand, reading glasses propped on top of her greying hair. 'I'm just doing the gravy . . . John! Ava's here!'

Ava followed her inside, the familiar chaos blasting her, along with heat from every radiator despite it being July. Her dad seemed to always be cold, Mum telling him to wear an extra jumper and stop sitting around.

Her mother, one hand on the bannisters, hollered up the stairs, 'John!'

'Coming!'

'Honestly,' her mum muttered. 'Man moves at a snail's pace. Grab a drink, darling, and catch me up with everything . . . and remind me to give you back that book you lent me before you go, I whipped through it . . .'

Ava felt her palms dampen. She gripped her bag as her mum rattled on. She had been waiting to tell her mother her news for more than eight weeks.

The kitchen was the same as ever: a round dining room table that would easily seat eight if the chairs weren't piled high with books and the surface wasn't covered in folded old newspapers; abandoned crosswords; a large, well-thumbed dictionary; leaflets about pet insurance; a fruit bowl containing no fruit but about one thousand paper clips, an elastic band and some loose change.

Ava's mother returned to stirring a saucepan on the hob. 'I've opened a bottle of wine . . .' She nodded at the fridge in the corner, which was plastered with photographs, terrible paintings of stick figures with a questionable number of arms, and various tradesmen's cards.

'I'm OK,' said Ava. 'What are you making?' She dumped her bag on the table.

'Toad in the hole. Can you stay? We've got plenty. Your father probably shouldn't have too many sausages anyway. Not good for him.'

'No, I—'

'Frances, stop giving away my sausages!' Dad interrupted in mock-alarm from the doorway. 'Heya, lass.' He moved inside the room and gave Ava a peck on the cheek.

'Hi, Dad. No, it's alright, I can't stay. I just wanted to pop in.' Ava took a breath. This was it.

'Pippa told me you're going around there later.' Mum continued stirring.

'Ah, that's nice.' Dad moved a pile of books off a chair for her to sit down. 'Glad you see each other, good for her after being stuck with the wee bairn all day.' He started searching the table for his cigarettes and lighter.

Ava mumbled, guilty that she hadn't seen much of her sister in recent months and nervous now that the moment she had been building up to was suddenly upon her.

Her dad lit his cigarette and sat back. 'So . . .' His eyebrows shot up. 'You need to borrow money or you just want to check on your elderly parents?'

12

'Speak for yourself, John!' her mum said.

'No one could accuse your mother of being elderly.' Her dad inhaled on his cigarette. 'She took Gus out for one of her six-hour power walks round the city. He's been lying dead still in the conservatory ever since, poor dog . . .'

'It wasn't six hours – oh, John, do use an ashtray! And, Ava, sit down. Really. Tell us your news . . .'

'I'm trying,' Ava said as her mum returned to the gravy, almost physically incapable of staying still for more than two seconds. Dad blew out smoke, narrowing his eyes as Ava took a breath. 'I came to tell you . . . I'm . . . pregnant . . .'

Her mum stopped stirring the gravy. Her dad's mouth dropped open, his cigarette forgotten in one hand.

'Twelve weeks,' Ava finished in a small voice.

There was a momentary pause and then her mum's face broke into an enormous grin. 'Oh my God, that's wonderful. John, did you hear that? A baby, another grandchild. Oh . . .' Tears filled Mum's eyes as Dad got up, moved around to Ava and put an arm round her.

'That is wonderful news . . .' His voice was thick with emotion.

'Don't smoke that around her, John!' Ava's mum started flapping her hands, a shocked expression on her face as Ava laughed, the relief of being open with them overwhelming her so that she sank into a kitchen chair.

'Take it out to the conservatory.' Her mum continued fussing around. 'We need to celebrate! Oh, I need to call your sister, John! Two grandchildren too. Ha!'

Dad had stubbed out his cigarette. 'Slow down, woman. Och, let Ava catch her breath.'

'Do you want to see the pictures from the scan?' Ava reached into her handbag for the well-thumbed envelope.

'Of course!' Her mum wiped her hands on her apron, her eyes sparkling as she reached for the images, pulling her reading glasses down to really inspect them. 'Oh, look! She looks like she's waving. Oh, are you going to find out if it's a boy or a girl? John, look . . .'

'Not sure,' Ava said. 'Fraser had to go back into school and we hadn't wanted to plan anything until we knew the scan was OK.'

'And it was OK?' Her mum looked up sharply, concern filling her eyes.

'Yes.' Ava beamed. 'He, or she, is in the lower percentile for weight, but nothing to be worried about . . .'

'You were small. Only just six pounds,' her mum said. 'Your dad was always worried he'd pull a finger off every time he dressed you.'

'They were tiny,' he said. 'God, I haven't thought about that for years.' His eyes misted over.

Ava reached and squeezed his hand. 'Don't, Mum. You know us as babies and the Rangers results make him cry.'

'Oh, another grandchild!' her mum said again. 'I can't wait. And you're telling Pippa?'

'Tonight.'

Her mum gave a satisfied nod, always worried about her daughters. 'I'm sure she'll be delighted. A little cousin for Tommy.'

'How is she?' Ava asked.

'Enjoying being back at work, although Tommy is playing up at nursery. I think it's probably because he's feeling unsettled – Pippa was a little prickly with me when I suggested it. "Mum guilt", I think they call it . . .'

'Well, I'll send her your love.' Ava didn't want to be accused of discussing Pippa behind her back. She started to slip the scan pictures back into the envelope.

'Oh, can we keep one? I'll put it on the fridge . . .'

Ava handed one over, still amazed by the tiny black and white image. She had spent weeks trying, and failing, not to think too much about the small cluster of cells growing inside her, not until they had a scan to reassure them that all was well. Now she felt a flutter of excitement at all the time ahead to prepare and make plans. Her mother rooted around in a drawer pulling out another magnet for the fridge.

'Actually, Mum, there were a few questions at my booking appointment that I couldn't answer and . . .' Ava coughed, realising that she was moving into largely uncharted territory. '. . . although the scan went well, I was hoping you could maybe shed some light?'

'Hmm?' Her mum had stepped back to admire the scan among the photographs and paintings on the fridge.

'Well, the nurse asked me questions about family history and, well, I couldn't answer all of them.'

Her mum had gone very still. Ava couldn't see the expression on her face.

Her dad looked over too and for a moment there was a crackle in the room as everyone waited for someone to say something. All the bonhomie of the past few minutes seemed to ebb away.

Ava's mum had been adopted and didn't like to talk about it. 'I've got a family of my own now,' she would always say and that would be the end of it. But this was different. Now Ava was having a baby, surely her mum would open up a little more?

Ava licked her lips as the seconds passed. The oven pinged, making her start.

'I probably can't help you much – all very normal, really. John, do lay the table. It's a mess . . .'

Her dad started out of his trance.

'Did you get a drink, Ava?' her mother said. 'You're making me nervous hovering like this!' She fussed past Ava, fetching a glass and filling it with water before she had time to reply. 'Did you work today? That's a nice skirt. You'll be needing maternity clothes soon, of course. Will you be on the news tonight?'

Ava took a breath. She couldn't let her mum off the hook as she always had in the past. Clutching her untouched water, she cleared her throat, aware of her mum's eyes sliding from her face. 'I know you don't like to talk about your birth family, Mum, but maybe now . . .' She trailed away, finding it too difficult to undo a habit of a lifetime.

Her dad stubbed out his cigarette on a side plate. 'What do you want to know?' His voice was gentle as he looked at her.

'Oh! I've overcooked the broccoli!' her mother announced in a too-loud voice, her back to Ava as she turned off the hob. 'I really loathe soggy broccoli. I should have timed it.'

'Ava?' Her dad gave her an encouraging nod.

'John, have you laid the table?'

'Frances . . .' His voice was soft. Her mum ignored it.

'Well,' Ava said, 'I wanted to know more about my medical history. I couldn't answer some of the questions . . .'

'John, have you seen the gravy boat?'

Ava looked at her dad, his pale brown eyes meeting hers. He glanced at his wife.

'Frances? Love?'

The silence stretched on – just her mum opening and closing cupboard doors and tutting. 'I was sure I put it in here.'

At that moment Gus, her mum's Wauzer, a ball of black fluff, wandered into the kitchen. As laid-back as her mum was frantic, dragged endlessly around Glasgow by his energetic owner, he padded across the room to Ava. She put down her water and reached to pat him, her hand disappearing into the springy curls as he gave his familiar piggy grunts of happiness that usually made her smile. Her mum pulled out the gravy boat.

'Who put it there?'

'Do you know what . . .' Ava stood up. 'Pippa will be waiting for me. I'm already late.'

'It's fine, love. Stay on a while,' her dad said.

'Let her go, John, if she's late. Pippa will probably want to eat after a long day with Tommy. And she'll be thrilled by Ava's news.' Her mum's voice was high and strange.

Her dad stared at her mum.

Ava wished she had just kept quiet. 'Yes, you're right . . . well, I'd better go . . .'

Ava had never pushed, had respected her mother's silence on the subject. She knew she'd had a difficult childhood, estranged from both her birth and adopted families. But now it felt important to know more about her family history. This wasn't just about her mum any more, she thought, as she placed a hand on her stomach. She almost pushed on, but the strained muscles in her mum's neck and the wary expression on her dad's face pushed the questions back down. She plastered a smile on her own face and picked up her handbag. 'Enjoy your dinner. It smells great.'

'You could stay.' Her dad's voice was lower, more serious.

In that moment Ava wanted her mum to stop her, to tell her to cancel seeing Pippa. She wanted her to look less troubled, her words less stilted. Instead she stirred the gravy. 'Lumpy; I'll have to sieve it . . .'

This was not how Ava had envisaged her announcement going. With a heavier heart she left the house without another word, the front door clicking shut behind her.

it waited with me. I shifted on the bed, the movement prompting the strong smell of mould. I wondered how long the bedroom had remained empty. Finally, I heard footsteps crossing the hallway outside and he returned holding a candle. I made a tiny noise and then sucked in my breath as he crossed the room towards me.

He was wearing a nightcap and nightshirt and I couldn't help staring at his feet and calves, the hair thick and dark and making my heart hammer furiously.

He looked disappointed. 'You're still dressed.'

I knew I'd already goofed. Dragging my tongue over my lips, I felt my throat constrict, my reply stuck somewhere within me. I didn't have the first clue how to behave and I so wanted to be a good wife. I followed his instructions to the letter, hoping he was pleased with me.

'There, there,' he said as I covered my breasts with my arms, the chill in the room making my nipples poke out, my flesh soon covered in goosebumps. I truly believed I might die of the humiliation as he laid me back and examined my body. I was terribly still, because Susan told me that it was shameful when women moved or seemed to enjoy marital relations. Hamish had climbed under the bedclothes, beckoning for me to do the same, and I dived gratefully beneath, alarmed at the sight of him, freckles on his shoulders. Staring at the canopy over the bed and wishing the room was cloaked in darkness, I closed my eyes and I spent my first night with my husband. It hurt horribly and I tried not to cry out.

Chapter 4

CONSTANCE, 1949

I have to stay here while they are outside cleaning. The dust makes me worse. My lungs are one of the things wrong with me.

I am wearing my white nightgown with the button missing, thick woollen socks and my pink cardigan. I wonder if today I will wear my other clothes and my shoes and be allowed upstairs. Perhaps I'm too ill today.

I am sick. I was born with things wrong with me and then I got polio when I was a baby. I don't remember not being sick. I'm six, so that means I have been sick for six years. I'm learning my numbers. Six plus six is twelve, which is really old. I hope I will be twelve one day but maybe I will die before then.

Someone drops something nearby. It clatters as if it's metal. There are tiles with different colours on in the hallway and it sounds like something has hit them. I want to see and I press my hands against the door to peer through. My eyelashes tickle the keyhole but it's all black – the key is in it today. I sink to the floor because it makes me sad. Sometimes I can see all the way through to the legs of the brown bear and count the different coloured stripes. Six plus six plus six is eighteen which is really, really old.

There's a cough and someone is moving in the corridor. It might be Annie or the other woman who helps her some days and calls her 'hen'. I think it's Annie because the footsteps are gentle and I imagine I smell oranges. Sometimes Mr Hughes has to come inside with his gardening things and his boots are heavy and he clicks his tongue once, twice, three times. It makes me giggle. He looked over at my door one day and I wanted him to come inside because I wondered whether his big boots would make a different noise on the wooden floorboards.

But he can't come inside. Nobody is allowed in my room. Not even to clean it. I have to stay away from other people or they could make me so ill I might die. And if you die then you don't wake up the next day.

Mother cleans my room with me but some days I can't help because it's a bad day and I'm tired and my tummy aches and aches and stuff comes out of my mouth which she takes away in a bucket.

I don't feel like things will come out of my mouth today and I get back up and lie on my bed so my head tips off the edge and my hair nearly touches the floor when I put my feet up on the wall. Above me is a small shelf of books. There's a tiny spider underneath it and I say hello to him today. Rabbit is sitting on my pillow and she has one floppy ear and one eye and two arms but on one the stitches have come out and Mother says she can mend her. I had stitches once but not in my arm, on my tummy. And the doctors mended me but not really well because I'm still sick. I talk to Rabbit and tell her things that I make up. I am good at making things up. I think of the pictures in the books I read and pretend that I am in them. In my books the children go outside lots and that is where the real adventures happen.

Mother visits me when they are gone. I hear the key turn and something makes me put my legs down and twist so I'm lying back on the top of my bed. She nods as she appears, her hair in soft waves today. She isn't holding my shoes in her hand and that makes my stomach hurt – not with something coming out of my mouth but with a sad feeling because I don't think this is one of the days I get to go upstairs.

'They've finished,' she says and I sit up in the bed.

Lots of things spill out of my mouth because it isn't the same as with Rabbit; I feel like I need to tell her everything in my head because she might not stay long and then I'll be alone again. And sometimes she answers my questions and sits on the wooden chair on the other side of the room with sunshine diamonds on her cheeks from the pattern on the window and helps me with my numbers and letters.

'You should rest,' she says. She tucks me back in under my sheet even though I'm definitely not tired.

I almost say no, but she doesn't like it when I refuse and I like her visits. I hate it when she doesn't come back for hours, sometimes a whole day, and I don't want that. I feel a hole inside me today that scares me. I swallow down the words, the idea that we should play a game. A few weeks ago she taught me a card game. Or we could read together. I like it when she reads to me best, so I haven't told her how much more I can read myself now.

'Close your eyes,' she says in her whispery voice. And I do because this normally means that she will stroke my head and I love when she does that. The bed creaks and I tip slightly to the side as she sits. I can smell fish, mackerel from breakfast, as a shadow passes my face. I feel her hand, warm and soft on my forehead as she murmurs a song. I know the song and sing it with her in my head.

Hush a bye, baby, on the tree top . . .

The song always ends the same way, though. I think after the fall the baby will need to be mended like me.

Chapter 5

AVA

By the time Ava arrived, Pippa had put Tommy to bed. 'Come in, I was just putting stuff away,' she whispered. Ava followed her down the hall, noticing the couple of inches that had been lopped off her hair.

'I like your hair.'

Pippa rubbed her neck self-consciously. 'Bit short.' She kneeled down on the red rug in the living room, a glass of almost-finished white wine resting among toys in every colour and size. 'Sorry. I wanted everything tidy for you but then I started drinking. Grab some. It's in the fridge . . .'

Ava walked through to the kitchen, dumped her coat and bag and opened the fridge. A triangle of parmesan cheese slipped forward. The contents were crammed in as if Pippa was preparing for the apocalypse. Pippa's house, like her parents', was always full to bursting with stuff. Was Pippa's comment about tidying meant to be a dig? Ava poured herself an orange juice, wishing it was wine. She felt her nerves build as she returned to the living room.

Pippa didn't notice the juice; she was busy, bent down, picking up marbles and tiny cars to throw into a burgundy box. 'So, how have you been? How's work?'

'Work's fine, thanks.' Ava perched on the edge of the dark brown sofa. 'I was out at a biscuit factory today.'

'Lucky for some.'

'Not exactly . . .'

Garry, her producer, had allocated her the biscuit job at that morning's briefing. Ava had been far away, worrying about the upcoming scan, and would have agreed to anything anyway. She was lucky in that, as one of their longest-serving reporters – coming up to fifteen years – she was often allowed to pitch her own stories. She'd gained a reputation for getting people to open up and she virtually monopolised the light-hearted or quirkier pieces in the final segment of the show.

'One of their workers was arrested for deliberately contaminating one of the machines. There's a massive recall of two of their products.'

Pippa wrinkled her nose. 'Ugh. That's gross.'

'Well, I managed to get through the whole piece with no biscuit puns at least.' Thoughts of poisoned biscuits were making Ava's stomach turn. 'So, covering the usual hard-hitting news . . .' She lowered herself onto the rug and helped out by reaching for random toys: a plastic Spider-Man whose arms moved; a small car that looked like some kind of child's computer; a plastic pig with a large stomach. She found herself staring at every item, imagining for a second her sparse flat littered in this way.

'Well, I went to soft play – so you still win.' Pippa picked up a dog in a police uniform and waggled it at Ava. 'This guy has always given me the creeps.' Then she stopped and tilted her head to the side. 'Is everything OK? How's Fraser?'

Ava hesitated. 'He's fine. Yup . . .' *Say it, Ava! Spit it out!* Why did this seem so much harder than telling her parents? 'He's sorting stuff for the end of term. He's starting a new role in September – head of sixth form – so he's doing a handover and . . .' She noticed that Pippa's eyes were glazing. 'How's Tommy doing?'

'Alright.' Pippa picked up her wine glass. 'Well, alright or weeping about something. Today his banana pancake wasn't in the shape of a square. But when I made him a square one he cried louder because it wasn't a big enough square . . .'

Ava couldn't stop her hand touching her stomach, her bark of laughter a second too late. 'I'm pregnant,' she blurted, a momentary relief that she had said it out loud.

Pippa's eyes, the same light brown as their dad's, widened. Then a brief, uncertain shadow crossed her face before she crawled towards Ava, the last of her wine sloshing onto the rug as she reached out one arm and drew her into a hug. 'Oh wow, congratulations . . .' Pippa's cheek bumped against hers. She smelled of lasagne and had a fleck of blue plasticine on her nose. 'That's why you've come over. I've been wondering the whole day!'

Ava felt a sliver of guilt. When had she stopped popping round for a drink in the evening?

'I can't believe it,' Pippa continued, 'I knew you guys were trying but I was worried . . .' Pippa sat back on her heels. 'It's great news.'

Ava felt something loosen in her chest. 'We had the dating scan today. I just told Mum and Dad.'

'Bet they were pleased.'

'They were.' Ava thought back to her mum's initial delight and excitement. Why had she messed it all up?

'Well, that *is* great news,' Pippa said. 'And you're not drinking. I should have guessed.' Her speech seemed a little faster than normal.

'How's the new job?' Ava suddenly felt a need to change the subject.

Pippa flicked a hand as if batting something away. 'Oh, it's fine, but I want to know *more*. How have you been feeling? Nauseous?'

'A bit.' Ava felt a tentative warmth enter her.

'Isn't it the worst? And the tiredness . . . nothing like it.'

'I napped in the editing suite the other day,' Ava admitted, gratified to see Pippa's mouth lift at the corners. She wondered for a moment what she had been nervous about. She *wanted* to share stuff like this with her sister.

'And I always wanted savoury food – peanuts . . . salt and vinegar crisps . . . stuff like that . . .'

'I haven't really had cravings yet.'

'Oh, I used to make Liam go out and get me stuff. Sometimes just because I wanted it . . .' Pippa grinned.

Ava took a sip of juice, glad she had come over, glad it was going well.

'Are you excited about being a mum?'

'Yes, definitely. I mean, I haven't thought about it a lot – you never know, do you, in those first weeks. But now the scan has gone well . . .'

'I wondered if you were ever going to be a mum.' Pippa sipped her wine.

Ava bit her lip. Not sure if the words were meant to carry a sting. 'Well, I am. And it might be nice not to have to work for a bit . . .'

'It *is* work, though,' said Pippa, a familiar bristle in her features.

'Oh, I know, I know . . .' Ava said, backtracking immediately. 'But you know what I mean . . .'

Pippa didn't reply, just scooped up another toy and threw it in the box. 'And goodbye lie-ins.'

'Yeah.' Ava felt the air shift. Since Tommy arrived, Ava had often said the wrong thing. She and Pippa had always been close, but in the last couple of years they had somehow lost that familiarity. Ava felt awkward and bumbling again.

'Is Fraser excited?'

Ava couldn't stop her face relaxing, her insides warming. 'He really is. I shouldn't be surprised – he loves kids. They're why he went into teaching but, still, it's nice . . .'

'Superhero teacher and dad,' Pippa said.

Ava didn't know how to respond. Was she being friendly? Pippa liked Fraser; she knew that. Why did she end up overthinking everything about her sister these days?

'I was about to chuck a pizza in the oven for Liam. Do you want one?'

'No thanks. I've got stuff at home.' Ava's stomach flipped and for a moment she felt a tide of sickness rise up within her. She probably should eat, but suddenly she didn't feel like staying. 'There was one thing that came up when I was at Mum's . . . I asked her about family history . . .'

She could almost hear Pippa holding her breath. 'How did that go?'

'Yeah, not well.' Ava pulled at a loose thread on the red rug.

Pippa's eyebrows pulled together. 'She doesn't like to talk about it.'

'Yes, but now I'm going to have a baby it would be nice to know there wasn't heart disease or some other weird condition in the family.'

'Well, if there was she'd have said something to me, wouldn't she?'

'Would she?'

'Of course,' Pippa snapped a little too quickly. 'She loves Tommy. She would have said.'

'Maybe.' Ava's voice wavered.

Pippa pressed her lips together, not meeting her eyes, and Ava knew she had got it wrong again. Pippa was a lot closer to Mum these days. They had Tommy to talk about, to fuss over together. Their mum was devoted to him, dusting off old board games he was far too young for, dragging him off on too-long walks. It had made them closer in the last few years; before then there had often been a suggestion that Ava was Mum's favourite. Somehow the tension between Ava and her sister always came back to Mum.

The key turned in the lock and they both looked at the door. Seconds later, Liam appeared in the living room, too-bright tie askew, orange-red hair sticking up. 'Oh, hey, Ava.' He drew up short, only half-disguising the annoyance that someone else was there. 'There was a visiting lecturer,' he said to the air, as if justifying the late hour. 'On the future of large-scale cellulosic biofuel production.'

'Hi, Liam.' Ava got to her feet with a light laugh. 'Sounds like a ball.'

A blush crept up from Liam's collar. 'It was interesting,' he mumbled.

Oh God, had she messed up again? Ava had gone to the same school as Liam. He'd been in her year, although Ava had almost no memories of him other than of somebody diligent, freckled and earnest. She had a vague recollection that he'd fallen off stage playing his trumpet but couldn't remember if that had been him or another boy with freckles. She hadn't even recognised him when Pippa had introduced them seven years before. Ava stood to give him an awkward kiss hello. He blinked twice. He smelled strongly of diesel. Were all her senses heightened now?

'Pizza's in the oven, Liam,' Pippa said. She didn't tell him Ava's news.

'I'll go out and grab some wine.' Liam didn't wait for a reply and the door soon closed behind him.

'I didn't mean to scare him away,' Ava said.

'You didn't,' Pippa said, an edge to her voice. She tucked her hair behind both ears.

'I should get going, too,' Ava said quickly. 'Don't want to disturb your night . . .'

'Yeah. And congratulations again.' The words seemed hollow this time.

Ava fetched her stuff from the kitchen, glad to be leaving, going back home to Fraser, where she couldn't get things so wrong. 'Bye then,' she said.

Pippa was putting the last things away. Ava didn't approach her for a hug.

Outside, there was a noise in the street. Ava turned and squinted towards the sound, unable to see anything other than an empty road and a line of parked cars. Getting her keys out of her bag, she walked down the short path and pulled the small wrought-iron gate open. *Families*, she thought, as she stared at Pippa's silhouette showing behind the living room curtains. *So many complications.*

Chapter 6

MARION

I never dreamed it.

We are engaged.

I am to marry Hamish West. I will be Marion Eveline West. Isn't that a scream?

How that birthday trip to the Savoy changed my life! And thank goodness, because I was quite despairing that, at twenty-four, my chance at marriage was over. Susan, who lives in the house two down from us, is twenty-seven and absolutely on the shelf. I am trying desperately hard to downplay my excitement in front of her, but of course she knows – I can't stop hugging myself. It's all just the cat's pyjamas.

Hamish has been so attentive these last few weeks. It's been such a wild romantic time. I feel like one of the plain heroines in the novels I read who is finally about to experience her life beginning. I had truly started to believe I'd be stuck in Barnes forever, an endless cycle of laundry, a walk in the park with Susan, both of us moaning about being old maids, strained meals where the only sound is the cutlery scraping on the china, endless identical jigsaws with Mother to stave off the interminable boredom.

He wrote to Father in the week after my birthday, which was very proper, and Mother invited him to the house. I cleaned the whole place from top to bottom, fussing over the brass fender of the fireplace as if I was a scullery maid. I wanted things to be perfect. He noticed the snowdrops I had placed in a small vase and told Mother her rock cakes were out of this world. And he said terribly nice things to Father, thanking him for his service to the country and making him go quite pink.

He has taken Mother and me out on a couple of occasions. We visited the Lyons' Corner House in Coventry Street, where an orchestra plays on every floor, and he bought me a burgundy felt hat that I just adore. He is so dear. His stories are fascinating. He has a most thrilling job in the City, dealing with stocks and shares for an American company. It is quite beyond me but terribly impressive.

Father thought him a little smooth, but I think that's rather unfair. Father often says things that are meant to hurt, so I don't hold much sway by them and I won't let him get me down, not when things are going so marvellously.

And poor Hamish has had a terrible time, losing both his parents rather suddenly only a few years ago. Mother and I felt tears lining our lashes as his head drooped onto his chest. How I wanted to reach across and stroke his hand, staring at the fine hairs on his knuckles, my own skin tingling with the thought.

Then I was quite distracted as he drew from a rather shiny leather wallet a scalloped-edged photograph of the most wonderful-looking house – like a castle, the warm sepia colour making it look like the most romantic destination. It has a square tower, turrets and crenellations.

And, extraordinarily, he is now the owner of it. It is on an estate in Scotland called Overtoun and was built by his grandfather, who did something terribly clever with chemicals.

'It's looking a little tired these days,' he said as he slid the photograph back in his wallet.

I was barely listening, imagining for a strange second a haunted look on his face, something dark and unknowable passing across his features.

It seemed unreal to me: a prince and a castle. How could someone I know be the lord of a manor? He isn't a lord but he certainly lives in splendour if the fancy stonework and a hundred windows are anything to go by. And now I am to be mistress of it all. I feel like Lizzie in *Pride and Prejudice*, too happy and excited to believe what is happening. It is impossible. To be plucked out of Barnes, dull little Marion Foot, and taken off to such a glamorous setting with such a faint-inducing husband. Susan is practically sick with jealousy and, even though she can get on my nerves with her endless prattle, I do feel desperately sorry for her being left behind.

We are to be married in Chelsea and then we will travel to the estate just north of Glasgow. I've never even left London. Susan is rather sad at the prospect, but I have assured her I shall write and invite her to stay in the summer. Oh, what larks I am about to have! Scotland has many treasures. Hamish tells me there are streams so cold they make you gasp when you trail your feet in them, and beautiful walks. I imagine walking hand in hand on the edge of a rippling stream, sunlight glistening on its surface.

I will miss Mother and Father, of course, but I can't help looking around my tiny bedroom with the faded flowered curtains and the singed rug from the fireplace that spits when the logs are wet and feel my chest explode as I ponder my future. What a grand life I shall lead! They have dances called ceilidhs that Hamish tells me he shall teach me, and dinners and waiting staff, and children and more. And Hamish, like a prince from the books I read by gaslight as a child.

I can't stop smiling.

Chapter 7

AVA

She felt exhausted by the time she walked up the first flight of stairs to their flat.

'Hey,' Fraser called as she opened the door, light from the corridor spilling inside. He sat in the semi-darkness on their sofa, still in his work clothes with a beer in his hand and an empty tray of food on the floor. She moved to close the curtains. He looked up at her. 'I didn't wait. Sorry. I made spaghetti carbonara. It'll be OK in the microwave . . .'

'Thanks.' She moved into the kitchen and put the plate in the microwave.

'Give me two minutes!' he called.

She leaned back against the counter, waiting for the food to ping. Fraser had already washed up and wiped every surface down. She thought of Pippa's remark about tidying as she glanced around the utilitarian kitchen. Maybe it was growing up in a house full of clutter that had given her a taste for minimalism: the white counters gleamed; the light grey cupboards with their glass fronts showed rows of polished glasses and mugs; a calendar on the wall displayed the correct month of July; a shopping list on a small whiteboard instructed one of them to pick up cornflakes and bananas. It was ordered, clean, calming.

She removed the plate and stepped over to the small round table with its brushed steel legs and glass top. How would they cope with the chaos of a baby?

Fraser appeared in the doorway, his dark hair ruffled, a mark just below the collar of his shirt. He lifted the beer bottle to his lips, stubble on his face. 'How did it go?' He pulled out the other chair. 'I'm sorry I didn't come with you; just taking the afternoon off for the scan meant I had to catch up . . .'

'Of course. I just wanted to tell them in person . . .'

'How did your mum take the news?' His mouth lifted into a smile.

'She was chuffed.' Ava grinned, recalling her mum's wide smile when she'd told her.

'And Pippa?'

'Yeah. It was alright.'

Fraser nodded once, not sharing his thoughts. He took a sip of his beer. 'I can't wait to tell Dad when I see him next. It feels weird, doesn't it?'

'Yup,' Ava said, her fork poised. 'I know we've known for ages but today made it feel real.'

Fraser ran a hand through his hair, the bags under his eyes bigger but his blue eyes bright. 'Good weird, though.'

'Very good.'

'I'm glad I'm off in a couple of weeks – our last summer holiday before we become three.'

Ava swallowed her food. She always took a decent amount of time off work to coincide with Fraser's holiday. They made last-minute plans – cycling, hiking, picnics, paddle boarding. Last summer they'd explored the west coast, taking ferries to obscure islands, staying in campsites and B & Bs. Endless memories of still blue water, soaring landscape, purple heather, rose quartz rocks, shingle beaches.

As if reading her thoughts, Fraser leaned forward in his chair and smiled. 'We're going to have the most fun introducing him – or her – to the world.'

Ava felt a warm glow all over.

'Although I might not let you jump off any cliffs this summer.'

'It wasn't dangerous.' Ava laughed. 'Mum took us there as kids!' She made to stand up with her empty plate.

'I'll do that.' Fraser stood, dropped a kiss on her shoulder and took it from her. 'And it was like a thirty-foot jump, Ava. It's called *tombstoning* for a reason. Anyway, we both know your mum's a bit mental. Remember her sixtieth? She made us all go white water kayaking in February.'

The thought of danger made Ava shiver a little. She put one hand on her stomach. 'Do you think the baby will be alright?'

Fraser looked over his shoulder at her from the sink and frowned. 'Of course . . . And the scan was good.'

Ava bit her lip. 'It was.'

The furrow in Fraser's brow deepened. 'So why would you think the baby might not be alright?'

Ava fiddled with the button on her shirt. 'I don't. I guess. It's just . . . I wish I knew a bit more. I asked Mum about her family history and it went down like a sack of shit.'

'Well, you know your mum . . .' Fraser turned off the tap and moved back to the table. 'A closed book. You always say so.'

She nodded glumly. Mum was bubbly and charismatic, the beating heart of their small family, the sun around whom they all orbited – but notoriously private. 'I just wish she'd been a bit more reassuring.'

'I'm sure she would have told you stuff if it would affect a baby,' he said.

She nodded. 'That's what Pippa said.'

'Well, there you go.' He leaned back on two legs of his chair – something he'd probably tell his teenagers off for in his class. 'Great minds . . .'

Ava wanted to laugh but she couldn't shake the image of her mother's pinched face. 'I never push her on it, though, and now I'm having my own child it would be quite nice to understand a bit more, you know?'

Fraser rubbed the stubble on his chin. 'Well, go easy. I taught a kid last year who was taken into care. He hated talking about his family – practically lamped anyone who tried. It's hard if something grim has happened. From the tiny things she's told me in the past, it sounds like her dad was pretty violent . . .'

Ava's heart lurched. 'Violent? When did she tell you that?'

Fraser's voice dropped low. 'After Mum died.' His mum had died almost three years before, the anniversary just a couple of months away. An aggressive breast cancer had spread quickly to her brain. 'We were talking about some things. It came up.'

'I didn't know that – how could I not know that?' Ava tried to swallow down a stab of envy. Her mum rarely opened up, and she had told Fraser that.

'Maybe she found it easier to tell me because I'm not family, as such.'

Ava could barely look at Fraser now. Not family. It stung a little more these days.

Chapter 8

AVA

Sunglasses on, scurrying into the building under a milky blue sky, Ava tried to keep down her decaf coffee and toast. In the newsroom, the morning team were watching the rehearsal on monitors. There was a low hubbub of voices as she strode past them. Ava glanced up, noting Claudia's glossy lipstick and her blow-dried blonde hair. She should find her after the programme and tell her too, although she would have to swear her to secrecy; she didn't want everyone at work to know just yet.

The newsroom was busy, a bank of monitors on hot desks, heads bent over work, a balcony running above their heads, more people moving about. Over at the sports desk a couple of colleagues were hunched around a computer, a laugh from one of them, a slap on the back. Beyond them, another journalist entered the editing suite, balancing a mug on top of a folder of papers, a pen in her teeth. In the corner of the room, a bearded intern, new last week, stood at the water cooler next to a tall stranger with a yellow visitor's badge on his lapel. He smiled across at Ava as she caught his eye.

It was a moment before she realised her mobile was vibrating in her bag. She searched inside, smiling at the banana that Fraser must have popped in, always concerned that she was too busy for breakfast, particularly now she was pregnant. Pulling out her mobile, she frowned at the name: DAD. Dad never really called her. They swapped the odd text message, but it was always MUM or HOME that cropped up – Dad in the background, annoying her mum: 'I'm trying to talk, John!' Ava's hand hovered over the phone for a moment before she answered.

'Dad?'

'Ava. Good. I thought it might be too early. Your mother's gone out for milk . . .'

The noise of the newsroom seemed to fade. Why had he waited for Mum to go out? 'No. Actually, I'm late for work if anything.' Her laugh sounded strained.

'It's about last night . . . the questions you had. I was sorry about the reaction. I think your mum was caught off guard.'

'That's OK. I know she's private.' Ava's grip on the phone tightened. 'She is.'

Ava sank into her swivel chair, a black one she'd ordered last year to help support her lower back. It was as if the moment she hit thirty-seven she suddenly noticed more things aching. 'She always has been.' Ava felt the breath suspended in her body as he continued.

'I always respected the fact that she didn't want to talk about things, but maybe I should have tried harder . . .' His sigh when it came was weary and made Ava's heart ache.

'It's OK, Dad. We don't need to talk about this . . .'

'No. It was fair to ask. Your mum might not have been close to her family, or her adopted parents, but it's only natural – wanting to know a bit more now you're going to be a mum.'

'Fraser said her dad was violent,' Ava blurted suddenly, encountering silence at the other end. 'Dad?'

He cleared his throat. 'I don't think he was a nice man, no. Liked a drink.'

'What else do you know?' She realised as she heard her voice, high and fast, that she thirsted for knowledge.

'Not a great deal. When I met her, she didn't want to talk about it. Told me he had died . . . that her adopted mum and her didn't speak . . . no siblings, no idea where her birth parents were and she didn't care either . . .'

Ava listened. Some details she had known: she only had uncles and aunts on her dad's side; she knew her mum had been adopted as a baby; she knew her mum avoided her eyes on the few occasions she had asked her anything more about her past.

'Your mum has always wanted to live in the present.'

'The past's the past,' Ava intoned – a line that her mum often came out with if Ava ever asked for an old photograph or a story from Mum's childhood. 'But it obviously still affects her.' Ava didn't want to sound churlish, but nor did she want to just give up as she had always done in the past.

'Perhaps. But that's what she wants. I just phoned because I wanted you to know that she would never conceal anything that would harm her girls. We both love you a great deal . . . both of you.'

Her dad's voice was low and Ava felt warmth rushing to her cheeks. Dad wasn't the gushy sort. 'We know you do.'

'Aye. Good. Well, that was it. And your mum will be back shortly so . . .'

Ava nodded despite him not being able to see her. 'Thanks for ringing, Dad. I appreciate it.' She knew it would have taken some courage on her dad's part. She doubted her mum would have liked it much. She sat back in her chair, absorbing the things he'd said. Why had she prodded something that she had grown up knowing was taboo? Dad was right: her mum didn't owe it to anyone to tell her sorry tale. People dealt with things in different ways. She had covered enough harrowing stories – victims of domestic crimes who had hidden the truth for years, some who never spoke of them.

She was meant to be researching but she couldn't settle to anything, scrolling down over a list of possible stories to develop. She found herself breaking off to search baby websites on her phone, wondering about what kind of mum she'd be. Glancing up, she saw Neil, one of the cameramen, looking down into the newsroom from the balcony overhead. On catching her eye, he looked quickly away, pushing back his long dark hair, stumbling a moment before moving out of sight.

Ava was still looking up when Claudia appeared in front of her, her studio make-up more orange than tan in the harsh strip lights, the magenta-pink lipstick making her teeth sparkle.

'Morning.' She smiled, pulling up the chair opposite and dropping into it with a theatrical sigh.

'How did the programme go?'

Claudia waved a dismissive hand. 'All fine. We interviewed the wife of a man who has badly injured himself quad biking so not the most upbeat way to start the day.'

'How grim.'

'It really was.' Claudia rotated in the chair. 'Where are you headed to today?'

'Nowhere,' Ava said, finally opening her computer. 'Research day.'

'Slacker.'

'Ha. You can talk. You're off now for the day.'

'Ava . . .' Claudia leaned forward, her voice dropping seriously. 'I have an appointment.'

'Oh?' Ava's eyebrows raised.

'With a nail technician, but still . . .' Claudia laughed and stood up. In her powder-blue dress she looked every inch the face of breakfast news. 'Can you escape for lunch later?'

'Probably. Actually, there was something I wanted to tell you.'

Claudia immediately sat back down. 'What? What is it? Gossip?'

Ava started laughing. 'Oh my God, wait till lunch.'

'You're pregnant!' Claudia guessed.

Ava couldn't disguise the startled expression quick enough.

'Oh my God!' Claudia covered her mouth, her oyster-shell nails impeccable from where Ava was sitting.

'*Don't* tell anyone else,' Ava warned, leaning forward and whispering. 'We had the twelve-week scan yesterday.'

Claudia's hand still covered her mouth; her smile was wide as she lowered it. 'Oh my God. Amazing. And I won't,' she added hastily.

Ava felt a thrill at sharing the news. It was a relief after so many weeks of carrying the secret around the newsroom. 'Not even Daniel.' Ava arched an eyebrow.

Daniel was one of the camera operators on the breakfast show, tall, swarthy and divorced.

'Why would I tell Daniel?' Claudia stopped rotating, crossed and then re-crossed her legs as Ava appraised her. 'Ha ha! OK, fine. I won't.' She got up and smoothed her honey-blonde hair at the temple before glancing down. 'I can't believe you know about Daniel,' she whispered, then glanced over her shoulder. 'It's only been a couple of weeks. Don't tell anyone else about that and I'll keep your secret, too, Preggo.'

They linked fingers as if they were still twelve and Claudia turned back, flashing a last amused look. 'I'll text you about lunch. And, Ava . . .' She lowered her voice again, her mischievous blue eyes for once serious. 'You're going to be a great mum.'

Ava couldn't help the smile that split her face, watching her friend sashay away.

God, she hoped she was right.

Her thoughts returned to her own mum, her own childhood. Family had been everything, Mum right at the heart of it: bundling them into the car in pyjamas for road trips, exploring every part of Scotland; playing endless games with them – jigsaws, chase, stuck-in-the-mud, bat and ball; the beach, even in winter, screaming along wet sand; hot chocolate in flasks; scooping them up and spinning them round. Her mum had always had a magnetism, an energy. It drew Ava's friends to their house, the laughter around a crowded table. Her mum was cool. How would she measure up?

She noted the time on the computer and realised she really must try to do some work. *Focus, Ava.* Her eyes roved over the stories, the places on the list. One place suddenly nudged at her memories, the phone call from her dad returning in a rush: Dumbarton, a memory that jarred, that seemed part of the other side of her mother, the side she didn't like revealed. They had travelled there. Ava must have only been five or six, waiting in a car as her mother stood at the entrance to a churchyard, a small crowd dressed in black standing in a semi-circle in the distance. Her mother loitering, glancing back at her and Pippa in the back seat of the car, tears streaking her face. Ava wanting to go to her and undoing her seat belt but the car door was locked. Her mother turned and moved quickly back to the car, wiping at her face. What had made Ava remember this?

She looked up Dumbarton, a place she had driven past a hundred times, halfway between Glasgow and Loch Lomond. As she clicked on the links in her research file, the newsroom faded around her as she finally lost herself to work. She had saved the story a year or so ago, something that had piqued her curiosity, the place less than twenty miles out of Glasgow. One of the links led her to a local blog, large purple text on a pea-green background; blurred photos accompanied the posts, news articles from fifteen years before. A bridge, built at the end of the nineteenth century, which had a macabre reputation. As many as five hundred dogs had leaped to their deaths from it into the gorge below. The Dog Suicide Bridge.

If she could persuade a producer it was worth covering, Ava would have an excuse to explore the nearby town. As she stared at one of the photos on the blog, the same feeling she'd had a year ago came back to her: a burning instinct to hunt down a story.

Chapter 9

CONSTANCE

I'm feeling heavy in my body today, head sunk into my pillow as I watch the rain blur the windows. Mother has a small clock on a chain and she has started to teach me about minutes and hours which are shown by big and small hands and I think I watched the rain for a thousand minutes.

My porridge is on a tray on the floor by my bed, sticking to the sides of the bowl, turning grey. I only had two small spoonfuls, as yesterday I was very sick in my mouth and my tummy still aches. Mother told me she had to go into town and normally I ask her if I can come, even though I shouldn't be near other people because of the germs, but today I didn't ask because my legs and arms are tired and my mouth tastes all horrible, like rotting vegetables.

When I sit up, my head feels all strange, as if I am on a boat on the sea, and I put my hand on the cold, white wall, tiny flakes falling from it, until everything feels normal again. It has stopped raining and the sun has come out all pale, making the drops shine like on the ring Mother wears.

The windows have lots of diamond shapes in the glass made with black lines, so the outside looks all broken up and pointy.

From my bed, I can see the green bushes and lots of sky. If I pull the chair over to the window, though, and stand on it, I can see one corner of the bridge. I like to stay there and watch for the people. Some days no one comes, but other days, especially if the sky is blue and the sun turns the stone bridge a pale grey, there are a few.

Mother has told me not to move the chair so I always drag it back to its place so she doesn't know, even though I am not sure why being near the window would make me sicker.

My legs shake for a moment as I stand, the wood scratchy on my bare feet. A noise like a gasp makes me sit straight back down but I think it is the house and not Mother. Sometimes it feels like the house spies on me for her. Crossing the room, pulling on the chair, which makes a loud squeak as I drag it, makes me feel strange again and I have to sit down for a lot of big-hand minutes.

Carefully, I step onto the chair, the strawlike seat tickling my skin. My eyes are right next to the window, hands on the white windowsill as I stare out. I almost fall backwards because there is a boy right there on the bridge! I can see his head popping up above the grey stone, his arm pointing at something. He is young – younger even than me. He is not as thin as me, though, and his skin looks a bit different too – pinkish, the same as one of the stripes on the tiles in the hallway.

He is leaning forward, looking over the edge, and for a moment I press my palm to the glass, worried he will lean too far and topple. He needs to be careful: Mother has told me it is a long drop down to lots of rocks. On quiet days, I can hear the water splash over them and once, when I was in the garden when I was about as small as the boy, it was really loud, like it was in my head and not under the bridge at all.

The boy is calling to someone over his shoulder but I look and look and can't see anyone, so they must be standing farther along the bridge out of sight, or it is like when I talk to Rabbit and there is no one really there. My mouth hurts where I chew my lip, worrying about the little boy.

This boy has something in his hand, but when I move even nearer the window my breath makes the diamonds go all steamy and I can't see out. When I look again, the boy has bent his right arm back and I see what he is holding. He is going to throw it over the bridge onto the rocky bit below. It is a stick and I see his mouth open as his arm moves quickly and his hand lets the stick go so it spins in the air and drops out of sight. He is looking down again and I wonder what it looks like as it hits the rocks below. Did it break? Did it float away?

I am wondering so hard, I miss the boy stepping down out of sight, so it is just the blank stone wall of the bridge again, his head and arms gone. I wish I had watched him longer because it might be ages, maybe a few circles of the small hand, before another person comes along. I press my nose to the glass and pray for more people. I stare at the bridge and the steps until my eyes ache, but no one else comes.

Chapter 10

AVA

Ava felt guilty as she looked in the rear-view mirror at an innocent, contented Gus, no doubt imagining himself off on one of the trips she and Fraser sometimes took him on. Would they be romping up a hillside or burrowing on the forest floor?

Her mum had been quieter than normal when Ava had gone to pick him up, her gaze focused somewhere to the right, her words mumbled. They had hardly spoken in the last few weeks, her mum out at endless book clubs or watercolour classes or hikes. Ava felt punished for probing into things she knew she shouldn't. All the things she had planned to say died on her lips as Gus trotted out to greet her. It was awkward, her mum thrusting the lead at her before Ava could hug her goodbye and she could have kicked herself for stirring things up. She had memories of such silences when she and Pippa were younger; they had learned what caused them and were able to avoid them.

Neil was meeting her there, when he finished filming something at Celtic Park, and she was glad to have the car to herself and her thoughts. When she crossed the Erskine Bridge, she never failed to admire the soaring steel pylons, remembering Fraser telling her that the bridge had been the longest of its kind when it had first been built. He had been on holiday for a week now, already getting fidgety, and she'd promised him they'd make plans that evening. Fraser wanted to take a trip and to sort out the flat while he had the time off.

She was almost sixteen weeks pregnant now, the slight curve of her stomach hidden under a loose cotton shirt. She drove on, the silver ribbon of the River Clyde behind her, almost missing the faded sign on the road that pointed visitors to Overtoun Estate.

She had persuaded Garry that the piece was relevant, an interesting segment they could put at the end of the programme on a quiet day. She knew she was lucky to have been there long enough to be allowed to cover the things that interested her. This was the first slow news day in a couple of weeks and Garry had been true to his word.

Turning off the road, she climbed up the hill past rundown terraced cottages and abandoned houses, leaving civilisation behind her. The driveway was long and pockmarked with holes, the uneven ground making the car rattle. To her right, an imposing line of crags loomed suddenly, an impenetrable wall of greys and greens. Gus raised his head and whimpered as the car slipped into shadows.

'It's more than a hundred acres,' she told him, wanting to talk, to make noise. 'Well, that's what the Internet said.'

Gus was alert, sniffing the air. As the driveway curved to the left, she strained to see the building, making out flashes of grey, the house obscured by a row of enormous dark pine trees. She parked, the only car in a small empty square made for the purpose, and switched off the engine, staring at her hands on the wheel. 'Hey . . .' She opened the passenger door and beckoned Gus out, suddenly glad he was there, not wanting to be alone. Glancing over her shoulder, she felt as if the crags had somehow moved closer, hemming her in.

He hopped out, so trusting, and she attached his lead with fumbling hands. 'Come on, Gus!' she called. For a second, he paused and sniffed the air, but he soon allowed himself to be pulled along. She moved towards the house, feeling something crackle in the air. The Internet articles were doing this, she thought; she found her feet taking on a life of their own while her body wanted to turn back.

Gus strained on the lead, nose to the ground as he explored the new surroundings. There was a slight breeze, clouds scudding across the sky, patterns rippling over the stretches of green all around her. Rounding the corner, she couldn't help a sharp intake of breath, her jaw dropping open as she craned her neck back. The house was immense, rising up in front of her like a terrible surprise, the grey facade streaked with dark patches, hooded windows and intricate stonework. The towers and fish-scaled slate turrets seemed straight out of a Grimms' fairy tale. As she moved nearer, she could make out more detail: faces carved into the stone; inscriptions displayed at intervals; the archway of a grand entrance up ahead.

A sudden gust of cold wind that seemed to almost emanate from the house itself made her wrap her arms more tightly around herself and she wished she had brought a cardigan. The windows ahead seemed to wink in recognition as she passed beneath them. A chill entered her blood despite the July sunshine. Looking up, she noticed one of the inscriptions etched into the stone: *Ye that love the Lord hate evil*. She pulled Gus closer.

He had stopped, the lead taut as he crouched low, eyes fixated on something in the distance.

'Come on, Gus,' she said, her voice encouraging, with a lightness she didn't feel.

Gus didn't budge. His body was stiff as he stared ahead, a low growl building in his throat.

In that moment fear coursed through her and she turned, determined to leave. There was something alive in this place, something she needed to escape.

But as she turned, another car bumped its way up the drive. She walked quickly towards it, retracing her steps. Garry's dark blue car spat stones as it turned in to the car park. There were two figures inside. She waved a hand.

'Hey, Ava!' Garry got out of the car. 'I thought I'd come along too.' His blonde hair gleamed as he stretched. His thin, bottle-green jumper lifted a fraction to show a flat stomach.

'Hey!' Ava said, her voice too loud, the relief at seeing a friend palpable.

'All OK?'

Was he asking because she looked different? She tugged on her shirt. 'Fine.'

Neil had stepped out of the passenger seat, his long hair frizzy, looking at her as he banged the equipment on the roof of the car.

'Watch it!' Garry called, giving Ava the smallest roll of his eyes as Neil stuttered out a hello.

'He didn't talk all the way here,' Garry murmured in an undertone. 'Just ate three sausage rolls.'

She suppressed a smile as Neil walked towards them, carrying the equipment. In his mid-forties, he looked like an ageing rocker in his ripped and stained T-shirt that strained over a small paunch.

'Well, this is cool!' Garry said. He looked round, hands on his hips. 'I had no idea it was here. I drive past on the way up to Loch Lomond. I love getting up there.'

'Me too.' Ava smiled, wishing for a moment that they were all on the shores of Loch Lomond, looking out over the still, velvety water. Garry grinned back before Neil managed to interrupt the moment with a phlegm-filled cough.

'You alright, Neil?' she asked.

'Asthma,' Garry told her.

Neil pulled out an inhaler and pastry flakes fluttered to the ground.

Garry looked around. 'So where's the bridge?'

'The other side of the house,' Ava said. She hadn't made it that far and the thought of moving past the house again sent a shiver through her.

They planned the shots as they walked around the corner. Ava avoided looking at the house but felt safer flanked by her colleagues. Gus seemed more relaxed, too, as they moved past the big projecting stone porch with its arched door flanked by sleeping stone lions. A couple of cars lined a field that climbed up and out of sight – a good place for a dog walk, Ava thought idly. Were the owners aware of the supposed danger that lurked nearby?

She stopped. There it was, straight ahead: the bridge that she had read about online. The photos had failed to do justice to the impressive Victorian structure. Thick stone walls lined a short walkway. There were semi-circular refuges on one side with raised stone steps acting as viewing platforms out over the estate. Ava could make out the sound of the water moving below it as they approached and the air above the bridge seemed to quiver with the noise. Gus had slowed and Ava wasn't about to risk taking him off his lead. Her skin prickled at the thought. Bringing him felt suddenly reckless.

As they neared the entrance to it, all of them fell silent. Ava peeked at the two men, wondering if they were affected too. Gus seemed reticent to cross, attempting to pull her in the opposite direction. Garry seemed oblivious as he marched into the centre, turning back to face them all. 'Let's set up here for the introduction.' He took a notepad from his rucksack.

Neil was peering over the edge of the thick stone wall into the gorge below, then started fiddling with the camera.

'Is the water going to be a problem?' Garry asked him, his voice loud over the noise of the burn below.

Neil shook his head. 'No.'

Ava gripped Gus's lead tightly as she watched the two men moving on the bridge. It was as if there was a veil, a barrier between them and Gus and her. It was the strangest sensation; she just knew, somewhere deep inside, that she didn't want to step forward and join them.

'Ava, you ready?'

Gus still tugged in the other direction and Garry glanced down at him. 'We should get that on camera, Neil,' he said, pointing at Gus. Garry stepped forward just as the sun emerged from behind a cloud and Ava was momentarily blinded by the sudden shift in light. For a mad second it seemed that Garry wasn't Garry at all, but an indistinct figure made of whites and greys moving towards her.

Ava took a step back. 'I'm . . . I'm not sure we should . . .'

Neil was ready to go, headphones around his neck, camera at his side. Garry was in front of her, his features familiar, the light returned to normal. Ava could feel her heart racing, her skin dampening as she looked at his bemused expression. 'Not sure we should what?' Garry said.

The birds chirruped in the trees, the atmosphere cleared and it was as if the last two minutes hadn't happened at all. 'Film at this angle,' she suggested faintly. 'Maybe here?'

'Alright,' Garry said slowly, his eyes watchful.

As she stepped onto the bridge, she felt a swooping sensation as if she suddenly had no centre of gravity. She blinked and put a protective hand on her stomach. Gus edged closer as she felt the ground, solid – not shifting, as she'd imagined – under her feet. A breeze lifted her hair from her shirt collar as she focused on the things she needed to say.

Her words, when they came, were stiff and formal. 'Built in 1895, this bridge has gained a fearsome reputation. With sweeping views out to the River Clyde and plenty of paths to explore nearby, it has attracted visitors from all around the world. But it is here, amid this stunning scenery, that tragedy has unfolded.' Ava paused, staring into the lens, trying to imagine, as she always did, that she was telling a story to the viewer at home. 'From these crenelated parapets' – Ava moved towards the nearest one as Gus tried to tug her back and Neil captured it all – 'it has been said that hundreds of dogs have leaped over the side of the bridge to their deaths.'

She shivered as she finished, a glance over the granite wall to the sharp rocks and rushing water. She stepped back, her breath catching in her throat. Bending down, she drew Gus to her. 'Good dog, good boy.' She patted and stroked him, feeling the normally laid-back dog quivering. What did cause the dogs to leap to their deaths? What lured them onto the rocks below? Did the others feel the strangeness of this place?

Garry had moved away, talking to Neil about the next set-up. For a moment, Ava stood on her own and stared out at the greyish blue of the river in the distance, sensing that something was moving in the corner of her eye. She knew she'd been avoiding looking at it but she found she couldn't help herself, her head twisting once more to the house. Her eyes roved hungrily over its features, strangely familiar to her already: the glass of the different-sized windows reflecting sunlight; the shadows of the trees as if the windows were alive and drinking it all in. She found herself drawn to a latticed window on the ground floor in the shade of the house, part-hidden by thick tendrils of ivy, the glass black as if the room behind had sucked any light away. She felt nausea roll within her and swallowed, a sudden stench, like curdled milk, forcing a hand to her mouth.

'Let's film from beneath the bridge,' Garry said. 'Ava . . . are you coming?'

'I am,' she muttered, taking a last look back. Gus growled, unbiddable as she tugged on his lead. Normally placid, he seemed alert to every sound and sight, staying close to her, almost tripping her. 'Good boy,' she said again, the lead still tight in her fist, hating the feeling of turning her back to the house as she followed the two men off the pebbled deck.

Garry had discovered a path that fell away steeply and then twisted back on itself, disappearing underneath one of the enormous arches of the Victorian structure. Neil followed him and their shoes made muddy prints in the path as they dropped beneath the level of the road and into the cool shade of the trees.

Ava followed, the sun lost behind a canopy of larch, beech and pine, all blocking her view. Beneath the bridge, the atmosphere seemed desolate. Moss clung to the stone walls and the smell of damp filled her nostrils. Unease nudged at Ava as she stared at the burn moving past. How many bones had shattered on the jutting rocks? Why had she ever wanted to come here and film? This place felt devoid of hope.

Gus was barking now, staring at the space beneath the archway where Garry was standing. Garry gave Ava a perplexed look. Ava bent to comfort Gus, a hand on his springy fur. Could he sense the menace too?

Neil appeared suddenly at her side, making her jump. 'I just need to fix your mic,' he said.

'Sorry.' She laughed, trying to lighten the mood. 'It's all this weird history. It's making me edgy.'

Neil reached for her collar, his ears pink as he spoke. 'I read that this is one of the thin places,' he said, as he fiddled with the small microphone. He was so close Ava could see a spot of blood on his chin from where he'd cut himself shaving. For a moment her head seemed filled with the sickly scent of it, as if the river running past them was flowing with it.

'What's that?' She tried to disguise the tremble in her voice. Gus shuffled near her feet.

'It's a Celtic term. About places where the gap between heaven and earth is closer.' His dark brown eyes seemed intense as he stared up at the bridge, the three arches, the blackened stone.

Normally, Ava might have laughed at this explanation but instead she just swallowed.

'Right, come on.' Garry made them both jump. Even he looked put out.

Ava rolled her shoulders and cleared her throat. She needed this to be over, despite it being her idea in the first place. 'It is reported' – Ava swept an arm across the setting – 'that dogs first started to jump from this bridge during the 1950s, with some stating that as many as five hundred dogs have followed since. One report claims that some dogs survive the fall only to get back to the top of the bridge and leap again. So, what has caused these dogs to lose their minds in this way and jump, apparently without fear, into the gorge that runs beneath?' Ava felt dwarfed by the vast bridge and she had to raise her voice to be heard over the roar of the water, an endless accompaniment as it flowed past.

Relieved when Garry told her they'd 'got it', Ava followed eagerly as they all retraced their steps back up the path. Scooping up Gus, she plunged her face into his body, taking comfort from his warmth, the tickle of his fur, his familiar smell.

'Actually, let's do a last segment on the theories before we leave,' Garry said. Ava's mood plummeted. Neil eyed the bridge warily, his gaze resting on the sign reminding walkers to keep dogs on a lead. 'Neil, get a shot of that!' Garry called from over his shoulder. 'Right, Ava . . . how about you stand up here?' He indicated the raised stone step of the parapet and Ava looked nervously back at him, still cuddling Gus in her arms. 'Trust me, we can get a shot with the tower of the house behind you from there. Look . . . I'll take the dog.' He held out his hand for the lead. He seemed tetchy today, or was the atmosphere of this bridge getting to him too? Ava handed the lead to him, a prickly sensation building at the back of her neck again.

Standing on the step Garry had indicated, she took a breath, ready to finish the piece. Neil angled the camera towards her.

It happened so quickly that afterwards none of them were sure how.

Gus raised his head, ears pricked, and streaked towards the furthest parapet, his lead trailing behind him. Garry swore, Neil shouted and somehow Ava managed to jump down and pin the leather strip with her foot just as Gus sprang up onto the next parapet. Practically garrotting him, Ava tugged him backwards. He scrabbled at the stone wall as if possessed with a fierce energy and it took all her strength to hold him back. Reining him in at last, she bundled his trembling, tense body to her. He was panting excitedly, still focused on something beyond the wall. As she held him she could feel his heart hammering beneath the thick fur.

'What the—'

'Ava, I . . .' Garry began a stream of apologies. 'I thought I had hold of him – I'm so sorry – he just lunged and . . .'

Neil watched them both and Ava felt his eyes on her.

'Are you alright, Ava?' Garry's face was filled with concern.

She nodded, still not sure how she had gone from one moment to the next. She realised she was crouching on the slimy stonework of the bridge. 'I just. This house . . . this bridge . . .' She clutched Gus to her again and squeezed her eyes closed. Neil's words about the bridge replayed in her mind.

One of the thin places.

Chapter 11

MARION

Where to begin? I have barely had time to fill these pages and things have moved at such a terrific pace.

It was a short engagement: Hamish was keen to 'have me installed' in the house as soon as possible. He arranged everything, and Mother and Father were swept along in it all too. It was reassuring to have him decide things for me. He is so worldly, whilst I felt totally at sea. I was terribly frightened too that he might change his mind, discover my lack of education and accomplishments and cast me back to a lifetime of suburbia in Barnes, where I would surely have died an old maid. I was so grateful when the day arrived, my mother's lace dress, yellowed from the attic, adjusted to fit me.

We were married in Chelsea, with just my parents and Susan and a few chaps on Hamish's side. I don't remember the service – only Hamish's low voice as he spoke the vows and that the smell of the roses I was holding made me want to sneeze. We kissed on the steps outside and a photograph was taken, which I shall cherish.

Then, with barely a pause to celebrate, we were walking down the steps to a waiting car. Mother clung to me and I froze solid; she is always so stiff-upper-lip but, beside the grey face of Father,

I could tell that she will miss having someone else in the house. Father shook my hand and wished me well, and when he nodded, the coin-shaped bald patch on the top of his head made me want to weep for him. The Great War has a lot to answer for, I say. I had a sudden vision of a much younger man with a confident gait and a straight back sitting in our small square of garden, amusement etching his features as he filled in the crossword, throwing some remark to me with a smile. But, that day, he hunched in a too-small suit that smelled of mothballs. He cut such a tragic figure that I found myself, rather shamefully, wiggling away from him into the car where my husband was already waiting.

My husband. I really can't believe it even though I write the word. Hamish West. My husband. Oh, it is so thrilling! I have spent countless hours practising my new signature, a looping, rather theatrical flourish on the 'W' to befit someone of my social standing. Susan thinks it rather silly, but then she doesn't seem much to like any of the new developments in my life.

We took the non-stop *Flying Scotsman* to Edinburgh. Hamish told me it was so much better now that it could get all the way there in one go – something about the extra ton of coal capacity – but I couldn't take anything in, too busy admiring my hand with the new gold band catching the light, the smeared glass and wonderful countryside flashing past. What a big wide world! And I was off to live in it.

I blushed as Hamish reached across the table and took my hand. The gentleman across the aisle, only just returned from the on-board barber's shop, was nose-deep in a newspaper but I still felt terribly shy at the strange damp loveliness of Hamish's flesh on mine. It was so peculiar to be alone with him and I stayed awake as the day darkened and his head lolled to the side, his curls tickling the collar of his coat.

We were met by car at Edinburgh; Hamish wanted to get back to the estate without stopping over in a hotel. I couldn't make out anything in the dark and it felt desperately chilly, my thin coat no match for this northern wind. The driveway to the house threw me around horrendously and I fluttered apologies as I woke Hamish from another rest. Once we'd drawn up, with dry mouth and tired limbs, I stumbled out nervously.

It was enormous, and nothing like the fairy-tale castle I had conjured in my daydreams. In that moment I felt a chill wrap itself around my insides, icy fingers attaching themselves to every organ as I craned my neck backwards.

For a mad second, I wanted to scream, to step backwards into the automobile, beg the driver to take me away. This house, this place, was all wrong: I wanted to be anywhere – anywhere but here. I imagined my small room in Barnes with its comforting wallpaper and the soft light from the fire. Why had I ever thought to leave it?

My body wouldn't move. I stood rooted, unwilling, as Hamish barked impatient words from beneath the looming stone portico.

I was jolted out of the peculiar moment. It was down to the journey, to the nerves of the first night. This was my home now. I let out a laugh, high and quick – silly.

I stepped forward and the house, like an enormous black monster, swallowed me whole.

Inside was barely any warmer and our footsteps resounded in the tiled hallway, as if it was more than just Hamish and I stepping across its surface. The air seemed to stick to us as we moved, the musty smell entering my nostrils, making my nose twitch. Everywhere were closed doors, dark wood, portraits I couldn't make out in the shadows, but whose eyes I could feel on me, as if they all swivelled to watch us pass. A staircase bannister glinted real silver, freezing even through my gloved hand. The only one of its kind, Hamish told me as I snatched my palm away. I nodded, eyes like saucers, following him up and around. The darkness tripped me up as I stumbled on the top step – the darkness, I told myself firmly.

Our luggage had come on ahead and a suitcase stood waiting outside my bedroom. I had my own and Hamish's room was directly opposite. I didn't glimpse his room as he lit the gas lamp by my bed with a hiss. The wallpaper was busy with ivy that looked as real as if the outside had tangled through the walls.

'I will visit you in a while,' he said, making my heart leap into my mouth.

He left with a glance back and I lifted a hand as he closed the door behind him. Standing inert, I looked around, the lamp showing a room four times the size of my bedroom at home, furniture gobbled up by dark corners. A four-poster bed dominated the centre, initials, not ours, carved into the dark wooden headboard, its heavy drapes tied back on the poles. There was a step leading up to it, and I wasn't sure which side I should lie on when he returned.

What did one change into, or did one wait for one's husband to remove their clothes? I wished I knew, feeling utterly wretched that I would be a disappointment.

I did ask Susan about the expectations of the wedding night. It was all horrifyingly embarrassing, but I simply couldn't ask Mother and I felt so overcome with fear as to how to prepare. Susan's answers were brief and rather too focused on pollination to be useful. She didn't look me in the eye once and we never spoke of it again. A couple of years before, I had watched two foxes copulating in the garden under a full moon. They were circling each other and licking parts. The vixen made the most shocking sounds. But I wasn't sure humans would be much like foxes, and knew I'd be totally in thrall to Hamish.

I decided to keep my dress on and waited, perched on the edge of the bed, hands slippery with every distant cough or noise, imagining for a strange second the house inhaling and exhaling as

Chapter 12

AVA

They sat on a bench overlooking the river in Dumbarton, clutching takeaway coffees and not speaking a great deal. Gus was in Ava's lap, making her much too hot, but guilt meant he stayed there, rewarded with constant rubs of his head and mutterings of 'Who's a good boy?'

She had insisted on heading into Dumbarton. Memories of her mother outside that graveyard had fuelled her curiosity, reminding her why she had just put herself through that ordeal. The town was unremarkable. Once a centre for shipbuilding, it was now a commuter town for Glasgow: non-descript shops, a green, a town hall. She had felt sure she would recognise something. Now that she had shaken off Overtoun, she wished she could be left alone to explore.

'We should ask some locals about the bridge – see if anyone has any first-hand accounts,' Garry suggested. He threw his coffee cup in a nearby bin from a sitting position. He seemed more awkward with Ava and she felt guilty that he obviously blamed himself for what had *almost* happened.

Neil moved to stand at the rail that separated their small patch of grass from the river. Various boats idled in the water on the opposite bank, shifting reflections on their hulls. Orange and white buoys bobbed half-submerged in the water that sparkled silver in the sunshine. Ava hadn't drunk her coffee; caffeine wasn't good for babies but, because she wasn't ready to tell everyone at work she was pregnant, she had let Garry buy her one.

'Let's go,' she said. She got up, nudged Gus from her lap and threw her full cup away.

There weren't many people about, and most eyed the camera equipment with suspicion as Ava and Garry targeted passers-by. Gus trotted obediently by Ava's side. Two women approached, one unfathomably holding an umbrella despite the bright July sky and the other wheeling a tartan shopper crammed with groceries.

'Excuse me. Are you local? I wonder if you could help.' Ava fixed her most winning reporter smile in place.

'We both are. I own the B & B on West Street,' the lady with the shopper said with a twinkling smile in a lurid pink lipstick. 'Mary.'

'We're reporters. We wanted to ask locals more about Overtoun House?'

The smile dissolved and Mary seemed to recoil a fraction. Ava felt her skin tingle.

'Everyone knows Overtoun.' The woman with the umbrella spoke in a slow, careful voice, her eyes flicking quickly to Gus.

'We should get going, Jeanne,' Mary with the walker said. 'Overtoun isn't a news story.' She gave a firm nod to Ava as if that closed the matter.

'We're covering a story about the bridge,' Ava ploughed on.

Neither woman replied.

'We've heard reports that dogs have been known to jump off it, that they've died,' Ava said.

Mary bit her lip.

Jeanne said, 'Superstitious nonsense.' The words didn't match her nervous expression as she smoothed her iron-grey bob.

'Is it, though? Five hundred dogs in the last sixty years. Do locals have any thoughts as to why?'

A shadow crossed Mary's face. 'That's an exaggeration.'

'But *some* dogs *have* jumped,' Ava insisted.

'It's not news,' Jeanne huffed, 'and it's ghoulish. You should stay away. There's a sign there now that warns people. Locals know not to go up there.'

Mary touched her friend's arm. 'Come on, Jeanne,' she repeated.

'Why do people know not to go there? Because of the danger?' Ava asked.

'There's no danger.' Jeanne shuffled her feet and her voice dropped low as if somehow the house and bridge might hear her even from down in the town.

'We just don't want you sending a load of ghost hunters up here,' Mary interjected, a bright pink lipstick mark on her front tooth. 'My mum cleaned there when I was younger. It's just a house.'

'She cleaned there!' Ava said, eyes widening. 'So she went inside. I'd love to ask you more on camera?' Ava attempted.

'She barely mentioned it. It was a lifetime ago.' Mary moved her shopper from one hand to the other. 'Place is a wreck now. Has been for years.'

Ava could see that Mary was intent on leaving and knew she wouldn't get anything on camera. 'Do you think it's haunted?'

'Some people will believe anything,' Jeanne said, looking over at her friend.

'I heard that people call the bridge one of the *thin places*,' Ava added. 'A place where the worlds meet.'

Mary bristled. 'We really do need to get on.'

'Do you know anyone who has lost a dog up there?' Ava asked, curious as to why these two women, easily in their seventies, were so obviously afraid. What might they have seen or felt? Why didn't locals go up there?

For a second it looked like Jeanne was wavering, as if she might talk more. Ava could feel Neil and Garry waiting behind her.

And then the moment passed. Jeanne made her excuses, both women moving off. Mary checked over her shoulder to make sure Ava wasn't following before craning her neck to speak to her friend.

It only got worse from there. The footage they had would barely add a minute to the segment; the locals they stopped moved on quickly once they realised what they were being asked. The afternoon was disappearing and Garry's frustration mounted with the twentieth refusal to speak.

'It's like it's a bloody cult or something.'

Neil didn't respond, shy at the best of times. Ava didn't reply, remembering her own reaction to the house and bridge, feeling menace in the stones, the ground, lurking in the air. The memory stopped her talking too. Perhaps it was the power of the house itself?

Garry and Neil left soon after and Ava returned to her car. Gus settled in the back seat. She started the engine, glad to be leaving the place. The more she had heard, the more uncomfortable it made her. The house and bridge seemed to infect the whole town.

She drove back through the streets towards Glasgow, her mind filled with the day, the town taking on an even gloomier quality now the sun had gone. Trees obscured her view to the left, climbing higher. Somewhere within them she knew Overtoun lurked, and she shivered as she kept one eye on Gus in the rear-view mirror.

She was about to drive past when she saw it, tucked behind a row of shops, a small car park edged with the low stone wall of her memory, black iron railings enclosing the graveyard and a small lychgate through which she could see a narrow pathway to the church door. She pulled over in a hurry and someone honked at her from behind; she'd been lost in a memory from more than thirty years ago. She was so sure of it that she could almost see her mother's slim figure, hunched as she gazed through the railings.

This was the graveyard that had brought her to Dumbarton.

There was no one around as Ava stepped out of her car and moved, as if sleepwalking, towards the entrance. The tombstones were slanted, some in the shade of small trees, some crumbling, some moss covered, some well tended with the marble polished. She stared at the spot where she remembered a small semi-circle of mourners. Who had they been burying and why had her mother been there that day?

Her eyes were drawn upwards, something urging her to look. Forming a background to the scene was a thick, dark green line of trees and then the grey stone of Overtoun House, perched above the town, its windows like eyes looking down at it all and the silhouette of the towers pointing into the blue sky as if they were able to touch heaven.

A sudden series of barks made her whole body jerk. Gus, normally inert, had pushed his head out of the half-open window, barking frenziedly at her.

'I'm coming, boy, I'm sorry . . .' She turned back to the car. She could still feel the windows of the house watching her. *A thin place*. She turned on the ignition and, despite the heat in the car, shivered as she took a last look.

Chapter 13

AVA

The drive back to the studios was frustrating. Traffic and queues, wilting drivers leaning on their horns. As someone cut across her, a little too close and a little too fast, she swore out loud, her hands tight on the wheel. She glanced at Gus stretched out on the seat behind her. It had been reckless to bring him, her head filled with images of his compulsive run and his rigid body. Their beloved dog. What had she been thinking?

She barely stopped at her parents', dropping Gus back with a quick kiss of her father's cheek.

'Ava, come in,' he encouraged. 'Your mother's out at the hair-dresser's and we haven't caught up in a while now.'

The urge to stay was strong and sudden but she didn't want to admit where she'd been, that she'd headed to a strange town on the back of a distant memory. 'Sorry, Dad, I've got to turn this edit around quickly.' Her eyes slid from his face.

He tried to hide his disappointment and she felt a pang as he turned slowly, a hole showing at the elbow of his chequered jumper, and closed the door.

The newsroom was an utter contrast to the day she'd had: jaunty bright colours; the blue trim of the plastic tables; the glossy white-toothed photographs on the walls; a modern, bustling workplace full of chatter, the buzz of phones, bubbles from the water machine and fingers clacking on computers. She moved into the editing suite and pulled up the large swivel office chair, still warm from its last occupant.

Removing the SD card, she uploaded the footage, racing through it, trying to reduce the minutes they had captured into a short segment. Two clueless tourists in Dumbarton who'd never heard of the house or the bridge, their mouths moving at rapid speed, a man who had told them there were fairies in the grounds there, his wife pulling him away. There was Ava with Gus, some exterior shots and then the house. She paused. The Scottish Baronial manor loomed on the screen in front of her, filling it up. She stared at it, before moving to a shot of the bridge. Just a normal bridge, a wide walkway, thick stone walls. She remembered then the strange shimmering quality of the air as she stood on it, as if things were shifting just out of sight. On screen the bridge looked like any other, as if her memory was tricking her.

She felt unsettled, her recall already unreliable, *thin* like the air of the place. And yet when she put on her headphones, the hairs on her arms bristled to attention. Her body reacting to the sound.

She adjusted the headphones, listening to her introduction, cutting, adding background noise, still shots from the archives. She had been staring at the same twelve-second clip when she saw it behind herself – easily missed: in a third-floor window of the house, movement in the glass. She paused, leaned forward and strained her eyes, feeling her stomach plunge as she made out eyes, a mouth, the indistinct outline of a person. She blinked; the image blurred. Was it leaves reflected in the glass, moving in the breeze? Was it a face?

She moved to cut the clip and replace it with another shot, her heart thrumming in her chest. When someone tapped on the door of the suite, she pulled off the headphones, her palms sticky. 'Twenty more minutes!' she snapped.

The door opened and Claudia appeared silhouetted in the doorway just as Ava opened her mouth to say more. 'Hey. All OK?' Claudia said, her voice light. 'You look pissed off.'

Ava's head was spinning with Claudia's sudden appearance. 'Yeah, sorry, just . . .' For a moment, Ava wanted to ask her to take a look, tell her what she saw. 'Just on a tight turnaround.' Ava indicated the screen.

'This is why I only do stuff in the studio now,' Claudia said.

'Why are you back here anyway?' Ava asked, her eyes flicking back to the screen.

'Meeting.' Claudia rolled her eyes. 'Three-line whip.'

'Oh, right . . .' Ava's mind was still on the window.

'All alright?'

'Sorry, just tired.' She didn't want Claudia to see how rattled she really was.

'OK, well, let's catch up soon?' She lowered her voice. 'We need to celebrate your news.'

'Hmm?'

Claudia laughed and motioned to her stomach.

'Oh yeah.' Ava's response came a second too late, and Claudia's smooth brow puckered.

'I'll see you tomorrow? After the morning show.'

'Great.' Ava dredged up a smile.

The door clicked closed and Ava returned to the screen, unease rising, wishing for a moment that Claudia was still in the room. Neil had taken shots of the bridge from below, the soaring arches transporting her back there. Even in the safety of the studio, Ava felt threatened by the moving images. From the top of the bridge, he had filmed the drop to the rocks below. Ava's stomach lurched as she recalled peering into the gorge.

She watched again the blur that was Gus's determined run towards the edge, his hop onto the parapet. The horror on her own face as he passed her, the foot that pinned his trailing lead. Would he have dived over it? She put the headphones back on her head and rewound the footage, fiddling with the volume.

The crackle was unmistakeable. Her voice loud and disjointed and then disappearing into the roar of water that Neil had insisted would be alright. It was more than just water, though. She had been fifty feet above the gorge. As she strained to listen, she heard the disturbance, her voice lost. She saw lines leap erratically on the monitor in front of her as a low persistent hiss, like a television that had lost its aerial, interrupted the clip. And then, through the white noise, came another sound that chilled her blood.

She squeezed her eyes shut, plunged into something dreadful. Wishing she could block out what she could hear, fumbling for the volume once more. But it was too late. It had filled her head now. The high-pitched sound of a baby crying, one mewl that bled into the next, on and on, louder even than the distorted thunder of the water.

Ava pulled the headphones back, pushed herself away from the desk, her chest rising and falling as she felt the room darken around her. She needed to get out, needed the reassuring brightness of the newsroom, the normal noises of the day, not that unearthly sound.

She must have pulled the headphones from their jack as suddenly the small square room reverberated with the sounds, as if the river was about to burst through the wall in front of her, as if the rocks were around her. Then the high-pitched wail, like a terrible siren. The scream of a baby over it all.

For a second she imagined the flutter of something inside her own body, inside her womb – something she had yet to feel . . . She put a hand on her stomach, imagining the baby inside her as she stumbled from her chair, surrounded still by the cry that seemed to fill the room, fill her own head. Then it stopped as abruptly as it had begun.

Chapter 14

CONSTANCE

The doctor is coming to see me today and I am to say my leg hurts. It is very important that I say this. I touch the leg that is hurting. If I say it is, I can sleep in the bedroom with Mother. I really want to sleep in her bedroom with the green leaves on the walls. It is so nice in the bed with four poles. I lie on the soft pillows on one side of the bed but sometimes in the night Mother turns and her arm is right next to me so I can snuggle my face next to it and feel the tiny hairs on her arm tickle my cheek. Last time I didn't sleep for ages, almost all night, waiting for her to turn, trying to remember the shapes of the furniture in the dark for other days, the smell of Mother sleeping, the sound of water gurgling, owls outside, my head full of all the things.

The view from Mother's room is different too. It looks out over the walled garden and you can see the big cliff rocks called craigs making the house seem a hundred times smaller. When the sky goes a dark blue, they are completely black, a solid nothing that could suck us all inside. For a second it is like the green leaves in the bedroom are shifting and curling, reaching to wrap around me, to keep me close and stop me disappearing. I'm pleased when Mother pulls on the tasselled rope that draws the thick velvet curtains closed.

I have my breakfast on a tray as usual, but Mother waits as I eat, her head tipped to one side. My hand shakes as I lift the spoon to my mouth. I hope I am doing it right.

The porridge tastes different today. Sweeter. And I feel strong enough to put my different clothes on. I don't tell Mother that, though, as I like when she dresses me, feeling her warm breath on my cheek as she leans over me to button my blouse and help me put my arms in the sleeves of my cardigan. My heart skips when she appears with the shoes with buckles on, as I know I will be allowed upstairs in the house. They feel tight as I squeeze them on, but I don't mind. My heart beats faster at what lies ahead.

Mother frowns at me as I hop from one foot to another, my insides not hurting so much. When she lifts one eyebrow, I remember my leg and stop moving.

'How long has your leg been hurting?' she asks.

I rub it; it doesn't ache more than my other leg really and today they don't feel weak or wobble and there's no pain in my stomach that makes me want to be sick. 'More than a week,' I say, remembering what she told me and beaming at her.

The eyebrow is lifted higher and I fix my face again – no smile.

'And your other pains?' she asks.

I don't have to really think hard this time. 'I still hurt in my tummy on most days and feel dizzy and most days I am sick from my mouth.'

Mother nods once and I feel pleased that her eyebrows are normal and she looks happy. I know she'll talk to the doctor because she always does, but it's good if he asks me a question for me to explain it the right way.

'It's time, then.' She moves across to the door and I want to jump up and run straight there with my too-tight shoes and my heart leaping from my chest. But I move slowly, one hand on my leg like she showed me, and I see her nod again and I can't help smiling now – but she smiles back, and when she does I think it is just the two of us in the whole world and it is wonderful, and I'm going upstairs into the house, across the stripy tiles and into the smart drawing room with the peppermint walls and the babies that smile from the ceiling and the huge windows that show the sun all day and I'm going to spend the day with Mother and not be alone in my room any more looking at the diamond windows.

For more than a week, this leg, I repeat in my head because the doctor will come soon and I must get it right so I can stay upstairs all day and play and explore more rooms and then spend the whole night with Mother. And maybe, if I am really good, I won't have to go back to my room on my own any more.

The bliss of the door opening, the air changing as I step into the corridor, my shoes loud when I normally have bare feet. It is always colder, the air swirling around me in the house, not stuffed into my room with nowhere to go. Ahead is the big brown bear, taller than Mother. I stay close to her legs, afraid he's not really dead but only pretending.

I follow Mother into the drawing room and move slowly to the long sofa that's curved with no back and sit on it with my feet together, my shiny shoes squeezing me, and cross my hands in my lap waiting for the bell to sound in the hallway and the doctor to arrive. Mother is smoothing her hair in the mirror over the fireplace, her blue eyes bright, her movements quicker. *More than a week, this leg,* I repeat in my head as I rub at it.

The bell sounds in the hallway and Mother glances at me, nods again. It is time.

Chapter 15

AVA

She had returned to her desk with trembling legs, barely acknowledging another reporter moving past her into the editing suite she had just left.

The colours and sounds of the newsroom were muted as she lowered herself into her chair. For a moment she simply sat there. What had she heard? The insistent wail of that baby clouded her thoughts. She felt the strange darkness wash over her, the same sensation she had felt when she had stood on the edge of that bridge.

'Ava!' Garry was crossing the office towards her, a pen and paper in his hand. 'Ava, have you sent the piece to Alex? Ava?'

Ava felt herself returning to the room. 'I was about to email her, sorry. The footage we got, it's . . . the sound in places . . . it's . . . not right.' She licked her lips, feeling silly as she attempted to explain.

'Did Neil screw up?'

'No. No one screwed up.' Why didn't she tell him what she had heard? 'Even if I replaced the bits with voiceover, I'm not sure we have enough anyway – and we never did find a dog owner. I think I'd like to re-film one day . . .'

Garry's eyebrows drew together. 'We could just drop it. A dog hasn't jumped for a while and—'

'No.' The word came out sharper than Ava had intended. Something about the place had got under her skin. Despite her body almost instinctively wanting to arch back, she could feel a tug inside her. 'No, I want to go back there. I don't mind going on my own. I'll self-shoot and use some of the stuff from today . . .'

Garry shrugged. 'If you like.' He was always accommodating – the producer Ava most liked to work with. Claudia teased that he let her do whatever she wanted. Ava had always protested the fact. Perhaps Claudia had a point.

'Well, I'd better tell Alex to come up with something else, then.' Garry tapped the pen on his teeth.

'Great. Would you?' Ava was already packing up her bag and drifting towards the door. 'Thanks.'

She had bought herself time, storing the SD card in her top drawer to use at a later date. She shivered as she thought of returning to Overtoun by herself.

She didn't remember the drive home, her mind catching up with everything that had happened. The flat was immaculate. If Fraser was cleaning, he was definitely bored. The thought left her head as soon as she kicked off her shoes and slumped onto their pale grey sofa. Taking out her phone, she had a thought and then started to type. *Thin places . . . Celtic myths . . . fairy circles . . . jumping dogs . . .*

She didn't hear Fraser walk up the stairs and push open the door to their flat, but he called out and she glanced up, the sky outside now streaked with cloud.

He was laden with shopping bags and started pulling cupboard doors open and closed. 'Have you been back a while?'

'Hmm . . . what's that?' Ava was back to staring at the small text on her phone.

'Doesn't matter.' Fraser poked his head through the hatch between the two rooms. 'I thought I'd do a barbecue?'

'Hmm . . .'

'Thought I'd make that sauce.'

'Hmm . . .'

'The one your mum always makes.'

'Really?' Ava mumbled, not quite concentrating.

Fraser's voice was closer now. 'Yup, because I've always really fancied her . . .'

'Great.' Ava scrolled down her phone, opened up new windows and made random notes on a pad.

Fraser put his hands on her shoulders. 'Ava!'

She jumped, the phone slipping from her grip. 'Fraser, what the hell?'

He laughed as she fumbled to retrieve it. 'I knew you weren't listening. Angry Twitter rant? Who's done what?'

Ava had momentarily misplaced her sense of humour. 'I'm working.' She waved the phone at him.

'Alright.' The laughter fled from his eyes. 'Well, I was just saying I thought I'd make that barbecue sauce your mum makes.'

'Thanks.' Ava squirmed, her eyes still drifting back to the information on her phone. She didn't move from the sofa as Fraser moved past her to open the double doors to their small iron balcony. He lit a round barbecue they hardly ever used and soon smoke was billowing into the air, the charcoal smell filling the flat. She was barely aware of him moving back and forward from the balcony to the kitchen, lost in local council reports, historical houses, photographs of ancient stones, trying to make sense of her day.

The amateurish blog about Overtoun Bridge contained theories about why the dogs jumped: a strange scent; a terrifying frequency only dogs could hear; they were lured to it by the ghost of a White Lady; and, lastly, a brief mention of a *thin place*. What *were* those? She discovered more articles about thin places, nodding to herself as one writer described them as *mesmerising*.

That bridge.

The air, the atmosphere had been different. Other. She trembled as a little glimmer of how she had felt by the bridge returned to her.

'Could you grab the plates and things?' Fraser hollered sometime later, the sizzle and spit of the meat behind him. 'Ava?' She eventually dragged her eyes away. 'Plates!'

'Coming, coming. Sorry.' She went into the kitchen and loaded a tray with plates, cutlery, a cloth and carried the tray outside, itching to get back to her trawling for more information. A baby's cry made her start, the tray wobbling before she steadied it. She felt an icy chill in an instant. 'Do you hear that?'

Fraser looked around, confused. 'What?'

'The baby?'

'Oh yeah, think they've been trying to get the poor thing to sleep for a while.'

Ava felt her shoulders slump with the relief that the noise hadn't been in her head. Fraser had turned back to the barbecue, prodding at the meat, the delicious smell drawing her towards him. She encircled his body, solid and familiar. He put one hand on hers.

'Thanks for cooking,' she said into his T-shirt.

'That's alright.' His voice was gentle as he removed her hand. 'I need to check on the sauce.' Fraser rarely stayed annoyed with her for long, quick to forgive.

She started to wipe down the white wrought-iron table and chairs and lay the table for them, still thinking of the White Lady: a figure wandering those grounds. She shivered as she thought back to that desolate spot beneath the bridge.

The sun sank from the sky as they ate. It was ribboned with bluish purple hues and a couple of stars had emerged. Ava smeared a chunk of bread in the dark sauce on her plate. It was thick and tangy.

Fraser rested back in his chair. 'You seem quiet.'

She almost didn't say anything, was unsure how to put her disjointed thoughts into order. 'It was a weird day,' she said, finally.

'How so?' He chewed on a last mouthful, his eyes searching her face.

'It was a piece we were doing . . . on an estate in Dumbarton. Supposedly dogs died by suicide at a bridge there.'

'Suicide?' Fraser's fork hovered over his plate.

Ava nodded. 'They jump. There's a sign there warning people.'

'That sounds horrible.'

'It was.' A bolt of hatred for the place coursed through her and yet, underneath it, that familiar current that drew her further in. 'It was the creepiest place – a *thin* place. Have you ever heard of thin places?'

Fraser shook his head. His lips screwed up.

'I've read a bit more about them. It seems there are some places where two worlds sort of . . . *merge*.' Fraser's face twitched. She knew he was sceptical about anything supernatural. Perhaps her tone was serious enough for him not to interrupt her. 'So normally the real world and the eternal world are far apart but in thin places they cross over.'

Fraser moved his arms up and down. 'Woooh.'

Ava found a smile lodged somewhere inside her. 'It's just . . . this is going to sound odd, but I did feel something. Something I've never felt before.'

Fraser's arms dropped. 'OK.' He seemed to select his next words carefully. 'Maybe you felt things because you were expecting to be scared, your body already reacting. Like when it's dark and we see things in the shadows?'

Ava bit her lip. 'Maybe.' How could she explain what she had seen and heard? Out loud it would sound absurd. Crying babies . . . quivering air . . .

'It does sound like a weird day, though.'

She smiled weakly. 'Yeah.'

'Hey! I bought us ice lollies!' Fraser stood up. 'And then I thought we could talk about this weekend?'

Ava was already glancing back into their living room, wanting to resume her research. 'That's great,' she mumbled. 'Cool.'

Fraser went inside, taking their plates with him. Ava stared out at the sky, looking north in the direction of Dumbarton, flinching as a moth brushed her cheek. She stood up, her chair scraping. As she left their balcony, she heard the baby cry once more.

Chapter 16

AVA

Her mum had barely messaged her of late. Usually she sent something almost daily: animal GIFs, links to websites, photos of the watercolours she had painted in her weekly classes or pictures of Gus in over-sized sunglasses or a perky bow tie. Now the messages were perfunctory, polite. Ava had asked to meet her after her next midwife's appointment. She couldn't refuse that.

They met in a cafe around the corner from the GP surgery. It was a miserable day, unseasonably cold, and Ava scurried inside for protection from the north wind. The cafe was full of families with the same thought, kids on their holidays scribbling in colouring books as their parents looked on.

'Hi, Mum.' Ava felt a pang when she saw her. She had dressed in a navy top and cream cropped trousers. Only one eye was properly made-up, as if she had left in a hurry. It made Ava's hug that little bit tighter.

'I got us a table by that wall,' her mum said. 'I had to ask the girl to wipe it down.' Her voice sounded a little too high.

'I'll get the coffees,' Ava said. 'You sit down.'

Her mum didn't fuss or argue and Ava felt the unusual awkwardness between them. She returned carrying mugs and a slice of carrot cake with two forks.

'So how did it go at the doctor's? All alright?' Her mum's knees looked a little too high as she struggled in the bottle-green velvet armchair.

'Just about.' Ava removed her denim jacket and flung it over the back of her own. 'Pretty standard, I think. She told me about some prenatal vitamins I might want to take and I had a urine test. Everything was normal.' She didn't mention her blood pressure – a little high. Her mum would worry or attach some meaning to it and Ava couldn't face defending herself.

'Did Fraser not want to go with you?'

'He's staying with his dad.' She didn't reveal that she had also wanted the excuse to see her mum on her own, fix whatever it was that had broken down between them. Fraser had gone to spend a couple of nights with his dad in Perth. Fraser was more aware of a need to get up there to see him these days; since Fraser's mum died, his dad had struggled a bit. Fraser had messaged Ava to tell her he was sticking around an extra day or so. The washing machine had packed in and his dad had thought he could fix it. Fraser had ordered him another one and wanted to be in to sort the delivery and installation.

'He's a good boy.' Her mum's face softened as it always did when she spoke about him. *Butter wouldn't melt* . . . Ava often teased.

'He made your famous barbecue sauce the other night, Mum.'

Her mouth lifted. 'Did he?'

Ava took a sip of her decaf coffee, relieved that her mum seemed to be relaxing. 'We've got the twenty-week scan coming up in a few weeks. That's where they can tell the sex of the baby, apparently.' She picked up her fork and divided the slice of carrot cake into two pieces.

'Are you going to find out?'

'I'm not sure.'

'What does Fraser think?'

'I . . . You know, I'm not sure.' She took a bite of the carrot cake, feeling guilty that she hadn't asked him. She had barely thought about the pregnancy lately, or made the promised plans. 'There's still time to decide.' Was that to make herself feel better?

'Well, as long as the baby is healthy.'

For a second, their eyes met . . . the past conversations . . . the elephant in the room. Ava felt the cake sticking in her throat as she swallowed. She felt as if the noise in the cafe, the chatter of customers and the hiss from the coffee machine, was melting away.

'Look, Ava . . .' Her mum struggled to straighten in her chair. 'I know we haven't spoken a great deal in the last few weeks . . .'

'That's OK.' Ava's voice was small, as if she was a teenager again, wanting to avoid the black cloud that crossed her mum's face on occasion.

'No.' Her mum smoothed a loose tendril of hair. 'No, you had every right to ask me what you did and I haven't handled it very well.' She coughed; apologies were hard. 'But you're an adult now.'

'Mum, I've got grey hairs.' Ava laughed, trying to lighten the tense atmosphere. Her mum's half of the carrot cake was untouched. Ava took a sip of cooling coffee as her mum took a deep breath.

'The thing is, it's been so many years now. But when I think of that time, it still hurts.'

'I . . . I u-understand.'

Her mum's eyes had clouded with pain.

'Honestly, Mum, it's fine. It's none of my business.'

'No.' Her mum put her mug on the table. 'You were right. My history is yours, too. I've been selfish in the past for not wanting to talk about it.'

'It's OK, Mum. Really.' This was clearly difficult for her mum and a lifetime's habit was hard to break. But Ava *did* want to know. Awareness of becoming a mother herself had awakened a dormant desire to know more about her own.

'No, I should have told you.' Her mum's eyes were planted just over Ava's shoulder. Ava's whole body stilled, not wanting anything to interrupt. 'You know I was adopted when I was a baby . . .' She cleared her throat.

Ava pressed her lips together, desperate not to interrupt. She nodded.

Her mum smoothed her trousers. 'I didn't get on very well with my adoptive parents. My father was . . . difficult.' Her voice dropped. Some children at the next table squabbled over a cookie. Ava wanted to twist around, plead with them for silence. 'He had a temper . . .'

'I'm sorry.' Ava reached for her mother's hand, imagining her as a young child.

Her mum's eyes stared fixedly at the table. 'I was lonely, mostly. No brothers or sisters. I used to dream of having my own family.' Her smile was weak as she finally caught Ava's eye before averting hers again. 'I left when I was sixteen. I met your father a few years later. He was a bit older, very kind, very loving. He gave me such confidence. And I never saw my parents again. Never wanted to.' She had finished. Her eyes filming just slightly when Ava squeezed her hand. 'Anyway . . .' Her mum's face cleared and her shoulders straightened. 'It was selfish of me to keep my past to myself. I just wanted to reassure you that none of this should have anything at all to do with your baby.'

'I'm sorry, Mum.' Ava's throat felt thick with the emotion.

'It was a lifetime ago now.' Her mum's voice wobbled.

Ava tipped her head to one side. 'Thanks for telling me a little more.' She swallowed down more questions, could see that even this small step had been a momentous moment for her mum. 'I'm sorry you had a miserable time as a child.' Ava placed a hand on her now unmistakeable bulge, a reminder that she would soon be a mother too.

'The past is the past,' her mum intoned. And she took up a fork and took a bite of the carrot cake. 'And Fraser will be a great father. He's a loving boy.' She quickly stirred her cappuccino that was surely cold by now.

'I know.' Ava wanted to lighten the mood. 'As long as I don't mess it up.'

Her mum placed her teaspoon down, her eyebrows knitted together. 'What's that supposed to mean?'

'Nothing. Bad joke.' Ava waved a hand. 'I pissed him off the other night. I've been a bit distracted.'

'With the baby?'

Not wanting to shatter their fragile peace by mentioning her trip to Dumbarton, she nodded slowly. 'Yup . . . baby . . . work . . .' She didn't want to lie to her mum.

'Remember, a job is a job. You've been there years – you don't need to prove yourself.'

'I know. It's not that. It was just there was this place we went to. It got under my skin . . .' She wanted to confide in her mum, wanted to tell her more.

'How so?' Her mother's fork was poised over the plate.

'Well, it felt . . .' She half-closed her eyes, replaying the feel of the place all over again. Her body recoiled, as it always did when she thought of being on the bridge – then followed a compulsion to relive it. 'It felt like nowhere I've ever been before. It's just a bridge, but it's thought that dogs jump to their deaths from it.'

Her mum's face drained of colour. She had always adored animals, fussed over them like children, had never been without a dog. 'How horrible! Why would you want to cover that on a news programme?'

'Well, it's interesting. Why do they ju—'

'Oh my goodness!' Her mum's eyes widened, realisation dawning. 'Is that where you went with Gus?' Gus was spoiled rotten. With her empty nest, her mother doted on Gus like a beloved third child, sent photos of him on endless walks, videos of him rolling on his back demanding to be stroked, her laughter in the background. The family at the next table looked up as her voice carried. 'Did you take him there?'

Ava felt her toes curl. 'Well, I . . . I had him on the lead. Although . . .'

She knew she should tell her mum what had happened, but perhaps the eventual piece didn't need to include his sudden run. She felt things taking a turn for the worse. Her mum made no attempt at keeping her voice down and her fork clattered onto the plate. 'I can't believe you would endanger Gus like that!'

'Well, I didn't really believe any of it . . .' Ava tried to conjure up the feel of the place, sitting in this warm cafe miles away. A thin place. She *had* endangered Gus. She hung her head. 'But you're right, Mum. I'm sorry.'

Her mum nodded curtly and Ava wished she'd never mentioned it. Her mum might never have found out. Unlike the early days when Ava was a young reporter, her mum rarely watched the news. She didn't watch television at all, really, berating her dad for wasting his life sitting down. Maybe the final piece wouldn't have to include Gus. They talked a bit more – about Tommy, about the baby, about Fraser's new job in the autumn, about Dad and his garden – but the atmosphere had altered and soon her mum was reaching for her jacket.

'Do you have to go already?' Ava felt bereft. They had only just made up and now she had ruined it all.

'I should get back. I need to finish the book for the book club. I'm hosting tomorrow night. And I should check on your father.' Her mum was suddenly brisk and no-nonsense. 'And Gus,' she added, making Ava feel guilty all over again. 'I'm glad the appointment went well,' her mum said, relenting. 'And I hope you can spend some proper time with Fraser. Remember what's important, Ava. You're pregnant now. You've got a wonderful partner, a great job . . .'

'I will, Mum.'

'Good.' Her mum leaned down and gave her a quick hug. Then she turned and left and Ava sat alone, staring at the half-eaten carrot cake, her appetite gone.

Chapter 17

MARION

He reached for me in the morning, daylight edging the bottle-green curtains, his breath smelling sour. I so wanted to please, embarrassed by the pants and sounds that he made, my head thrust into the pillow. I never dreamed it would all be so frantic. I hope I shall learn to get used to it; it is a strange and novel feeling to feel bare flesh next to my own.

My cheeks flamed as I watched him stand and stretch, all of him on display, unapologetic.

Breakfast in the dining room. He was sure I could find my own way. I nodded.

The door clicked shut and still I remained there, staring up at the once-white ceiling, the corners streaked with yellowed damp. I stepped down gingerly from the bed, horrified to feel dried blood between my legs. I wondered if I should strip the sheets. I bit my lip, pulling back the heavy velvet of the curtains, a wash of greys and greens blurring through the glass.

I washed myself as best I could and the water in the bowl turned pink.

When I emerged from my room, I gasped. It seemed that the corridor went on forever, a hundred closed doors on either side, as if I could walk and never remember which room was mine. The threadbare blue runner seemed to absorb my footsteps and, with a shiver, I glanced over my shoulder, as if someone could be following me in the silence. All I could see were more closed doors and faded gaps on the walls hinting where paintings might have once hung.

I came across the shocking silver of the staircase suddenly, reflections bouncing off it, distorting the air, the walls, so that for a moment I was sure I would topple straight down it.

A clatter from downstairs made me jump, a hand on my chest, an admonishment to myself: it was the scale of the place, the lack of sleep, the strangeness of it all. I had no choice but to grip the silver, feeling its chill enter my skin, move through my veins, making me wrap my cardigan more tightly around myself as I descended.

The hallway was dominated at one end by an enormous brown bear, stuffed and watchful, its claws mid-scrabble in the air as I approached. I stifled a scream, as if it might step off its plinth and come at me, rearing up, its jaws clamping down on my neck, its claws tearing into my flesh. Holding my breath, I forced myself to put one foot in front of the other towards it.

The bear wasn't guarding a great deal: cabinets with a strange uneven scattering of figurines; a wooden pew; two golden chairs in desperate need of upholstering. The other end of the hallway seemed closer, as if the downstairs of the house didn't fit the upstairs. The tiles stopped abruptly, disappearing down a few steps to a heavy wooden door at the bottom, an inscription carved into the stone above it. *I will fear no evil, for you are with me.*

'Marion? Don't loiter.'

My head snapped back as if the bear had spoken. The voice was close, a doorway open to its right. I stepped inside, the high-ceilinged dining room with its blood-red walls making my grey, high-collared dress even duller, my whole self smaller.

'Good morning.' He smiled and lifted his curly head, the same rich brown as the bear.

I returned the smile, remembering my prince in the fairy-tale castle. How silly I was to be jumping at shadows.

Hamish sat at the end of a glossy mahogany table. Another place was set farther along. I felt my heels clack on the wooden floorboards, dust motes dancing in the shafts of light from the latticed windows. The grounds beyond looked exceedingly lush, the grass grown quite tall. How marvellous! I found myself drifting towards the window to take a better look.

He crunched his toast as I scuttled back to sit next to him.

We ate in silence, my body weary from lack of sleep and all the travel, but my mind racing with everything I had to explore. What plans might Hamish come up with now he was at home and able to show me the estate? I revelled in the sound of another person, the comfort of him biting, chewing, swallowing.

I was shocked when he told me he had business in Edinburgh and would be back the following day. The toast stuck in my throat. All I could do was nod.

'There's a woman who looks after the house, Miss Kae, who can answer your questions. She has a room beyond the kitchen. Many of the rooms are locked. We cannot afford the upkeep of a large part of the house.'

I thought of the sepia, scalloped-edged photograph, the romantic castle of my imaginings dissolving into dust.

I waved him off from the grey stone porch feeling a sudden urge to weep. The strange impenetrable line of the crags rose up to my right, a natural boundary. There was a verdant forest, fields and meadows hinting at long walks. How I wished I could walk down paths and see nature with my new husband. I would not mope, though; two days wasn't a terribly long time and we had a lifetime of each other ahead.

Miss Kae emerged as I moved back inside, feeling terribly small as I stared around the hallway. The bear was still frozen in his stance. Enormous oil portraits, Hamish's ancestors, looked down on me – a brief worry: had I already let him down? I searched their faces for answers. I could have asked him who they were, moved arm in arm around the estate as he told me the history. I shook my head, scolding myself for my self-pity. Miss Kae, a short woman in her forties with a left eye that drifted when she talked, showed me the other rooms that were open – faded furniture, gaps where things had once stood. She brought me tea on a tray with short-bread, crumbling and warm from the oven.

'You are kind,' I said. I wanted her to stay in the great room with me, unused as I was to the cavernous spaces I now inhabited.

'Mrs West liked this room,' she said, swallowing. She had known them, of course. I was reminded again that my husband was an orphan. I had never asked him how they had both died.

I unpacked, alarmed at how the light had failed so early that I had lost the chance to set foot outside. Trying to focus on my book, I twitched at the rustling of trees, clanking of ancient pipes, my own breathing. The sofas and armchairs with their plumped cushions seemed to be waiting for people to sit on them.

The sheets on my bed had been changed and they were cool to the touch, the bedspread thick and much needed. I brushed my hair for a hundred strokes, trying not to see monsters in the dark corners or hear insects chittering in the ivy that climbed my wall-paper, trying to silence my nerves. I pictured our own small house on Adams Street, my parents sleeping in the next-door room, the familiar street sounds outside – milk bottles, carts, bicycle bells. Getting up, alarmed at a blockage in my throat, I opened the stiff window and dusty flakes were dislodged onto the sill. Leaning out,

I could hear water running over rocks – and then the screech of an owl, startling me.

There was no moon, nothing for me to look up to or for Hamish to share with me. I willed him to return to his new bride as quickly as he could manage.

Chapter 18

AVA

'Thanks for meeting me here,' Pippa said.

'Is this some kind of test?' Ava joked as she drew up a chair. The red plastic table wobbled as she put down her bottle of Sprite. She scrubbed at the smears from the last occupant before she sat, and noticed a barely perceptible eye roll from her sister. 'It's gross,' Ava laughed, before chucking the balled-up tissue at her.

The soft play centre was sticky and loud. There were kids everywhere: shouting, appearing through holes, diving onto nets, chucking plastic balls at each other as they clambered over an enormous structure in primary colours.

Tommy had toddled away and Pippa was talking out of the corner of her mouth as she watched him navigate a small plastic tunnel, another child coming in the other direction. 'Sorry. He loves it, and I can't keep going to the park on the days I'm not working. I'm so bored of the park, and I didn't know it would be this busy.'

'Everyone's on holiday,' Ava pointed out.

'Yes, I thought they'd be away. Away on an actual holiday, not stuck in this sweat pit.'

Ava unscrewed the lid of her Sprite. 'Where's Liam?'

'Tommy!' Pippa called out suddenly. 'Play nicely.' Tommy dropped the ball he was holding and waddled off. 'Oh God, don't. Working on his PhD about molecules or stem cells or whatever. He's like 55,000 words in or something and might finish it in ten years or so – and that's probably a conservative estimate.'

Ava grimaced and raised her bottle. 'Commiserations.'

'I thought his long holidays would be great, but there's always some book to read or someone to interview or some way of getting out of, you know, actual parenting.'

It was a familiar rant and Ava felt sorry for her in that detached way because it was a world she didn't yet understand. She wondered then what Fraser would be like with their child. The thought, as ever, made her insides flutter.

'He came back the other day with a new camera – for interviews or something. For a blog he might do, he said. It looked expensive too.'

Ava smiled weakly. 'Well, at least he'll be a doctor.'

'Not a proper one,' Pippa scoffed. 'Anyway, enough . . . how's it all going?' Pippa still scanned the room. A tiny girl in a silver leotard and a pink tutu passed their table, clutching a Power Rangers football.

'Yeah, it's good.'

'Mum said you and her met up? We should sort a barbecue or something.'

'We should. What did Mum tell you?'

'Nothing much. Well . . .' Pippa twisted in her seat. 'Tommy! Let the other boy have a turn!' She turned back to Ava. 'Said you had a good scan, that everything was going well with the baby. It is, isn't it? You weren't just fobbing her off because she gets intense about everyone's health?'

'Well, I . . .' Ava paused at the appalled expression on Pippa's face. 'No, nothing too bad. My blood pressure was a tiny bit high, but I knew Mum would go on and on . . .'

Pippa relented. They both knew Mum could be over the top when it came to her involvement in their lives. 'Alright, but promise me you'll take it easy.'

'I will. What else did Mum say?'

'Not a lot. She was moaning about you taking Gus somewhere dangerous.'

'Oh for God's sa—' Ava bit her lip. It *had* been a risk. He had run for the parapet. If she hadn't managed to grab his lead . . . 'OK, it wasn't the most sensible thing I've ever done. But nothing happened. It was all OK.'

'Well, you know what she's like about Gus. She buys him actual steak for dinner. I don't think she buys Dad steak.'

Ava tried to laugh but, as ever, her mind seemed to be elsewhere, miles north of Glasgow.

'Where did you take him anyway?'

'Just somewhere for work. A bridge.'

'Doesn't sound dangerous.' Pippa's nose wrinkled, eyes as ever scanning for Tommy, who appeared to not have emerged from inside a plastic two-storey-high helter-skelter.

'Well, people claim that their dogs have jumped off it in the past. Jumped off it and died.'

Ava watched Pippa's shoulders drop a fraction as she spotted Tommy whooshing out of the helter-skelter, a wide smile on his face as he raced back to do it again. She turned again. 'God, no wonder Mum was cross.'

'Yeah.'

Pippa tipped her head to the side. 'So why do they jump?'

Ava shrugged. 'No one's really sure.' She felt something familiar building inside her. 'My cameraman said it was supposed to be a *thin place* – spiritual – a place where two worlds come together.'

Pippa's brow creased. 'And you believe that?'

Ava shifted in her seat, unable to dismiss the question, remembering her visceral reaction to the estate. She averted her eyes, probing her thoughts. 'It felt . . . like nowhere I'd ever been before.'

'Sounds like you're on one of your missions.' Pippa waved at Tommy through some netting.

'Not a mission exactly.' Ava bristled. 'I'm just interested.'

'You know you can get quite obsessive.' Pippa's voice was reasonable, as if the words didn't sting.

'I'm not.'

Pippa leaned forward as the whoops and screams threatened to drown her out. 'You only have to look at your flat.'

'What? That isn't being obsessive. That is being tidy.'

'It's just . . .' Pippa sat back in her chair, the red table wobbled again and Ava's Sprite made a puddle on the surface. 'You know what I mean.'

Ava fell silent, the muscles tight in her neck. 'Well, if you say so.' It was as if they were teenagers arguing again. She sipped at her drink and tried to quell the simmering annoyance at her sister. She wasn't obsessive, she just liked to get to the truth of things. Nearby, a baby in a pram started crying. It was quiet at first and then building . . . building . . . She pictured herself back in that dark editing suite, the primary colours of the soft play melting away as she recalled the fuzzy track, the jumping screen, the strange insistent wail. She wasn't obsessive. She just liked to get to the truth.

Chapter 19

CONSTANCE

I pick up my stick, which I sometimes forget. The doctor told me I had to use it to help my other leg get stronger. Mother doesn't like it when I walk without it. I don't mind too much but my leg doesn't ache any more than my other one so it is hard to remember sometimes. I'm allowed into the main house if I have my stick and Mother has started to unlock the door after breakfast. But I have to stay away from Annie because of the germs. Sometimes I see her crouched on the stairs rubbing the shiny bannisters and I want to talk to her so much I feel I might pop.

At first, I don't know where to begin, wishing there was another child I could play with. We could hide behind the furniture or the curtains and look for the other. I've seen children walking across the bridge on sunny days and I ache to join them. Once, the boy who is a little younger than me walked right past the window of my room! He was swept into a big spinning hug by Annie and then they left together over the bridge, his small hand in hers. I wonder about his life – whether he gets to be outside all the time, whether he gets pains that make him sick too, whether Annie is a loving mother, whether he'll be back the next day. I watch for him all the time in case he walks past again.

There are lots of very big, dark pictures on the walls of men in skirts with fluffy circles on them and hair down to their shoulders. They have been painted by someone, like when I saw the man who was painting the iron bench in the garden. I have asked Mother for paints. Christmas is coming and last year she gave me a china doll with a red velvet dress but this year I hope she'll give me paints so I can paint a big picture. One of the pictures at the end of the hallway is my favourite. I have to tip my head back to look at it. The man in the picture has reddish hair and is standing in a study with lots of books behind him. It isn't the man I love, but the dog that sits at his booted feet. The man's hand rests lightly on the dog's head. I imagine my hand stroking the fur. It is the look on the dog's face, like he will never leave the man's side. I stay cross-legged on the floor staring at that picture of the dog for hours.

Today, I am not interested in the painting because I have invented a new game. Mother has left me for a while to go and see about the garden. The apple trees are infested and she is worried; Mr Hughes is trying out a new pesticide. I have been allowed to stay crocheting in the drawing room. I'm not very good at crocheting. None of mine looks like Mother's. She can make the coloured threads turn into anything – a field of sheep . . . a steam train . . . a river sparkling in the sunshine.

I pretend the floor is a muddy bog that I will get sucked into and the cushions are the stepping stones that stop me falling in. I listen out very hard for Mother in case she comes back but I soon forget everything because I'm wobbling on one cushion and I'm definitely going to fall and I can almost feel the thick, wet mud all around me, covering my tight shoes, dirtying my white socks, until my whole body starts sinking, my legs trapped, the mud rising, so cold, up, up my neck so I lift my chin and strain everything but the mud gets higher until it pushes at my mouth and nose and then I can't breathe. The thought makes me wobble more and I try to stop my foot stepping on the swirled rug. I'm going to make it to the next cushion but then I see a face appear in the window opposite and I gasp and forget the game.

It's Mr Hughes, who's married to Annie. They used to live in the house with Mother, but now live in a cottage in Dumbarton with their son, who is the boy I see. Mother sent them to live in the cottage last year because of the bad germs. Mr Hughes has a big, wide hat that makes his face all dark but I can still see he has tanned skin and dark hair around his nose and mouth.

He's holding an enormous pair of scissors and, even though they look sharp, I find myself smiling right at him. I lift my hand and wave and he puts a hand on his hat, which I think means hello. I wonder if I can open the window and talk to him. My heart beats with the thought – I think it might burst right out of my chest. Maybe Mr Hughes will walk with me outside and tell me stories and be my friend? I jump off the cushion, wanting to search for how the big window opens because he is still there and I realise he is cutting some of the leaves from the roses under the window and I don't want him to move away and miss speaking to him.

'Please wait!' I call. There isn't a catch like the one on my window. He looks up again and I feel the same leaping in my chest. I wonder what his voice will sound like. I wonder if he is like the man in the book I just finished who gives his children rides on his back. My father got lost in the war. There's a painting of him and he looks younger than Mr Hughes. I wish I'd known him. Mother doesn't like me asking questions about him. I think she must miss him because he is dead because of Hitler.

I am halfway across the room to Mr Hughes when I remember. It's like ice in my stomach as I freeze, eyes wide. He looks at me, his bushy eyebrows meeting in the middle. I turn slowly to see my stick propped against the armchair on the other side of the room. He has seen me without it. Mother told me I must always use it.

I pause, not knowing what to do. I want to go to the window but I need my stick. I feel suddenly that I want to cry. By the time I've turned to fetch my stick he has moved away from the window.

I stare out at him as he disappears around the corner of the house with his big scissors. I'm not thinking good things any more, though. I'm worrying. Will he tell Mother? What will Mother do?

There is a noise above me and I rush around the room. Footsteps passing, doors opening and closing, feet on tiles, on stairs, over and above me. I strain to hear as I try to sit as still as possible. When she returns from upstairs, I have put all the cushions back and I'm bent over my crochet so she can't see my face. As I hear her footsteps behind me, there's pounding in my ears. Has he already said something to her? She puts a hand on my shoulder and normally I would lean into it but I jump as if her hand has burned me.

'You really do need to learn the bullion stitch,' she says.

I mumble a reply, praying that it will be alright, that Mr Hughes won't say anything to her. 'Could you teach me? I'd really like that.'

Chapter 20

AVA

Overtoun seemed familiar to her as she stepped out of the car. The grey towers and walls had found their way into her head, the atmosphere still menacing despite the smell of freshly mown grass and the sound of birds chattering in the tall pine trees. Straightening her loose cotton dress, she craned her neck upwards, taking in the scale of the place, wondering yet again at its strange pull.

The hot August sun was warm on her face and bare arms. In the last few days, she'd felt the tiny stirrings in her stomach more and more, butterfly flutters on her insides, often when she was lying awake at night, her thoughts elsewhere, as if they were nudging her to notice them. She picked up her camera bag and moved towards the house as a light breeze ruffled her fringe.

There was no one around as she skirted the house, shadows lying in thick stripes on the tarmac like long fingers reaching outwards. She shivered as she moved across them. There was no way she would have brought Gus again but she missed his presence, his chocolate eyes, his tentative nudges. She approached the bridge, feeling exposed, nerves already jangling as she placed one foot on the walkway.

Checking and rechecking her camera, she screwed it onto the tripod and began, her voice competing with the noise of the water below, a constant reminder that it was there, that it was waiting. She stumbled over the words and had to start again, a distant bark startling her, making her turn her head. There was no one around – just the house, ever watchful behind her, making her skin prickle with the feeling that there were eyes on her.

Unscrewing the camera, she moved slowly towards the worn parapet onto which Gus had jumped. As she looked down, wondering who else had stood there, it seemed as if the air itself became alive, the temperature plummeting as it lifted her fringe and swirled around her. She found her body tipping forward, an urge to place her hands on the stone, to peer down over the edge . . .

'You were here the other week,' a voice said.

Ava jumped, her hand shooting out to grip the stone of the bridge, freezing despite the heat of the day.

'Sorry, I didn't mean to sneak up on you.'

'It's OK.' Ava breathed with one hand on her chest as she turned to see a man in his late sixties or so, standing next to her tripod. 'I just . . . I was just . . .' She felt herself wrenched back to reality. 'I'm a journalist.' She stepped back down onto the walkway with him, tugging at the hem of her dress. 'I was filming a piece about the bridge.'

The man had thinning grey hair, copper at the roots, and a narrow face. He wore a creased, pale blue shirt. He glanced at the tripod. 'You are, are you?' He had a Glaswegian accent. 'Well, it's a free country.'

'Are you local?'

'Very.' The man smiled, eyes crinkling.

Ava felt her shoulders drop a fraction. The man wore a relaxed expression.

'I look after the house.' He stuck out a hand. 'Keven Hughes.'

'Oh.' Ava took it. 'Nice to meet you. I'm Ava Brent.'

'Nothing's happened at the bridge for a number of years now. So not sure there's a story. Old news.'

'Stuff like this is always interesting, though. Things out of the ordinary. I'd love to know more – about the house, the bridge?'

His weathered face seemed to be sizing her up. 'I've got a face for radio, I'm afraid.' He turned to leave.

'Could I come inside quickly?' Ava blurted. 'Not for long.'

His back stiffened before he turned. 'The house isn't really in a fit state for visitors.'

'I just need the loo.' She was desperate not to lose the opportunity.

He nodded. 'Aye, come on then.'

Their feet crunched on the loose stones as she moved into the shadow of the house. Her heart thumped as she neared the entrance porch, goosebumps breaking out on her skin. Keven held open a heavy, glass-panelled door. Beyond him was a hallway lined with coloured tiles. She hesitated, overwhelmed for a moment by an instinct to turn away. Nausea rolled through her, despite her being well into her second trimester now. It was as if her insides were repulsed by the prospect of entering.

Keven looked at her, a puzzled expression on his face. 'It's just inside,' he said.

Ava nodded slowly, the strange tug of the place overriding her caution, his mild manner melting any more resistance. She crossed the threshold.

'Excuse the mess,' Keven said as she followed him in. The light of the day was swallowed completely; the interior was tired and grey. 'I'm re-painting one of the rooms,' he explained. At the top of three steps she looked to her right, noticing an open doorway, a dust sheet just inside covered in dots of paint and abandoned brushes. The smell of turpentine competed with the musty scent of the house. As Ava glanced to her left her whole body jolted – an enormous stuffed brown bear with glazed eyes and patchy fur glared fiercely at her.

The corridor was draughty and gave the sense of being too big. There was a ripped-out fireplace, faded lines where pipes must have run along the wall, strange rectangular spaces where pictures must have once hung. The bear looked to be lording over nothing, just an almost empty glass cabinet thick with dust and a pathetic collection of china to defend.

Keven must have followed her gaze. 'Looters. They took what was left before I got the grant to renovate the house. Toilet's just there on the left.' He pointed to a doorway next to the bear and a small stack of chairs that needed to be upholstered. 'I'll be in here.'

Keven watched her turn left towards the bear before he disappeared into the room with the dust sheet. Once she was alone it was as if Keven had simply stepped off the earth, her footsteps echoing on the tiles, the bear's gaze following her as she opened the door she needed.

She didn't move inside, imagining herself becoming trapped in the small space, clawing at the walls of this neglected building. She backed away. She had wanted to come in to see what was inside the imposing grey house. It was a shell of its past self, spent and sad. It made her feel the same inside, an empty hole yawning deep within her. To her left she could make out the first step of a staircase, a surprising glint of silvery bannister enticing her to venture upstairs. Instead she padded backwards, away from the strange pull, the bear's eyes, the terrible loneliness of the place.

She could hear Keven moving around and a strange whir, like wheels on a wooden floor. Something he was using to paint, perhaps? For a second she sensed something scuttle just out of her vision, like claws on wood, and whipped her head around. A heavy wooden door stood at the other end of the corridor, down a few short steps. Anxious not to be caught snooping, she took a few steps forward, her feet careful on the tiles. She felt as if the corridor was narrowing, the door looming larger as she approached, pulsing with secrets. Ava imagined whispered words, a muffled giggle, a strange yap. A smell like rancid milk made her nose wrinkle as she moved softly closer. A wooden ramp rested upright against the wall. She couldn't drag her eyes away. The key in the lock seemed to quiver as she neared.

'Finished?' Keven's head appeared around the door, staring at her profile. She spun around, startled, the mood shattered by the word.

She could only nod a response.

For a second he opened his mouth as if to say more and then snapped it shut.

'Can I see?' she asked. She had noticed peppermint-green walls behind him, illuminated by large windows. The room was a relief when she moved over the threshold. A soaring painted ceiling lined with intricate plasterwork forced her eyes upwards. Fat cherubs playing among clouds. Keven was repainting a recess.

'You have to manage all this?' Ava looked round the huge room, a scattering of five or so rather shabby round tables circled by faded pink chintz chairs.

'I was thinking of opening it for afternoon teas,' he said.

Ava scanned the room, noticing the dark mould in the corners and the patches of threadbare carpet. Who would come here wanting a pleasant day out?

'Tourists might like it,' he said, as if she'd spoken out loud. 'When you're retired you need a project.'

'I'm sure you'll make it look lovely,' she said, trying to fake enthusiasm.

'And the house has got an interesting history. It was supposedly modelled on Balmoral. You could put that in your bit.'

Ava nodded. She had unearthed that already. 'Our piece will focus more on the supernatural, I suppose.'

'Of course it will.' Keven waved a dismissive hand. 'Don't all old houses come with a ghost or two?' He was clearly amused.

'Who's the ghost meant to be?'

Keven gave a small shrug. 'The Internet'll tell you Lady West – otherwise known as the White Lady. Came here after the First World War. English. She wanders the estate, supposedly.'

'You've never seen her?'

Did he hesitate a fraction or did she imagine it? 'Aye, I've never seen her. And I've managed the place for years now. And I used to come up here with my mum. She's dead now.'

'I'm sorry.'

'Long time ago, now,' he said, yet his face still twisted with pain. 'But I suppose, even at my age, you miss your mum. And my dad, he doesn't know much these days but he knows he still misses her.'

'I'm sorry about that, too.'

Keven shrugged. 'I'm always a bit down after visiting him. He's in his nineties now – care home down in Dumbarton. They're looking after him well. You got kids?' His tone suggested he was keen to change the subject.

Ava couldn't help the warm flush as she nodded. 'About to.' She placed a hand on her stomach.

'Congratulations.' His beaming smile made her feel lighter.

'Thanks.' She felt a flicker of shame that she had barely thought about her pregnancy these last few weeks. She recalled the terse silence from Fraser the night before when he'd asked her about birth classes. He wanted to book them early so they wouldn't clash with school commitments. She had fobbed him off, staring at a screen, numerous windows open: old photographs, reports on long-nosed dogs, Celtic myths. He had walked off with a muttered reply.

Keven moved back towards the door. 'Shall I see you out?'

'Did Lady West have any children?' Ava tried to keep her voice level though her heart thudded erratically.

Keven's mouth turned down. 'She did. A girl. A very sickly child.' For a moment the old man's face looked stricken. 'A terrible business. That's why many say Lady West did it.'

Ava swallowed, her mouth dry. 'Why she did what?'

'Why she jumped,' Keven said, his eyebrows drawn together. Ava felt her stomach lurch.

Keven bent to move a brush near the edge of the dust sheet. 'It was more than sixty years ago, now. Ancient history.' He straightened up. 'Best not to stir things up in my opinion . . . are you from Glasgow, then?'

'Yes, yes,' Ava responded, feeling her window of questioning dissolving. 'Is that why the dogs jump, do you think?'

'There hasn't been a dog jump in years.' Keven dismissed it all with a wave of his hand. 'Locals just enjoy riling each other up about the place. It would be a welcome change to have some positive stories, if you have to do something,' he added, a note of hope in his voice. 'Did you know the garden was designed by Edward Kemp?'

Ava let him continue, but out of the corner of her eye she could just see the top of the bridge. Behind these walls she couldn't hear the water. She thought of the child. A sickly child. She thought of a baby's insistent cries. And the woman who wandered the estate.

They say that was why she jumped.

Chapter 21

MARION

Hamish is not often at home. Work takes him to London. But I must not complain too bitterly. As Mother has advised in her letters, I am a wife now and must put the needs of my husband first. I think of Father in our darkened living room, the ashtray spilling over, the work she takes in, despite her arthritis, to make sure the bills are paid.

When Hamish is home it is wonderful, the gloomy grey stone walls touched by magic. Miss Kae has hinted that the house has made him sad, that he will be pleased to have a wife in it, a future now after all the tragedy. I try my very best to be cheerful, to arrange things well. Flowers in vases in the rooms we occupy, lavender sprigs on his pillow, polished surfaces and smiles.

I crave his touch, a hand on my shoulder as he walks by, an arm around me as we stroll through the grounds. These things don't happen often, but when they do I feel such a lightness in my soul. The nights are easier now. I undress, I lie in the bed, pull the bedclothes over me and wait for him. He appears, drawing back the covers so that goosebumps cover my skin from the cold air and the shock of him. He has shown me what I can do to please him and I try my best.

I want him to stay afterwards. I want to rest my head on his chest, on the carpet of wiry dark hair. I want to hear the beat of his heart and fall asleep to it.

Stay, my love. He doesn't hear it.

He doesn't stay. He gets up, replaces his nightshirt, complains of the cold, pads back to the room across the hall. The door clicks closed and I lie, eyes open, unable to sleep, twitching with my loneliness, rolling over to breathe in the smell of him, pretending he is still there.

He has been gone for more than two weeks now. I move outside, the house watching me as I wander the estate, the hooded windows like eyebrows lifted. Summer has turned to autumn, the trees a riot of oranges and reds, leaves filling up the gurgling streams. I take care on my walks, shoes slipping as I step over tree roots and uneven ground. I descend into a ravine of rocks and leaves, looking back at the house watching me like a concerned mother. The air smells of bonfire smoke and damp. Mud sticks to the hem of my skirt, a sticky layer over my boots.

I return when the light touches the tops of the trees and I know I need to get back, muscles straining, skin damp, skirting puddles on the road. This side of the house seems always in darkness, the thick stone bridge between me and it. My pulse quickens as I approach, as I step onto the rough gravel, drawn to the far parapet. I peer over the edge, the water roaring in my ears. It is a long way to fall and for a second I feel breathless with the thought of it.

I received a letter from him this morning telling me he will be another week more. My shoulders droop and I return to my bedroom, to a book I keep picking up and putting down.

I miss simple things. My mother and I standing at the butler's sink, staring out at the familiar patch of grass, washing hanging on a line as we passed teacups and saucers to be washed and dried. Leaving the house, basket over my arm, to the shops a short walk away: the butcher for a pie, the grocer for potatoes, the tobacconist's for Father's cigarettes, talks with Susan, a walk in the park, stopping on a bench, tilting my face to the sun, people passing.

Here you cannot step outside and see people; you need to navigate the long walk down into Dumbarton, the road pockmarked with deep puddles, wetting the bottom of my dress, stones digging into my boots. No passing traffic, just an occasional rambler. The motorcar is kept in Edinburgh, not that I would ever dare to drive such a vehicle.

I rest back on my pillows, stare at the heavy curtains of my bed. I hear a noise and frown; Miss Kae dusting in the hallway, perhaps, or even a noise I have simply conjured. Sometimes I believe my own mind tries to make-believe I am not lying here alone. I lay a hand on my stomach. My energy is depleted. Perhaps today I will not dress or go downstairs. I stare at the ivy that roams over the walls and imagine it reaching its tendrils into the room and stroking me before rolling me up and smothering me.

Chapter 22

AVA

Ava barely remembered the drive home, her head still back in Overtoun House.

That's why she jumped.

Standing on the parapet, that crackle in the air, the feeling as she looked over the edge into the water below.

Fraser was waiting for her as she arrived home, an expectant smile on his face. 'I thought we could go to the cinema tonight?' He was in his sunny spot on the balcony, an open book abandoned.

'Good idea,' Ava said, relieved to be forgiven for working that weekend. 'I'm just going to change into something else. I'm boiling.' She needed a few moments to return to the present.

'Notice anything?' he called as she walked down the narrow corridor.

She looked around at their small bedroom; it all looked the same: the king-sized bed made neatly, the grey and pink throw tucked in; both bedside tables tidy; clean glasses; a neat stack of books; a white wicker chair in the corner supporting a pile of laundered clothes.

'You ironed?' she called out.

Fraser appeared in the doorway. 'Not here.' He held out a hand to lead her into the small room next door that had always acted as an office.

She had walked straight past it and not noticed. The door was propped open with two bursting black bin bags. The room had been packed away, boxes filled with files and books, a desk dismantled and propped against the wall, barely used gym equipment piled up.

'Oh!' Ava turned to him.

He shrugged, looking around the small space. 'I'll keep the files and things at school and I've made a space for the cot, and a changing table could go here.'

A changing table. She hadn't thought about a changing table.

'I asked Pippa for a list of what we needed. She emailed me. It was . . . thorough.' He laughed.

'It's great!' Ava returned to the present as she stared around. It must have taken him all day. 'Thank you.' She gave him a hug, reminding herself of what was important. She had to concentrate on their burgeoning family, stop disappearing into the past.

And yet in the cinema, in the dark, she couldn't concentrate on the storyline. Sitting stiffly in her chair as the movie blasted on the screen, the sound all around her, vibrating through her, she found herself returning to the darkened corridor, the locked door, the feel of the air standing on the bridge. She couldn't taste the popcorn that Fraser passed her as she imagined once more peering over the edge.

That was why she jumped.

Was that why the bridge had such a nasty feel? Had others jumped from that height? Why did dogs feel lured to its edge? What would have happened to her if Keven hadn't appeared? She gripped the armrests, her teeth grinding as her brain leaped from one thought to the next, as if she was physically restraining herself even now.

'You OK?' Fraser looped his arm around her shoulder as they returned to the lobby, the smell of hot dogs, popcorn and grease butting into them.

She nodded, not trusting herself to speak. She hadn't told him about her day; the very word *Overtoun* now seemed to make him bristle. She felt herself pulled deeper into the story, startled by Keven's admission that there had been a child. Was that why she'd heard a baby? Had the baby grown up to be that sickly girl?

She felt removed from her surroundings as they left the cinema, blinking as Fraser asked her what she thought about the film. As he shared his own opinions, she made sounds of agreement, all the while distracted by other thoughts. They moved across an almost empty car park, Fraser ducking into the driver's seat as she opened the door. Her hand paused on the handle as the same prickling sensation she had felt on the bridge itself returned. She twisted to look over her shoulder, convinced that someone was watching. There was no one there. A row of cars but no people.

The next morning, she woke knowing where she needed to go.

Fraser wanted to join some of their friends for a pub lunch. 'We haven't really seen anyone since the news got out,' he said, his blue eyes on her.

'It's just that . . . if I don't do this now, I know I'll be sent out on another job tomorrow . . .'

'Is this going to be like Kenny Watson?' Fraser asked.

This was another story from five years or so before. A shop owner had called the police after a break-in. Kenny, a black man, had been arrested outside and had later died in police custody. She had talked to officers off the record. She had interviewed ex-police about the officers involved. Her dogged coverage, her insistence that his murder had been covered up, ensured the story remained in the local consciousness. Ava had become obsessed, barely sleeping, dreaming of the story, working all weekends, determined to help the family see justice. She had failed. She winced as Fraser reminded her.

'No. This is different.' How could she explain why this story had such a hold on her? 'If I leave now, I could probably join you all mid-afternoon.'

Fraser just shrugged.

'I really will race.' She felt guilty as she kissed him goodbye. And his cheek was stiff.

She had exhausted the Internet for information on the house. The same websites gave her acreage, tree species, discussed the landscaped gardens, the architecture. She could have given a presentation on the intricacies of Scottish Baronial mansions. But what made that bridge so special? It wasn't the masonry, the design or even the terrifying stone gargoyles that leered, almost leaping themselves from the stone to the river below.

She had stared at photographs of it taken from every angle. The previous night she had stayed up discovering more news stories, interviews over the years and tragedies, some avoidable, that plagued the area: owners of dogs who had jumped; a teenager who had toppled from a bank in the ravine, the ground giving way from under her; a local man found miles from where he was meant to be, dead, his shotgun beside him. She felt tugged back there with every story as the mystery deepened. The feeling when she thought of it was something she struggled to explain: dark undercurrents that swirled, the haunting sound of white noise, the insistent cry of a baby.

The drive to Dumbarton flashed by and she parked in a hurry, the back of her car at a slight angle. She scoured the high street for locals of a certain age, needing to know more about the child that Keven had mentioned, as if spurred on by the memory of that cry. No one knew about a child. No one wanted to talk. Hours passed with unreliable snippets and nothing else. *The woman had lived alone. I heard she jumped . . . I heard she was pushed by a man who knew her . . . I heard she's the ghost . . . No one goes there. No one likes to.*

Finally, bone-tired, Ava returned to her car, her spirits temporarily lifting as she read the sign for a nearby B & B. Her pace quickened as she approached, her tiredness evaporating as she opened the low picket gate and turned up the short path to the little porch flanked by pots of lavender. *Temporarily closed*, a sellotaped note on the front door said. *Family matter. Thank you for your understanding.* Ava squeezed her fists in frustration, wanting to scream out loud. Wearily, she turned and headed back to her car, out of ideas, just a wasted few hours to show for herself.

One of the thin places, she thought as she left the town, passing beneath the shadow of the house. Fraser's pub lunch was long over. She had missed it and she had discovered nothing more about Overtoun; her questions remained unanswered. What kind of things happened when this world brushed up against another? And why did she feel so compelled to discover that for herself?

Chapter 23

CONSTANCE

My wheelchair is folded by the door. Mother prefers it to my stick. The townsfolk raised money for it. I haven't wanted to leave my room for days now. Mother insists on carrying me out sometimes, resting me in the wheelchair that she has opened at the top of the small flight of stairs. The bear watches me. I stare at his strong legs, thick and powerful, as I tuck mine underneath me and let her wheel me along, listening to the whir of the wheels on the tiles.

When she leaves me in it in the house, I feel afraid. The hair stands on my neck and arms. It's always cold but now it seems as if the air is whipped up, carrying strange noises that rush round me – make me jump. As if the house is alive somehow, waking the moment I'm alone. As if it wants me back in my room or gone completely, to be left alone with her.

The big green room doesn't feel as nice any more. I notice the patches on the walls, the faded marks on the floor, the empty space with no people, no voices, no one to play with. The babies on the ceiling seem to flutter above me laughing with each other out of my reach. How I wish Mother would have a baby, a sister or a brother for me.

I sit in my chair, always too cold, and listen to the distant sounds of pans clashing, footsteps, a voice. I see Mr Hughes working in the garden. I imagine what his voice would sound like if he spoke. I'd ask him stories about his son, about the war that he was in and whether my daddy definitely got lost in it.

Today Mother leaves when I say I will stay here in my room. I sit kneeling up on my wheelchair that I have rolled to the window. There are tiny red circles on my knees where they press into the canvas. I watch walkers cross the bridge. I have to be careful to get down if she returns. I leave a book on the floor so that she will see I was just reading.

The weather is warmer now, my room stuffed with it, the days longer, and people walk early and late. I love to see them, to imagine their lives. They are so alive, so healthy. I hold my hand up to the glass, press my palm against it and wish I was one of them.

I have had my wheelchair for a year now. Mother took me back to the hospital in Glasgow when the doctor was worried my legs were getting worse. Mother told him that I was spending longer in bed, feeling more pain when I walked. He spoke to her about 'muscular atrophy' – from the polio I had when I was little. He spent longer with me. He liked Mother's shortbread, warm from the oven. They talked over me as I sat in the room. He thinks she does so much. A good Christian lady.

She has a stack of medical books filled with strange diagrams and long words that she told me are Latin. I am not to mention the books to the doctor. Mother says it is better if she speaks to him because she can explain things better so I can get help. She's right. Some days I just hurt everywhere and I can't imagine not being like this.

When the doctor comes, she has a list ready of some of the things wrong with me and his thick dark eyebrows with grey strands poking out pull together into a frown as he tells her that she was right to request a home visit, that I am a 'conundrum'. He is rewarded with her widest smile, her chin tilted higher as she offers him more tea, or a whisky before he leaves. She is a version of Mother I am not used to – her voice softer, lighter like one of the fairies in my books, flitting around the room as he taps and listens with his cold stethoscope and talks about more tests. I see Mother's eyes flash behind him. It will mean another hospital stay, a long recovery.

She is such a good mother, the doctor says. I am lucky to have her. Lucky to have someone dedicated to my care. I nod; I know I am. If Mother wasn't here, there would be nobody and that thought opens up something so black inside me it takes my breath away.

I have days where I can't get out of bed. I still wear the clothes I wore two summers ago. My hair is thinner now and Mother has made a cloth covering for me to wear. I think I need the chair. Sometimes, on days where I am not sick from my mouth and I feel strong, I walk up and down the room, kick my legs in circles on the bed. Once, Annie came to the door, drawn by the noise. 'Is that you?' Her voice was a whisper. I become a statue, waited until she moved away. Mother would be angry. My legs are weak and I mustn't wear down the bones or I will never be able to stand let alone walk again.

Today is not one of those days. I have been bent over the porcelain chamber pot with the purple flowers painted on the rim as I am sick from my mouth. My breakfast reappears in burning chunks that make my mouth sour. I touch a tooth with my tongue and the pain makes me cry out. It hurt last week and I told Mother, opening my mouth so she could see. Peering down, she quickly stepped back, eyes wide, hand over her mouth, nose wrinkled by the stench of me. All the vomit is rotting my teeth, the doctor says. I have new adult teeth but I have already lost one in the side so my tongue can slide into the space and tickle my gum. The tooth that still hurts is near the back. I don't want to lose that one too.

I hear Mother's footsteps and use all my energy to sit back down in my chair and lift my book. She appears and I quickly turn the book the right way up, feeling dizzy with all the movement. I don't say anything as she enters, hoping she doesn't say anything about being so close to the window. She doesn't like it. She once told me she might move me to the other side of the house and the thought of leaving my room made everything tilt. The stain in the shape of France, the way the room is always warm, the smell of porridge, the shelf of books, the swirls in the wood that look like eyes. And mostly not seeing the corner of the bridge, the trickle of walkers moving by, made me want to weep.

I look up from the book and see her mouth is pressed together.

'Shall I comb your hair?' she suggests and I agree, hoping she'll stay a while.

The nodding makes my tooth hurt again and for a second the room spins. The picture of the mountain looks blurry and I feel my insides clench. There is nothing left and the feeling passes as she wheels me across to the small table in the corner.

I meet her eyes in the mirror and smile at her, the gap in my teeth obvious when I do. When she draws the comb through my hair, my scalp hurts but I just smile again, wanting her to talk, to keep touching me.

'I think it will rain,' she says, and I imagine the sparkles on the stone of the bridge, the way the raindrops make the gutter rattle against the wall. I can't remember what rain feels like, water dropping onto my head. Would it hurt? I want to feel the rain, want to be outside, closer to the smells that seem to rise like steam when it does.

If I had a dog, I could walk it. If I had a dog, I could go outside.

I squeeze my mouth closed in case I ruin things by asking. I asked her last week, and the week before and the answer has always been the same. I have tried.

I wouldn't have to leave my chair. I would teach the dog to walk next to it, to fetch sticks, to stay at my feet. A playmate. My whole body aches to feel its soft, furry body in my arms. I dream about this so much, I sometimes wake and imagine it is true.

I can't help it. I ask again. 'Please . . .' I know what the answer will be before the words have left my mouth.

Her hand is frozen over me, the comb like a knife about to fall. Today feels different. There is the smallest pause before she bites her lip and says no.

'I'll be good. I'll stay in my chair. I'll wear the scarf so I don't breathe in the bad germs.'

No again. I am too weak. A dog would exhaust me. I am not well. Not like other children. She has to do so much for me. The people in the town have sent her a basket of fruit, a card. She shows me the words inside.

For a wonderful mother. In our thoughts.

Chapter 24

AVA

She was late back to work from her lunch hour, flying into the newsroom, aware of Garry swivelling in her chair and Neil next to him fiddling with his bag strap.

'Sorry, sorry, sorry . . .'

In between other jobs, and during lunch breaks, she had spent the last few weeks in the library, scouring old news reports for any mention of Overtoun Bridge, Lady West or a child and poring over anything on thin places. She dumped a pile of books on her desk, things she was planning to take a look at that night. Fraser was away, had rushed back to see his dad, who had burned himself cooking a shepherd's pie a few days before. He hadn't seen a doctor and his finger had got worse. He hadn't told Fraser either but a local woman who'd been close to Fraser's mum had phoned him.

'I've tried to get the stubborn man to the hospital but there's no telling him,' she'd said.

Fraser had left that morning. 'Not that you'll notice,' he'd said. He tried to keep his voice light but the hurt leaked through.

'Ava!' Garry grinned, reaching towards the notepad from her desk. 'We were about to leave you a note . . .'

'Garry, you know the piece that went out?' Ava began. 'On Overtoun?' In the end she had only produced a short, generic piece to camera. 'I think there's more there, potential for a follow-up . . .'

'Well . . .' Garry stretched his arms behind his head. 'Not today. That's what we were about to tell you. We're being sent to some haunted house in East Street – a poltergeist. We've become the resident ghost hunters.'

Neil stared at her as she removed her jacket. She looked down, realising that her bump was clearly on show in a top that had ridden up. He coughed and looked away when he noticed her panicked expression. She tugged her top down and the loose cotton covered her straining waistline. She wasn't ready to share the news at work yet.

Crossing her arms, she hoped Garry hadn't noticed.

'Ava – what do you think? Up your street?' Garry waited with an amused expression on his face.

'Sorry, sorry, that's good. Ghosts . . . Speaking of which, what do you think about Overtoun?'

Garry gave her a blank look.

'The dog bridge I was just talking about?'

'Ah.' His expression was amused, his mouth twitching. 'What about it?'

'I want to get back up there. We put that small piece out but I think we should go back, dig deeper.'

Garry ran a hand through his hair. 'I'm not sure, Ava. We haven't really got time to keep chasing rumours . . .'

'Honestly, Garry, you know I wouldn't ask like this if I didn't think there was something. And the manager's nice – it would be no problem, I'm sure, to sniff about a bit more . . .'

'Maybe. And if a dog jumps or something actually *happens* then fine. Today, though, let's go to the actual job we're meant to be doing, OK?'

'OK.' Ava remembered to smile. She would persuade him.

Garry moved away. 'I'll just get my bag.'

'I'll go back there,' Neil whispered urgently. 'I've got a drone.' His face blushed crimson. 'We could get some good aerial footage and you could do what you do best – talk to people.'

Ava looked up at him. 'Really?'

His eyes slid from her face to the floor as he nodded.

'That would be great,' Ava whispered. 'Thanks, Neil. I'll message you a good time.'

'Neil!' Garry called from across the room. 'Sign out the camera, OK?'

Neil mumbled something and then pushed away from the desk.

Ava opened her top drawer to look for the spare make-up she kept, wanting another pressed powder to take to the job. She was surprised to see an envelope addressed to her. She reached for it. She rarely got post other than junk circulars or local newsletters. The odd letter appeared, mostly from discontented pensioners wanting to know why they paid their TV licence or eager to correct her pronunciation. This looked to fall into that bracket.

It was flouncier than most: a flourish on the right-hand leg of the large 'A', flicking up flamboyantly. Disconcertingly, the envelope had been hand delivered. She opened it up, eyes widening as she read the few words on the single sheet inside: *You are being watched.* She turned over the sheet . . . blank. She checked the envelope but nothing else was inside. When she looked up at last, the office seemed the same: the balcony held a steady stream of people; the monitors all showed the same show on their channel, the latest news headlines on a ticker tape below. She folded the note back inside, feeling an ominous lurch. Claudia sometimes mentioned the odd strange letter; once she'd been sent her face stuck on the photo of another woman's naked body. There were some oddballs out there.

'Ava!'

She started at her name. Garry stood waiting at the door, eyebrows raised. She stuffed the letter back in her top drawer. 'Coming!'

The afternoon dragged on. Ava thought of the books she itched to get back to, a night ahead where she could fully immerse herself in the story that dominated every waking thought. She wanted this assignment finished quickly. There was no poltergeist – no story really, just a man in a string vest with a very cluttered living room. The filming made for slow going as Neil played around with different shots of the house and then their interviewee kept leaping up when he said he saw something move and Ava had to constantly stop-start. Even Garry, who was rarely impatient, grew more tight-lipped each time he had to tell Neil to start filming again.

'Come on . . .' Ava muttered to herself.

They broke for a bit to set up another shot. Neil brought her a coffee. 'It's decaffeinated,' he said, making Garry look up and frown.

Flustered, Ava thanked him.

'So do you want to be around while we get some spooky-sounding noises, Ava?' Garry said. 'Footsteps . . . moaning – that kind of thing?' He waggled his eyebrows comically.

'Actually – if it's alright – I was hoping to get home early,' she said quickly. 'I can edit it later if you send me the footage?'

Garry gave her a lingering look. 'Alright,' he said eventually.

'Thanks.' Ava scooped up her things.

'See you soon, Ava.' Neil kept his voice low as she passed him. 'Garry? If it's alright, I've got another job to get to . . .'

She turned back around and both men were watching her leave.

Her car was stuffy from the hot weather. Sliding the window down, she rested her head back on the seat, aware of the bag with the books piled inside. As she wound her way around the streets of Glasgow, she passed smiling, summer-infused people: a group of teenagers dancing, a boy at the centre with his arms in the air, head tilted to the sky; a mother cooing into a pram; a man with a child on his shoulders; two older ladies sitting on a low wall eating ice cream. She felt twitchy and apart from them. She turned up the radio and tried to summon the same relaxed energy.

As she stepped out of her car in her street, she felt an unmistakeable presence nearby. She turned around, sensing movement. The street was empty, and yet the hairs on the back of her neck stood to attention. She'd had the distinct feeling that eyes were on her again. But there were no twitching curtains, no faces at the windows. But she had heard footsteps; she was sure of it. She thought then of the letter in her top drawer at work. Maybe it was making her jumpy? There was a click, like the sound of a camera. Swallowing, she reached into her car to pull out her bag and headed for her flat. As she opened the door, there was the sound of another closing somewhere behind her.

She almost tripped over the brown leather bag.

'You're back!' she said, drawing up short.

'I'm here!' Fraser called from the direction of their bedroom. He stood in the entrance to the office, hands on his hips, before turning towards her. He looked like he'd been running: cheeks flushed, hair askew, breathing heavier than normal. 'Finished work already?' His eyebrows lifted.

'Garry's sending me the piece to edit from here.'

'Ah,' Fraser said. He took her bag from her, as he so often did. 'Woah, this is heavy.'

'It's books.'

He glanced at the top one – she was sure that a muscle fluttered in his cheek. '*Scotland's Most Haunted Places*. More about that house?'

Ava mumbled a reply.

'I only just got in. My dad's alright. Penny came over. I think she's got a soft spot for him. She sent me packing. Dad was pleased, felt like I was making a fuss over a finger.'

'That's good – about Penny, I mean.' She seemed to be always putting her foot in it with Fraser lately.

'Do you want a takeaway tonight?'

'Sure.'

Fraser moved back down the corridor. 'What do you think about yellow?'

Ava pulled the books one by one from the bag. She wouldn't get much time this evening. 'Hmm?'

'*Yellow*. For the walls. I picked up some samples so we could test a few and see what we liked?' He waited a few seconds as if for her to catch up. 'Then, if it's a boy or a girl it doesn't matter.' He must have taken her continued silence as something else. 'Not that a boy couldn't have pink walls, but . . . you know what I mean.'

'Right. Yes. Yellow. That could work.'

It was the wrong thing to say; Fraser pressed his lips together, his hands falling to his sides.

'Or pink, blue . . . sorry. What do *you* think? It doesn't matter, does it? It's still really early.'

'But . . .' Fraser gritted his teeth. 'Tomorrow is results day, which means I'm going to be tied up with kids wanting feedback . . . clearing . . . angry parents – the works.'

'Sorry. Of course. I forgot.'

He muttered something she couldn't pick up. 'Look, summer is almost over for me, Ava, I've got this new role and I'm going to be up to my eyes. It would be nice if you could show *some* interest.'

'I *am* showing interest. Yellow is great. I agreed. It's a good idea.'

'Fine. I'll do it in yellow.'

'Thanks.' She scooted past him.

Her mobile rang and she answered. It was Garry telling her he'd emailed the piece and wanted it edited for tonight's programme.

When she hung up on Garry, she said, 'Um . . . I've got to work.'

Fraser just nodded wearily.

'Let's talk more later. Alright?'

He had gone into the office and didn't reply.

Chapter 25

MARION

I am pregnant.

Hamish is delighted, summoning the doctor, a tiny man almost bent double and with a pointed white beard, who examined me in my bedroom and confirmed that I am with child. It is the most wonderful blessing, and I find myself breaking into laughter at the strangest times, poking my tongue out at the big brown bear as I pass. Hamish has spent more time at home, removing the dust sheet from the desk his father had worked from, installing a telephone in the house, which makes a shrill ring when London are in touch. Sometimes I hear him laughing with somebody. I believe his colleagues must be close friends.

He dines with me and asks after my health, ensures Miss Kae produces food that will help the baby and talks earnestly of the excitement and relief that he has an heir for the estate. At night he is gentle, his touch lingers, his palms splayed on my stomach that has changed shape, a rounded belly where before there was flatness. I feel a warmth emanate from it, through my whole body, to my very fingertips. Hamish tells me I am beautiful.

I picture a rosy-cheeked infant with wide eyes and Hamish's curly brown hair. Someone to hold close and sing lullabies to. A child to keep me company in this great house, a little boy who will grow up to make his father proud.

The whiskery doctor has advised no energetic walking or riding of animals. How I wish someone could tell me more. I have written to Mother but we never speak of intimate things and Susan has less knowledge than I. Hamish tells me to stay within the walled garden and I do. I walk backwards and forwards, the sound of the river that runs alongside it accompanying every step. Afterwards, I wonder whether even this was wrong, whether I should have stayed in bed, completely still. Whether that day I left the walled garden, bored and unthinking, into the paths of the estate, sheltering underneath the archway of the stone bridge as rain fell, was what prompted it.

Hamish and the doctor are not there when it happens. He is not meant to come this early. I am woken by a crippling pain that slices me in half. Clutching myself, I feel a terrible damp, a shocking sight on the ceramic tiles of the bathroom floor, blood streaking the basin of the toilet, an impossible amount. I am surely dying. I cannot breathe. I stagger and slip in it, my nightdress coated, my hands, a scarlet swipe on my cheek that makes me recoil when I catch myself in the mirror. Panicking as I feel him leaving my body, I sink to the floor, stay there, cradling my grey son in my hands, oversized head and too-small limbs, the feeling of the thin cord between my legs as we wait in a red puddle, back to the door, whole body trembling. Hamish is away and it seems like hours alone with him in the bathroom before I hear my name, a knock, a cry, as Miss Kae finds us. She gets me to my bed, her voice shaking, her gaze not able to rest on him. She leaves to summon the doctor on the telephone. Later she cleans the bathroom, the bedding, the floor. I listen to her from another bedroom with dark blue walls and the smell of mould and when I return to my bedroom two days later there is nothing different, and yet every time I open the bathroom door all I see is red.

I never ask her what the doctor did with him. I want to. I open my mouth but the question dies on my lips. No birth certificate, and yet he had been a baby boy. I had seen him, held him. He was my son. Even when I shut my eyes, I see the inside of that bathroom. I can't sleep. The days and nights merge. Red-rimmed eyes stare back unseeing in my mirror, my hair lank, my sagging stomach empty.

Hamish returns, summoned I think by Miss Kae, who leaves me food on trays. The flowers picked from the estate dry out quickly next to the untouched plate. White-knuckled and silent, I want to tell him about his son. He visits that night but I cry out when he enters me and he leaves soon after. Curling up in a ball under the bedclothes, my whole body quivers. I have failed. I am being punished. I have let down my husband, unable to provide him with the one thing he wants.

It is only two days later when I accompany him to a house on the Borders. A large estate, the owner a newly appointed lord, is welcoming in the new decade. My face is pale and washed out, hair dull. The made-to-measure dress is loose, disguised by safety pins at the waist. Hamish doesn't tell me I look beautiful today.

The party is loud, sparkling with the chandeliers overhead, the candles in brackets, polished floor. Everybody greets Hamish, resplendent in his family tartan that accentuates his brooding looks. There are squawks from a plumage of women in rainbow colours, headdresses, flapper skirts, bright lipsticks that leave marks on my husband's cheeks, gossip and laughter and drink and high spirits. I know none of the dances; Hamish never taught me them after all.

The hostess, Mrs Palmer, is a beautiful, willowy woman twenty-four years younger than her red-nosed husband. With a severe bobbed haircut and catlike eyes, she purrs around Hamish, pressing another cocktail into his hands.

'She makes the best sidecars in Scotland,' he tells another man.

'Have you known her a while?' I ask.

He doesn't meet my eyes as he says, 'Forever.' He asks her to join him in the Dashing White Sergeant.

I escape to the downstairs bathroom just as another woman pushes inside with a friend. Shockingly, she pulls up her dress and lowers herself onto the seat. I just about get outside the door when his name stops me in my tracks, one hand on the frame.

'That was his wife.'

'Christ, he's shameless.'

'Drab little thing.'

'Still. He is a rogue.'

'He picked her up at the Savoy.'

'Cecilia doesn't seem to mind.'

'Well, she's married too. She can hardly protest.'

No one notices me as I sit in the library next door. The band plays on in the distance. The wooden shutters in the library are pushed back, so the full moon is the only witness to the tears tracking my cheeks.

When we leave, Hamish bids farewell to our bulbous host, his pretty young wife just behind him. She has the lightest laugh. My feet and hands are numb with cold, scarf and hat forgotten. I step into the waiting car feeling more miserable in this new year than I have ever felt before.

'You must look forward, old girl,' Hamish slurs, slumped against the leather. 'A new year . . .'

He lies with me the whole night. I don't sleep. I see bloodied bathrooms. I see bright-lipsticked Cecilia. The next morning, he tries to make another baby.

He is gone by midday.

Chapter 26

AVA

Her parents' small garden was bursting with life, neat borders in a range of pastel colours, lush grass cut in regimented strips. They were all standing around the gas barbecue as Ava's dad, in a navy and white striped apron, prodded at pieces of sizzling meat.

Fraser and Liam flanked him, all with bottles of beer to hand, smoke billowing around them as they talked.

Pippa was inside changing Tommy, who had announced in a delighted voice that he had done 'a stinker'.

'Come on, John! Surely the meat's done!' Her mum bustled out with a tray of potato salad and cutlery. Pippa appeared with a pile of plates, hot dog buns balanced on top. Tommy wielded a bottle of ketchup. Ava immediately offered to help.

'You stay there,' Pippa said, 'you're pregnant.'

Ava sipped at her elderflower cordial and sat back. Gus moved beneath the table, his springy curls tickling her legs as he passed. 'Thanks,' she said, her voice uncertain.

Her dad started transferring the charred meat to a white ceramic tray. Soon they were all sitting in the wooden chairs, calling to be passed things. A high chair was dragged out and wiped down for Tommy.

'Cheers!' Dad raised his bottle to them all, smiling around, his face tanned, his apron still on. 'So . . .' Her dad looked at her, sitting next to Fraser. 'Have you two been making plans for the new arrival?' He picked up some tongs and served up chicken thighs, legs, sausages and burgers.

Ava clenched her jaw as she recalled the frosty exchange with Fraser a few nights before. He had been quiet around the flat ever since. The office looked lovely, a creamy yellow, the fresh paint smell making her feel guilty every time she passed.

'She spends all her time at or obsessing about a haunted house at the moment.' Fraser tried to sound cheery but his body was stiff in the chair next to her.

'Fraser!' Ava swallowed her mouthful of potato salad and turned in her chair towards him.

'You do!' he protested, something sad in his profile. 'But I painted the nursery,' he added brightly, trying to raise a smile at her dad.

'But your piece went out on that house,' her mum said. 'Why are you still going there?'

Ava hadn't realised they had watched it. They never normally commented on her reports these days; the excitement of a daughter on television had long gone.

'It was very interesting, love,' her dad put in. 'Bit gruesome, but still . . .' He coughed.

Ava bit her lip, aware of Fraser's brooding silence beside her. 'I don't spend *all* my time there.' She felt ganged-up on. 'It's just . . .' Her mum looked watchful, stroking Gus's head as he sat next to her. Fraser sipped at his beer. Ava felt heat creep into her cheeks. How could she explain her continued interest in Overtoun, her fascination with the feel of the place, the hidden meanings?

Liam sat opposite, biting into a hot dog, ketchup splurting out of one end onto his plate. 'Do you remember at school when you, Paul and Jenna did a Ouija board?'

'We didn't!' Ava turned to Liam, always amazed by his detailed recall from their schooldays. They hadn't moved in the same circles; it had been a big group and they'd only shared a couple of classes.

'You did. It was at Ben's party and you guys wouldn't let anyone in the room.'

'I don't remember that. I'm sure we wouldn't have.' A vague memory of her giggling over a glass and some cut-up letters suddenly came to mind. 'Well . . . maybe we did . . .'

'Liam and his mates never dared speak to you.' Pippa laughed, taking a sip of her wine. 'Too cool for school, wasn't she, Liam?'

'Well, that was twenty years ago.' Ava tried to ignore the edge in her sister's voice. 'And Liam and I talk alright now.' She smiled across at him.

Liam shifted in his seat and a blush crept up from the collar of his shirt, clashing with his orange-red hair.

'Alright, alright.' Her dad clapped his hands. 'No more ghosts . . .'

Pippa looked at her. 'Is that the weird bridge with the dogs?'

'I don't like talk like this,' their mum said. Her hand had stilled in Gus's springy curls.

Ava felt ridiculous. As if she was eighteen and not thirty-eight. Tommy squealed from the high chair that barely contained him these days and forced everyone's eyes away from her. Pippa cut up a sausage for him, looking around at everyone else. Ava shifted in her chair, her hips aching today. Fraser was biting his lip, guilty perhaps that Ava looked so chastised.

Ava's mum moved around the table. 'Fraser, I made the sauce you love.' She beamed as she put a gravy boat in front of him.

Fraser smiled and took it. Only Ava noticed the slight tension in his shoulders. Liam had a somewhat sour expression as Fraser passed it to him. Perhaps he didn't like her mum's sauce.

'And how are you both enjoying the holidays?' her dad said, turning to the other side of the table. 'Liam? You still writing that dissertation?'

Liam nodded. His mouth was full and there was ketchup on his chin.

Pippa rested a hand on Liam's forearm. 'He's almost finished. I'm really proud of him.'

'How about you, Fraser? Preparing for the new school year?'

Only Ava seemed to notice the light dim in Pippa's eyes as their dad's focus shifted to Fraser. Despite being the academic in the family, a professor no less, Liam never quite got the same attention. It didn't help that none of them could ever understand a word when he discussed his research.

'Results were alright but we have a few kids needing help with clearing. A boy in care has scraped enough to go into sixth form, which is great. So we've been looking at suitable A levels for him.'

'Sounds rewarding.'

Ava stared down at her plate. She hadn't heard about this boy. A wave of shame washed over her. She really did need to pay more attention. Suddenly, before she could add something, Gus had jumped onto the grass out of the reach of her mum, who had been feeding him a sausage.

Moving quickly across the lawn, he began barking furiously at the hedge that ran along the back wall of the garden. Behind it was a disused path between the garden and those of the houses opposite. It was deserted and crawling with clinging weeds and brambles. Ava grew perturbed as she watched him, his insistent bark totally drowning out all other sounds.

'Must be something.' Her dad twisted around in surprise. 'A bird perhaps?' He reached out to Gus. 'Come on, boy.' He beckoned, but Gus stayed planted to the spot, silent now. There was a rustle – a large animal? A fox or a badger? 'It's not like him,' her dad said. 'Come on, boy.' As Gus started barking again, her dad moved across and scooped him up. 'Hush, the neighbours won't be impressed.' He took Gus into the conservatory, Gus twisting in his arms like a big angry baby.

The rest of lunch passed in a steady stream of safe conversation: the neighbours' skip, which still hadn't moved; house prices and whether Liam and Pippa should sell; the garden – Dad was disappointed with his tomato crop this year.

Ava picked up the plates from the table, wanting to be inside for a moment. Gus had settled now, stretched out in his sheepskin bed as if nothing had happened. She stared at him as she passed. He didn't even bother to open an eye. What had he heard? Why did everything these days make her jumpy? She ran the taps in the kitchen.

'I'll do that,' Pippa said, bustling in. 'You dry.'

Ava shrugged and stepped back.

'All OK?' Pippa asked, her voice low.

'Fine.' Ava picked up the tea towel draped over the handle of the oven. As children, Pippa had always preferred washing to drying; they'd spend endless hours shoulder to shoulder as they cleared dinner. They moved into this familiar stance now.

'Seems like you and Fraser are a bit . . .' Pippa looked around and then back at the crockery in the sink. She handed Ava a dripping plate.

Ava circled the plate with the tea towel. 'We're fine.'

'Well, if you want to meet and talk, I'm around tomorrow.'

'I can't.' Ava was glad of an excuse. 'I'm filming.'

'On a Sunday?'

'Don't you start.'

'I didn't say anything,' Pippa protested.

Ava took a breath. 'I want to go back to that bridge. One of the camera guys is going to bring a drone. There's a story there, Pippa. I heard . . .' Ava bit her lip, the desire to tell someone who might understand overwhelming her. 'I heard a baby cry. After I filmed before. A baby who' – she couldn't help her body convulsing at the memory – 'wasn't there. And I felt . . .' She stopped, knowing she sounded confused, trying to condense everything into a neat description. It felt impossible. 'I felt . . . I feel like the bridge, the house, they're . . . alive. It's like they need someone to reveal their secrets – lance the boil.' As she put it all in these words, she realised the truth in them.

Pippa shifted nervously, an awkward sound emerging. 'That's . . .'

'There was a woman.' Ava was unable to stop now she'd begun. 'She had a child. I don't know what happened but I'm frightened, Pippa. Frightened of the place. Of the power it has. I'm frightened for that baby I heard.'

Pippa's eyes were round; she swallowed slowly.

'Mummy, Mummy!' Both sisters jumped as Tommy raced in, a plastic car in one hand, his dinosaur hat askew. Their mum followed, a big, dirty china bowl in one hand, drawing up as she saw her daughters at the sink. 'What are you two looking so secretive about?' She straightened Tommy's hat.

'Nothing,' Pippa said quickly.

Ava looked away.

'Ava was telling me about work, weren't you, Ava?' Pippa said, a nod of encouragement.

'I was.'

Their mum sighed. 'We're proud of you, Ava, but I'm not sure work should be your focus right now.'

'What's that supposed to mean?'

'Well, if you hadn't noticed . . .' She indicated Ava's growing stomach through the T-shirt she was wearing. 'You're pregnant.'

'I know,' Ava said slowly, 'but I also have other things going on in my life.'

Their mother glanced at Pippa. Since Pippa had had Tommy, it was sometimes as if they had a secret mum code, making Ava feel like an outsider.

'Well, poor Fraser . . .' Mum continued. 'It sounds like you've barely seen him these last few weeks.'

Ava threw up her hands in the air. 'My God! How is this anyone's business?'

Both her sister and mum bristled and Tommy scrambled to his mum's leg. An awkward silence followed in which there were only distant sounds and the tick of the kitchen clock.

'There's no need to shout,' Mum said, lifting her chin.

Ava curled her hands into fists. 'I'm fed up with being made to feel guilty about doing my job.'

'I don't understand you sometimes, Ava,' her mum said.

'Oh my God, you're one to talk!' The words had tumbled out before she could stop them.

'Ava . . .' Pippa warned.

Ava spun around to her sister. 'So you understand Mum, do you?'

'I . . .' Pippa's face crumpled, panic blooming in her eyes.

Quiet for once, Tommy stared up at them all like a referee in a tennis match.

'How can I be a mum when I don't even know my own?' Ava felt blood pumping to her head.

The bowl her mum was holding slipped from her grip, smashing onto the floor, glass spinning in every direction. Pippa cried out, whisking Tommy from the floor.

Ava's mum looked up at her. 'Now look what you made me do.'

Chapter 27

AVA

Neil met her in the car park, stuttering an apology for being late, unable to meet her eye.

'You're not late. I was early, I . . .'

She had raced out of the flat, the atmosphere stilted since the barbecue, a quiet goodbye to Fraser, not confident enough to put her arms around him. They were both practically falling off the opposite edges of their bed at the moment.

'I thought we could start along the path beneath the bridge,' she said, 'see if we can get some shots from there?'

'OK.' Neil hoisted a dirty brown rucksack onto his back.

They walked past the house, cutting across the shadows that sliced the ground, their cars parked next to the field on the right. Ava bit her lip as they approached the bridge and glanced across at Neil, whose face in the shade was still, jaw rigid. Did he feel the same strange sense of foreboding as they neared the stones at each end, as if a gloom hung over the whole scene? As she turned back to the house, she quailed for a moment – an outline behind the glass. Movement. She realised it was Keven, watching them from the first floor. Ava lifted her hand and he returned the wave before disappearing into the murk of the house.

They plunged down the pathway that ran along the river, leaving the bridge behind them. Ava felt more confident with someone else by her side, as if the place had less power when she wasn't alone. The land tilted down, dappled sunshine in the dirt, chittering in the bushes as the ground levelled out. They stopped by a shady bank on their left, almost totally black with shadows. The water flowed past, steering around stones, weeds trailing in the water like long green hair stuck to the slippery rocks. It was so much colder here. Ava drew her arms around herself, her baby jiggling inside her. As damp seeped into her nostrils, she cleared her throat, nerves jangling as she looked back at the bridge, its archways soaring behind them, the stone turrets lost to the trees that bent over the path.

'How about here?' she said.

Neil started as if her voice had been too loud for the moment. He gave her a nervous nod and reached for his rucksack, his own eyes swivelling backwards to the bridge.

'It's creepy, isn't it?' Ava said.

Neil fumbled with the zip of the bag, drawing out a camera. 'I can't help thinking about them falling.'

Ava licked her lips. 'Why do you think they do it?'

Neil held the camera to his chest. 'I'm not sure.'

'My mum was angry with me for bringing her dog.' Ava flinched as she talked about her mum, remembering the disastrous end to the barbecue: her abrupt departure, her dad's puzzled look as he appeared around the side gate to see Fraser and her leaving in the car. She rarely argued with her mum, but she had also kept quiet over the years and now she'd realised she needed more. She needed to understand.

'He did nearly jump,' Neil said, his voice almost drowned by the water. Ava looked at him, lost in thought. 'Your mum's dog,' he added.

Ava nodded. 'He did.'

Neil removed the drone from its case. 'What if' – his voice was low, most of his face hidden as he bent to press buttons – 'a sniffer dog came here. My friend Aaron has a dog like that. He used to be in the police but he left to be a fine art photographer. I read that people thought there might be mink, that the smell might be driving the dogs.'

'You read about it too?'

Neil peeked up momentarily. 'Yeah. I thought it was pretty weird.'

A bird screeched nearby, startling them both. Ava wobbled before finding her balance. She imagined water in her ears, around her head, her body tossing and turning in the foamy current. She swallowed hard.

'Maybe a dog could find a reason – find mink or something?'

But what if it wasn't a smell, something less able to explain so easily?

'Did you read about the lady who lived here?' Ava whispered. 'The White Lady?' A breeze ruffled the hedges and trees. They sounded as if they were moaning.

Neil nodded. 'There was an inquest into her death. Suicide.'

Ava hadn't read about an inquest. She looked back at the bridge, remembering what Keven had told her: the lady with the sick child. *That was why she jumped.*

'Do you know anything about a child? Or a baby?'

Neil shook his head. 'Not that I read.'

'Ava.'

For a second her throat went dry, pulse quickening as she thought she heard her name. She closed her eyes.

'Are you alr—'

'I thought someone . . .'

'Ava,' came the voice again. Her stomach lurched. Craning her neck upwards, the bridge looming behind her, she stared. Moss clung to the damp stone underbelly, brown and white streaks on the aged stone like fingers climbing its walls.

'Ava!'

She sucked in her breath as a face peered down over the top of the bridge.

'For fuc—' Her hand went to her chest as she realised it was Pippa. 'Sorry, sorry,' Ava said to Neil, her chest still leaping. 'It's my sister.'

Neil still held the drone in one hand but his face had turned pale.

They both laughed nervously.

'I'll ring my mate about the dog,' he said.

Ava walked back up the path and Pippa took a couple of steps down from the bridge towards her.

'What are you doing here?' Ava asked. Then a sudden thought hit her like a train. 'Are Mum and Dad OK?'

'They're fine,' Pippa said, batting the words away. 'I wanted to see you. I remembered you were coming here. I looked it up. I thought we could go for a walk somewhere new.'

'Mummy!' a voice called from above them.

'We?' Ava was horrified. 'Is that Tommy?'

Pippa looked at her, her face in the shade. 'Yeah, he's just here.'

'Oh my God.' Ava strode forward.

'It's fine.' Pippa put her hands on her hips. 'The bridge is safe. The walls are really high.'

'He shouldn't be here.'

'Ava, honestly . . . he's fine here. He's playing with pebbles.'

Although Pippa was close to the top and the bridge, she didn't seem to be turning back as Ava, her feet slipping, pushed past her sister, fear like cold water dripping down her spine. 'Tommy!' she called, her stomach strained, her hips aching as she half-jogged. Pippa turned behind her.

Tommy looked startled as Ava burst around the corner onto the top of the bridge, scooping him up from his crouched position on the floor, holding him next to her, his legs either side of her bump as her breath came in gulps.

Pippa had an unruffled but sulky expression on her face. 'Ava, he was like an arm's length away.'

'This is not a good place.' Ava tried not to be angry. She was just relieved that Tommy was alright. His pudgy hands were on either side of her face.

'Baby,' he said.

Pippa moved to take him from Ava, his sandalled legs chubby and smooth. She lowered him next to her. Tommy crouched to inspect the ground once more, pushing loose pebbles around.

Ava couldn't stop staring at him, remembering Gus, feeling the strange oppressive atmosphere swirling around them as they stood there. 'What are you doing here?' she asked again. She wished Pippa would snatch Tommy back up into the safety of her arms.

'Baby, baby,' Tommy repeated.

'I wanted to talk to you. You left yesterday and I didn't want to upset Mum any more by saying something then.'

'I don't know why *she* was upset.' Ava knew she was pouting. '*I'm* upset. How am I meant to be a mum when I don't even know her?'

Pippa pursed her lips. 'We *do* know Mum.'

Ava couldn't stop the small scoff from escaping.

'She was upset, OK, Ava? When you and Fraser left, she talked to me *at length*.' Pippa emphasised the last two words and it seemed to Ava that there was a hint of triumph there – that she had become their mum's confidante after all the years of feeling that was Ava's role.

Tommy had stood up, his little eyes wide as he put a hand over one ear.

Ava tried to concentrate, felt her body sway slightly, her words slurred. 'I didn't say anything that would upset her.'

'She's worried about you. Worried about Fraser and you – and this obsession.' Pippa swept her hand towards the bridge and house.

The light flickered; Pippa's words seemed to swim in and out. Ava felt blood rush to her head and the onset of nausea.

'You've tried for years to get pregnant, Ava,' Pippa said. 'What are you doing here?'

'It's not an obsession.' Ava's voice was weak, uncertainty in each syllable.

'But I thought about what you said. How absurd it all sounded. Hearing things. Of course you're hearing a baby – look at you! And I agree with Mum. It's just a bridge, Ava.' Pippa stared around at the grey stonework.

Ava almost expected the bridge to react, to reveal itself. She glanced at Tommy, readying herself.

'Liam said you were like that at school, too. Got a bee in your bonnet and never let go . . .'

'Liam and I barely spoke at school.'

'And whose fault was that?'

Neil's startled face appeared around the edge of the bridge then disappeared again. Ava wished he'd interrupted them. As she looked back at Pippa, she felt her insides roll and put a hand on her stomach. She was going to be sick. She leaned over and closed her eyes.

'Ava?'

'It's nothing,' she said as if to the ground. 'Blood pressure.'

Sounds faded as Ava slowed her breathing. She straightened up. Pippa looked less certain now and chewed her lower lip.

'Look, Pippa, I've got to get on, OK? We've got filming to do.'

'You can't film. You should have some water. Sit down.'

Ava batted her sister away. 'I'm fine.' She blinked, wanted everything around her to still, for the cotton wool in her head to dissipate.

Tommy tugged on Pippa's cropped trousers. 'Baby.'

'Tommy, don't . . .'

'Baby!' he repeated, one hand over one ear, the other still pulling on the fabric of her trousers.

'Stop it, Tommy.'

'Baby!'

'Yes, Auntie Ava's having a baby.'

But Tommy wasn't looking at Ava. Ava watched him as he turned in the direction of the house and ran a few paces. She started after him.

'He's been whingeing the last few days,' Pippa said. 'Molars.'

Ava bent down to Tommy's level.

Tommy, both hands now clamped either side of his head, didn't really register her. 'BABY!' he shouted, turning towards the parapet where Gus had made his run.

'Tommy, shh,' Pippa said.

Ava couldn't stop staring at him. He seemed some place far away and he kept saying 'Baby' over and over and over again.

Chapter 28

CONSTANCE

I am always tired now. I lie facing the wall day after day, week after week, not noticing when Mother pushes inside, not looking as she draws back my curtains or talks about the weather. I don't care about the rain or the sun or the shape of the clouds. I don't even care about the people passing on the bridge. My smiles and voice are stuck somewhere inside me and I wonder why God would let me be so sick. I must be bad.

The mattress dips with her weight; her hand tucks the wisps of hair behind my ears. 'Come on,' she says, 'let's get you dressed.' She encourages me into clothes, pulling them over me when I cannot find the strength. Lifting me, she carries me out and up the few steps. The wheelchair is waiting and she wheels me along the corridor. I wrap my arms around myself. The ceiling is too far away, the echoing sounds too loud. I see the bear and through a sliver in the door, an eye – Annie silently watching us both.

The chair sticks on the bump of the threshold to the drawing room and it hurts the bone at the bottom of my back when she jiggles it over it. 'I want to show you something, Constance West; you won't believe it. The townsfolk have raised some more funds – isn't that wonderful? – for us. It is hard to raise a retarded child. Now look!'

She moves inside with a flourish and I gaze around at the enormous room, the green walls so bright I want to look away. On the ceiling the painted faces of the baby angels peer down, chubby cheeks and arms and legs. So healthy. A new wheelchair is standing in the middle of the room with a cherry-red leather seat and armrests.

'They say it will be more comfortable. And I will get a carpenter.' She puts a finger to her lips. 'So that you can be more easily wheeled around. Won't that be nice? People are happy to help. They feel so sorry for us all alone and dealing with such hardship.'

I try to smile at her as she wraps her arms around my neck, lifts me onto the sofa next to her and brings me my lunch on a tray. Her face is watchful as I spoon my soup, her watery blue eyes always a mystery. Somewhere outside, birds chitter to each other in the tree. A child shouts, playful and excited. The noise makes me feel more lonely. I want to go and lie back down. I'm tired. Mother lifts me and takes me back to my bedroom. She stays in the doorframe for an age, and when I turn, thinking she has gone, I see tears on her cheeks and wonder why she's the one who is sad.

The next day, a strange wet sensation wakes me and I think I'm still in a dream. Waves, rocks, roaring water, a pirate with a hooded face. Scrabbling over my chest, his tiny claws dig into my flesh and I gasp.

'He's yours,' Mother says – and I can't believe it.

I don't spend days staring at the same patch of wall. Now I play with my puppy. I call him Crumpet. His light brown fur is the colour of warm dough. I used to see dogs from my window, on the bridge, jumping excitedly, returning to their owner for petting and smiles. I wanted one. I knew I would like having one. I hadn't expected the swell of love, the longing as Crumpet snuggles next to me, tiny body warm, heart beating next to mine. He lies on my chest, stares into my eyes then, out of nowhere, darts his tongue out and licks me on the nose, making me shake with giggles. He knows how much I love it and does it again.

He whines if I leave him, even for a moment, then spins with delight when I return, as if I'm the only good thing in his life. We take short walks to the walled garden. I watch him with a rug over my lap as he digs a shallow hole, sits in it until I call out that I've 'found' him and he looks delighted. He puts his head in my lap on the days I'm sick, his wet nose on my skin. If I get up, he gets up. If I go to the window, he puts his paws on the walls and looks at me until I lift him into my arms and we stare outside together, his breath hot on my cheek as he nestles next to me.

He is the great love of my life.

I stay in my chair and watch him endlessly as he spins and yaps. He comes to me with melting brown eyes, giving my hand and face the tiniest licks. I have so much love in my chest I could burst.

The days are full of him. Even when I am sick from my mouth I try to play. He makes me feel better. Never-ending games, fetch, catch, cuddles. Mother seems happier too. 'You look better,' she says, stroking my cheek.

'Oh I am. Thank you, Mama. Thank you for Crumpet.'

She brings him food in a bowl but he often eats it all up so I make him little treats, pieces I take from the trays of food Mother brings me. He loves my porridge, creamy pieces sticking to his whiskers. He gobbles it all up, his pink tongue reaching to take the food from my hand. I think I will explode with love for him; it seems to make the whole room throb.

Then one day Crumpet doesn't want to get up, doesn't want to play. He whines at me, rolling on his back, pawing at his speckled stomach. Panting, he rests in my lap, curled up in a ball, the strange sad noises still coming from him as I stroke his fur, his ribs bony beneath my hand.

I am scared, stroking and cuddling him, trying to make it all better. His fur is wet with my tears as I pray, pray, pray so hard that he will get better, that his little face will clear, his head rise, his eyes brighten, his tail wag. He doesn't seem to be able to hear me as I whisper soothing words. 'Get better, Crumpet. Please.'

Mother watches him from the doorway, biting on her lower lip. 'I'll fetch for the vet,' she says.

Everything here gets sick.

Chapter 29

AVA

They'd finished filming some shots, Ava's heart not in it as Neil showed her some aerial footage. Ava twitched as she sat in the car, replaying the argument with her sister and Tommy's reaction to being on the bridge. Pippa had dismissed it, a concerned look as if Ava was certifiable. Ava hadn't cared in that moment; she just wanted them all off the bridge. Pippa had scooped up Tommy and driven off in a huff, abandoning the idea of a walk.

The weather had worsened, clouds banking on the horizon. Neil had left and she wanted to drive away too, but she found herself frozen in her seat, gripping the steering wheel, looking out into the fields beyond. The house and bridge sat behind the pine trees to her left, their menace never far, and she shivered as she recalled Tommy's blank look, his repeated words.

Getting out of the car, she started to walk, not towards the house but through the gate ahead; a signpost indicated a path that skirted the crags. The baby was still now that she was moving and she put a hand on her stomach as she walked past fields, verges bursting with long grasses, dandelions and buttercups, overgrown stiles and signs pointing in different directions. Sheep bleated and a butterfly dipped in and out of view.

Disappearing into a copse of pine trees, the smell was strong and sudden, twigs and pine needles crunching underfoot. She blinked. Sunlight was barely able to find gaps through the canopy overhead. Weeds tickled her calves as she stepped gingerly over a gap in the deer fence to an empty field beyond that tugged the steep side of the crags. Stopping at a spot that looked down on the house, she wished she had brought water with her. Her lips were cracked and dry.

There were two missed calls from her dad. She sighed as she stared at her mobile and called him back.

'Dad.'

'Ava.'

'You called me.'

'I did.'

She looked up the path to the crags. It was moss covered and looked boggy in parts. She clung to the line of trees as she pressed the phone to her ear. For a moment, she thought he had hung up but then his voice returned. 'I'm in the spare room.'

This had to be serious. She felt her foot slip, regretting that she had put on her pumps. The toes were coated in mud.

'Your sister's just left. She told me you had an argument.'

'We didn't argue, Dad,' Ava huffed. This was more exercise than she'd had in a while.

'You had words.'

'She was the one who chased me up here in the middle of filming to lecture me.' Ava shot a hand out to hold a wooden post, skirting churned-up mud, scrambling up springy moss, her thighs aching.

'Well, she was upset. And your mother was too.'

Pippa must have gone straight there, which made Ava defensive. 'I don't know why.'

'Look, Ava . . .' Her dad's voice was weary. 'People are worried about you, that's all. She told me you had a wee bit of a turn. We're worried you're making yourself ill, lass.'

'That's not you talking, Dad . . .'

'It's me and your mother.' He didn't sound convincing.

Ava felt a stubbornness build in her. 'Why don't we all go back to not talking.' She scuffed the ground with her already-ruined shoe. 'It's what we're so good at.'

'Ava? What's that supposed to mean, love?'

Ava lifted a hand to her head, the start of a headache behind her eyes. Squinting, she tried to concentrate on her reply. 'Just that we don't talk about what's really important, do we?'

There was a pause and she could hear conversation in the background. This was ridiculous. The pain in her eyes was building. 'Look, Dad, I need to go.'

'Why are you up there at that bridge anyway?'

Ava sighed. 'Not you too, Dad. It's my job.'

'We're just worried about you,' he repeated gently. 'This doesn't sound like your normal job, love.'

'I've come for answers.'

She felt desperate. It seemed that her family was closing ranks against her. Her dad never took sides, never made her feel like she was in the wrong. She stepped out onto a grassy ledge, a gust of wind buffeting her. 'I've got to go, Dad,' she said. The edge was so close as she crept towards it and she had a dizzying sense of vertigo as she peered down the cliffside, trees and scrubs sprouting at strange angles from the cracks in the rocks.

As she turned in the direction of the house with its grey bulk, spiked towers and the dark stone, menacing even from up here, she felt an ominous tug towards it. There was the bridge where so many dogs had jumped to their deaths. She took a step forward.

'Ava?' Her dad was still speaking to her but for a moment it was as if the estate was calling her name. Then came a sudden jerk forward, like two hands on her back, a gasp, her phone slipping from her hand and bouncing onto the grass. Crouching in shock, she whipped around, only to see the steep incline of mossy rock and grass above her, nothing that could have pushed her in the back.

Reaching for her phone, she tried to steady her voice. 'I've got to go, Dad.'

She barely heard his reply as she ended the call and started the descent quickly. She needed to get away from the edge, out of sight of the house. She was breathless when she finally burst from the pine trees, her car a silver glimmer up ahead. She clutched her throbbing head as she stared at the people walking past the house as if this was just any other day. Her heart had stopped racing by the time she was back on level ground, her nails biting into her flesh, her shoulders tense.

As she moved past the front of the house, she saw one woman open the boot of her car. Three dogs leaped out, sniffing at the air excitedly, tails wagging after being cooped up. They raced in circles before setting off in front of her. Ava's heart was in her mouth as they headed for the bridge. She should call out. She should point out the sign. She should tell the woman that dogs were not safe there. She sped up, kicking up pebbles as she moved beneath the sharp shadows of the house, the air chillier in the sudden shade.

The dogs were almost there, the woman with them seemingly oblivious to the danger.

'Excuse me! Excuse me . . .'

The woman couldn't hear her. Ava felt her chest squeeze; they were almost on top of it. One of the dogs barked, spun about, then suddenly they were there on the bridge, as Ava stopped and stood stock-still, her eyes not leaving them, tense as she watched them. One leaped and sprang, one put his nose to the ground. Ava felt her body stiffen. She remembered Gus, his sudden run. Tommy, hands to the side of his head. What if they darted for the edge? What if she watched one of them fall? The woman was on her mobile, a lead trailing in her other hand, oblivious.

Ava watched them all cross safely, her breath rushing out of her with relief. She turned back, glancing up at the window where she had seen Keven. Perhaps he was in. She could tell him about the sniffer dog, the theory Neil had read about the scent of mink, ask him about the crags. There was no answer as she rang the doorbell. Not wanting to admit she just wanted to see a friendly face, she set off to search for him.

There was no one around now, the evening sky darkening, the sun almost lost behind the trees. Descending the stone steps that led down the side of the house, she noticed again the window almost completely obscured by ivy. She found herself staring at it for a while, moving slowly towards it.

She felt jumpy, aware that this felt like snooping despite being metres away from the public road. She could say she was looking for Keven, though. He wouldn't mind. He had been kind to her.

The ivy was a thick curtain over the dusty glass, only a few diamonds peeking through. She stepped towards it carefully; the panes were covered in decades-old grime. The smell of damp overwhelmed her as she stood right next to a part of the wall that the sun was unable to reach. Pulling aside a few tendrils of ivy, insects scattering, she cupped her hands to her face and pressed her nose up to the glass to peer inside. The glass was surprisingly warm, a strange cloying heat that felt unnatural.

It was a small square room with plain white walls and a simple watercolour of a mountain on the furthest wall. A low single bed stood in the corner, a shelf running above it. Ava was too far away to make out the different books. A china doll was propped up to act as a makeshift bookend. A threadbare rug, missing some tassels and curling along one edge, was laid along the floor next to the bed. In the corner was a small oak trunk next to a dusty red wheelchair.

She stared around the tiny space, feeling her whole body suspended. This was the room beyond that wooden door. The locked room. She stared at the items, dust covering everything, cobwebs in the corners of the room and hanging beneath the shelves. This was a child's room. A sick child. Her baby somersaulted, wild movements as she stared once more at the wheelchair.

Her eyes travelled down, noticing the thinnest gap along the bottom of the window. The wood had warped over time so the window couldn't quite close. She was about to turn away when she spotted something strange on the white windowsill. Scratched into the surface of the paint were the subtlest of lines, the white flaking roughly along the edges. But Ava could see clearly what was written in capital letters, neatly spaced out, the words facing the outside so she could read them.

HELP ME.

Chapter 30

MARION

I don't tell Hamish any more, so the whiskery doctor doesn't come. I know the sensation but I also know they won't last.

Sometimes they cling on; sometimes my stomach swells with the promise of them so that, for a few weeks, I let myself imagine and it becomes almost unbearably true. I tentatively start to hope, start to believe. Sometimes there is a little blood; sometimes it pours out of me and I drip for days. Sometimes I am forced to cut the cord, take their tiny forms and bury them – sons . . . daughters. I bury them beneath the bridge, in a place hidden from sight of the house, that I can go to. My babies. I think of the first baby. I wonder where he is.

Hamish rarely comes home. I sit and lose the hours, my clothes hanging, hair grey at the roots, nails peeling, fine hairs covering my arms. Miss Kae fusses so I hide the food, remove it from the dining room, tip it into the soil outside.

I don't roam the estate, walk up to the crags, stare out at Dumbarton Rock or across to Ben Nevis. It is all I can do to visit them, breathless by the time I have reached the spot beneath the bridge, kneeling in the grass that grows there. Above me the bridge casts its shadow, gargoyles leering out of the stone. Sometimes people walk across and through the estate; I see their faces peeking over, fingers pointing to the River Clyde in the distance on sunny days. I stay crouched on the bank in the shadows below until they leave, feeling my sadness absorbed by the soil.

Hamish has been forced to sell more things from the house: a portrait, a silver dining set, a wedding gift. The brown bear stays, scowling as the hallway is diminished in front of him. Pale spaces, dust piling up; he doesn't employ more help from Dumbarton – I am to make do.

Susan has stopped writing, angry with my silence and the rescinding of a proposed visit. Mother tells me Father will not manage the journey. I stay in the house. I am not alone, though. I am with my babies, the solid stones of the estate holding us close.

Every now and again, on the rare occasions Hamish is home, we are invited to dinner parties but he says he is alarmed by my appearance. The excuses follow: she has a head cold, she has a fever, she is unwell. He goes without me and returns with bright lipstick on the stiff white collar of his frilled dress shirt.

Christmases and New Years come and go and she is always there. The border community is small and I have struggled to make friends, aware of the whispers behind a hand, bug-eyed women watching my husband. Her bob has grown out. Her husband is older, carries a stick, has been on breathing apparatus for something on his lungs. She twirls and touches his hands, throws back the blonde hair that hasn't thinned like mine. He follows her always with his heavy-lidded eyes, brown irises swirling.

There are words for women like her: a free spirit, a mistress, a concubine. She has borne her older husband's children; rosy-cheeked and combed, they are presented to her before their bed-times; they press faces through the railings on the landing above our heads. They are bonny and gorgeous. Three heirs. So many. I see Hamish notices them too, lips tight.

He can't understand what is wrong with me. Exhorts me to eat, to take the air. He has no idea that I do get pregnant. But the babies refuse to stay. I am not a mother. I am a waste.

I stand on the stone parapet of the bridge, dizzy with it all, the wind jostling me, whipping my hair across my face, turning my hands blue. I stare at the jumble of slick rocks below, pointed, sharp – a long way. And yet I cannot leave them. I see the spot where they are buried and I find myself stepping backwards onto the tiny pebbles of the bridge, slipping down the stone steps at the side towards them, wheezing as I make my way over and join them on the grassy bank where they lie.

Chapter 31

AVA

'You're serious?' Fraser came inside from the balcony.

'Sorry, I thought I'd told you!' Ava pulled on a different pair of trousers. They still didn't fit.

Flinging them to one side, she reached for a green chequered shirt dress, the buttons straining a little over her body. She looked down, surprised by her size. She had to shop for maternity wear. 'I won't be that long,' she said, pushing the fabric belt through the loops and tying it quickly.

She emerged back into the living room. 'Have you seen my white cardigan?'

'Ava, it's a bank holiday,' Fraser protested.

She stared up at Fraser, dressed in shorts and a T-shirt, the sun brightening the white muslin curtains that billowed behind him. 'I know. I didn't realise when I agreed but I can't cancel – he's Neil's friend. I don't have his number for a start.' She didn't add that she absolutely didn't want to cancel. The thought of a sniffer dog exploring more of the area around the bridge made her skin tingle with anticipation. Would the dog find a scent? Could the bridge just be explained away like that – mink or something else purely logical? 'You could come if you like?' she said, moving towards the mirror that hung above their sofa, pulling her hair into a ponytail. She leaned forward, noticing the thin strands of grey in her brown fringe. She should book an appointment with the hairdresser's too. The lack of enthusiasm in Fraser's reflection was disheartening. She met his eye. 'I really am sorry.'

'This is the last weekend of the holidays and I feel like I've barely seen you,' Fraser said, a weariness washing over his face. 'I wanted to relax this weekend; I wanted to . . .' His fists curled by his side, knuckles whitening.

Ava felt a lurch. She had neglected him, and had broken so many promises these last few weeks. Wavering, she considered calling Neil, telling him to go on ahead without her. They surely wouldn't discover anything new. She glanced at her mobile on the coffee table, imagining cancelling, not heading to Overtoun. She picked it up and put it in her handbag, mumbling an apology. 'It's important,' she said, convincing herself too.

Again, she felt that strange fascination seize her as she pictured her destination. She wanted to be back there; she wanted to see the house and bridge again, to walk around the estate. She didn't look at Fraser as she promised, 'Look, it really won't take up too much time. I'll call you when I'm on my way back. I'll tell Neil we need to be quick.'

Fraser slumped down on the sofa. 'Fine.'

'Make some plans for us.' She tried to keep her voice bright and kissed the top of his head as she swept past. 'Ah, found it!' She picked up her white cardigan from where it was draped over a stool.

Fraser didn't reply.

She reached to unlock the door. 'OK, so I'll see you later!'

He grunted, which was probably the best response she could expect.

She left the flat and drove out of the city, over the Erskine Bridge and off the road at Milton. She bumped up the dusty road to Overtoun House, her pulse quickening as she spied the grey towers through the pine trees, felt that strange sense of being enclosed as the crags hemmed her in on the right. Neil and his friend were already there. Aaron smoked a cigarette with one hand, held a scruffy golden retriever on a lead in his other. She lifted a hand to wave as she pulled in alongside them. The dog looked up, long yellowish fur lifting in the breeze.

Ava shook his hand and bent down to pat the dog.

'This is Bella,' Aaron said, his Scottish accent broad.

'Hello, Bella.' Ava reached to pat Bella, making her yearn suddenly to see Gus. Her mum used to send regular videos and photos of him, but she had barely messaged her in the last few weeks. Ava noticed Bella's white whiskers. 'She's gorgeous.'

'She's my best friend,' Aaron said simply, grinding his cigarette into the ground. 'So where's this bridge then?' His eyebrows lifted, lines appearing on his forehead as he hefted a rucksack onto his back.

'It's around the other side of the house,' Ava said. 'I'll show you.'

They walked together, Bella trotting beside Aaron, oblivious to any encroaching danger. As they stepped into the slices of shadows, the house blocking out the morning sun completely, Bella's ears pricked up. The sound of water grew louder and Ava's mouth went dry as she remembered the last time they'd brought a dog here.

'You will keep her on the lead?' she checked.

Aaron raised a pale eyebrow at her. Behind him, Neil stayed quiet.

'Neil must have told you about it. I'd hate for Bella to be at risk. There's a sign . . .'

'I'll be keeping a good hold of her.'

Neil moved to one side of the bridge, his eyes not leaving the dog, who seemed to be listening intently to Aaron as he bent down and talked to her. Ava joined Neil. A blush crept up his cheeks as she thanked him for arranging this. 'I wonder what we'll find out,' she said brightly, her projected demeanour at odds with the feeling she always got as she looked across the parapets, over the estate and into the distance. It was stifling and sad, everything a contrast to the sun that shone brightly, making her wish she had remembered her sunglasses.

Neil pulled out a small camera and started to film. Ava wondered briefly if she should stop him, see what they discovered first.

Bella sniffed urgently and Aaron followed, keeping the lead long. Ava wanted to caution him once more. They wouldn't be able to stop her if she . . . She swallowed down the warning. Bella returned time and time again to the parapet where Gus had made his run, the ivy-covered window of the house in view, the shadowy verge below. For a second, Bella leaped onto the stone, her body quivering. Her ears pricked as she seemed to sniff the air, a sudden, loud bark making Ava jump, almost treading on Neil's foot, their arms clashing. She took a step sideways, the tension mounting within her.

Then, just as quickly, Bella seemed to make up her mind, leaping off the parapet back onto the bridge, racing around the corner, almost garrotting herself on the lead as she strained to get to the path that ran alongside the bridge. Aaron took off after her as she tore down the speckled pathway into a tunnel of leaves, the trees bent right over the water in places. Ava and Neil followed. Ava paused as she stepped onto the path, watching Bella circle one particular patch up ahead. Aaron let her explore and sniff.

The river grew louder as they moved farther down the path, the long grass tickling their legs, water tumbling over rocks and around boulders, hurtling downstream. Bella had stopped, almost frozen, a little way off, a foot or two from the path on a steep slope that led back to the house, pockmarked with overgrown plants. As Ava reached Aaron, she could just make out the grey stone walls of the house at the top of the hillock. Her heart quickened as Bella seemed to emerge from her frozen state and a continuous low gurgle sounded in her throat as she started to scratch one paw along the ground, tapping at the earth. It didn't look like a home for an animal nor a place for mink. It was simply a grass bank with patches of dark green and spotted with weeds. Ava pulled her arms about herself; the bank was shadowed and cold.

'We could dig here,' Aaron said. He tugged a spade from his rucksack. Yellow nails clutched the handle as he turned to look at Neil.

'Dig?' Ava hadn't imagined this: the insistent pawing at the earth, the electric atmosphere that seemed to crackle in their small group. She laughed nervously. 'I didn't think . . .' What *had* she thought? She hadn't imagined the dog would find anything. And what would they find if they dug? 'Do mink live underground? What . . . I'm not sure we should . . .'

Aaron lifted his eyebrows at Neil as if exasperated.

Neil lowered his camera. 'What has she found, do you think?' He sounded uncomfortable.

'She's telling me there's something here. She's pretty adamant. And Bella here can sniff out things hundreds of years old.' Aaron's gravelly voice was full of pride and his gaze insistent.

Neil shrugged.

'I . . . I'm not sure,' Ava said. They weren't quite on the path; this was technically the grounds of the house. She looked over her shoulder at the deserted space. Even someone walking past on the bridge wouldn't see them unless they peered over. Her curiosity overwhelmed her. 'Alright,' she relented.

Neil raised the camera again. Aaron stuck the spade into the earth at an angle and pressed his weight on it. Bella remained rigid and stared at the spot. Neil had stepped up behind Ava. She could feel his breath on her neck and shoulder as he filmed. The dappled light, the sunlight on the water, seemed at odds with the dull bank, the muddied pile of soil and grass. Bella barked once and Ava felt her flesh fizzle with the sound.

'Stop, girl, stop,' Aaron said gently as he kneeled down. 'There's something here,' he said urgently. He bent over to work at the ground with his fingers. 'Bloody hell . . .' he whispered.

Ava drifted forward and saw Aaron lift something out and lay it on the grass.

'You said they first jumped in the fifties?' Aaron said to Neil as Ava continued to stare.

It was a bone, at least twenty centimetres long. *A bone.*

'It looks like a leg bone,' Aaron said. 'Certainly a limb of sorts, a . . .' He frowned up at Ava. 'A dog's femur?'

Bella growled, padded past the churned-up spot and pawed at the ground again, insistent, the gurgle growing. Ava kneeled on the dry ground and reached for the bone. This didn't seem right. This wasn't what she'd imagined at all. She'd thought the dog might pick up a scent, something driving other dogs wild enough to leap to their deaths. Not this. Why would a bone be found here? It wasn't beneath the bridge. Could it have been buried?

She found herself reaching for it, flinching once it was in her hand. She turned it over. The surface was gritty with clumps of dirt still clinging to it. She felt her face twist with revulsion. Neil stepped forward and filmed her examining it. 'I think . . .'

But whatever she thought was cut off by a shout from the top of the path. She straightened quickly, hiding the bone behind her in one hand, brushing at her white cardigan with the other. Keven was already on the path, looming like a giant. 'I heard the barking; you gave me the shock of my life. I thought—' He finished abruptly, making his way down to them.

Ava was disquieted, unable to step forward and speak. *A bone?*

'You're on private property.' His mild affability abandoned, Keven stood in front of her, patterns on his face from the leaves over his head. He scowled at the churned-up earth and scarred grass. 'I'm not sure what that dog's doing, but I don't want you here – making the house look bad, stirring up all the old wives' tales . . .'

Ava felt the hard nub of the bone in her hand and said nothing.

'I think you should go, Ava. You did your story. I've tried to be helpful but it's disrespectful to be coming back here like this, filming it again when we haven't had a dog jump in years. Trying to find something that simply isn't there.'

Neil had lowered the camera, and Aaron didn't say anything. Bella still pawed at the ground.

'We'll go.' Ava coughed, half-relieved to be interrupted, half-wanting to stay and watch Bella. Keven looked surprised, as if he had expected her to protest. 'We'll go,' she repeated.

A bone?

Chapter 32

CONSTANCE

Crumpet woke me this morning for the first time in days, wriggling down the sheets like a hairy snake, paws straight up, making me scoop him to me with a laugh. His claws scrabble at my skin as his hot breath clouds my face. I squeeze him tight. Forgetting everything else, I get out of bed. My bare feet move quickly over the wooden floorboards as I chase him in delight. We can spend hours like that some days. His yapping is loud and my laughter joins it. Kneeling on the floor, I make silly noises, watching him skip and growl as my fingers chase after him. He steals my sock, scuttles under the bed. It dangles from his mouth like a huge tongue as he crouches low, a ridiculous growl, loving my laughter as I tug at it.

I miss the sound of the key in the lock until it is too late. Mother stands in the doorway, her eyes wide as she sees me in the middle of the rug, scratching Crumpet's stomach as he writhes.

'Oh, Mother!' I get quickly to my feet, rush over to her, still forgetting, 'Look, look, I think he's better. He's up and . . . look!' Crumpet tugs on my abandoned dressing gown and shakes his head back and forward, dragging it to the floor and looking back at me so I might tell him 'good boy'. Rushing back down to bundle him up, I cover him in kisses.

I stop as suddenly as I began when I realise.

Mother has still not spoken and I see her staring at the wheelchair next to my bed. My muscles are so weak, my left leg will grow useless, the bone might break. I must always use it to stop making myself much worse. I know that. But this morning I have forgotten.

'I . . . I . . .' Crumpet is still in my arms, his warm little body giving me strength to find some words. 'Sorry, Mother. I forgot.'

It is for my own good. I will never get better if I don't follow the doctor's advice. I stand and drop into the chair, reach for the leather strap around my waist and buckle myself in. Wait for her to wheel me out of the room and up the wooden ramp she had installed. Crumpet wags his tail, looking up at me as if there is no danger.

She still says nothing and I feel the hairs on my arms stand up as she steps inside the room. She walks over to me and I repeat how sorry I am. 'My leg is alright today, though, Mother.'

It isn't the right thing to say.

Reaching down, she grabs Crumpet. With a frightened yelp, he twists back in her arms, his brown eyes trained on me.

'No!' I go to stand, but the leather strap means I drop back into the chair. My fingers wrestle with the buckle but she has already walked back out of the bedroom door. The lock clicks and her heels tap loudly on the wooden ramp that leads up to the hallway.

'No!' My fists bang on the arms of my chair. 'No, no, no, no! Please, no!' My screams tear out of me, the tears already streaming. 'Please, please, no!' My lap and chest are cold without his tiny body next to me. It feels like she has removed part of me. It is like no other pain I've known, like this time the doctors have cut into my chest and are squeezing my heart.

I am finally out of the chair, back on my feet and I race to the door and pull pointlessly at the handle. But I know it's locked. I pummel my fists on the wood, over and over until they feel bruised, knuckles bleeding. I can hear Crumpet whining somewhere nearby. 'Mother, please . . .' I sink to my knees and rest my head against the door, my body shaking with tears. I cry for I don't know how long. Then I strain to listen for noises in the house. I can't hear him whine. I can't hear his padding footsteps. Where has she taken him? Will she give him back?

'I'm sorry, Mama,' I plead, using the name for her that she likes best. 'Please, Mama, please . . .'

When I peer through the keyhole I can only see tiles, the claws of an angry bear, feel an icy blast that seems to be a warning shot to get back inside. The house is angry too: I am sure of it.

I wait by that door for the whole day, my stomach aching with hunger, loss and fear that I will never see Crumpet again.

Chapter 33

AVA

She knew she had to go home but she found herself turning right at the end of the driveway, back into Dumbarton, the town that had started this whole thing. On a busy bank holiday Saturday, it was thriving. She noticed the remnants of a market: cabbage leaves, squashed coffee cups, bruised fruit being swept away. People sat on benches or meandered next to the river.

What could she do with the bone? How could she find out where it had come from, how old it was? She had put it in a tote bag and glanced often at its peculiar lumpy outline on the passenger seat. She flinched, wanting to scrub her hands clean. With more distance she started to think more logically. No one had buried anything. It wasn't related to the bridge. Was it that unlikely to find an old animal bone? It didn't necessarily mean anything sinister. She was being dramatic, had watched too many movies. Still, she now knew where she was going.

She parked her car outside and glanced one last time at the bag before stepping out. This time, there was no sellotaped sign on the front door. She pushed it open into a dark panelled corridor lined with watercolours of the River Clyde. To one side was a small, unstaffed reception desk. The air smelled of burned toast.

'I'm in here!' a voice called from a room on the right. Ava followed the sound through two glass doors into a small dining room. There were four square tables with sprigs of yellow flowers propped up in vases. The woman from the high street held a bunch of cutlery in her hand as she looked up. She wore the same shade of pink lipstick.

'It's you,' the woman, Mary, said wearily. Ava couldn't help but stare at the knives gripped in her hand.

A bone.

'I'm sorry to burst in like this.'

The cutlery clattered back onto the table in a pile. 'I thought we made it clear that we don't want to talk about it.'

'Please . . .' Ava held out both palms. 'I'm not here with a camera. I'm not here for the news.' She took a step forward. 'I just need to know what you know.'

The woman stood stock-still for what seemed like an age, her fingers worrying at the sleeve of her blouse.

'I promise . . .' Ava sensed a chink in Mary's armour. 'It's not for a piece, it's for me.'

'We don't talk about the house,' Mary said. There was a tremor in her voice. She collected a pile of napkins and started to fold them mindlessly.

'Can I just ask you one question? When we met, you said your mother cleaned there.' Ava recollected the sound of the baby, felt her own baby inside her. 'I need to know about the child in that house. I've seen the room. I've heard . . . things. I was told she was sick.'

'Who told you that?' The woman's head snapped up sharply, napkins abandoned.

'Keven. He lives up there.'

'I know who Keven is.' Mary didn't comment on what he had said. She worried again at her sleeve, twisting a button until Ava thought it would snap.

The silence stretched on, the quiet hum of traffic passing as Ava waited.

'She was sick. Very.' The words were so quiet that Ava thought she might have misheard. Mary looked up, her pink mouth pressed shut tightly. 'My mother's friend, Annie Hughes – Keven's mother – told her about the girl. My mum only saw her the one time. A birthday party, she said. She sat in a wheelchair with a dog. I remember that because I'd always wanted a puppy. Annie said she'd been ill for many years. That she'd died.'

'She died?' Ava hadn't meant to speak so loudly.

Mary nodded. 'Died, poor hen. And then her mother . . . to do what she did? No wonder the place is cursed.'

Ava felt her legs wobble and had to lean on one of the breakfast tables.

Help me.

'Annie was so upset. My mother said that. She didn't like to go back there. And after . . . with the rumours about her poor David . . .'

Ava was one step behind as she looked up at Mary. 'The rumours?'

'Nasty maliciousness.' Mary's voice was hard, her eyes narrowed. 'Annie's husband couldn't hurt a fly. I remember him from when I was a child, gentle as anything. Gave all us kids conkers from the estate. But some say they saw him that day, on the estate, and that he'd been shouting at the lady of the manor. It dogged him for years. The police investigation cleared him, but still people talked. It upset my mother. She said the lady of the manor didn't seem quite right.'

'How did the girl die?' Ava needed to know.

'I'm not sure,' Mary said, looking uncomfortable. 'She'd had operations for all sorts of things. The town raised money for her, paid for some equipment and such, for the house. She was young, I'm sure of that.'

The shrill ring of a telephone jolted them both. 'I need to get that,' Mary said, turning to leave. She looked relieved.

'I can wait,' Ava said.

Mary turned. 'There's nothing else to say. It was a sorry business and no one wants it all brought up again.'

'But . . .'

'You need to leave now.'

She left her standing in the small dining room, a carriage clock chiming four. Mary's distant conversation could be heard in the background as Ava let herself out.

Dazed, she wandered out of the B & B and into her car, pulling away from the kerb without even clicking her seat belt.

The baby she'd heard . . . it had to have grown up to be the girl who'd lived in that room – and who'd died. Her mother had killed herself. So much sadness.

The drive took her less than a minute; the church was around the corner from the B & B. She parked haphazardly outside then spared a single glance up at the turrets of Overtoun House, looming over this part of the town. She stepped out of the car and moved quickly towards the iron railings, opening the lychgate. The scent of roses was sweet as she passed under it. Flattened grass pathways made tracks between the stones and she imagined what was buried beneath them, her mind full of death and bones. Reading a myriad of names and ages as she passed, she found herself wondering at the lives of Beloved Mothers, Granddads, Sons. Dead flowers leaned in dirty jam jars in which dried insects curled up in the glass.

There were cracked and sloping stones under a small beech tree, the inscriptions no longer legible.

Somewhere in the distance a baby cried, a wail in a direction she couldn't make out – muffled but persistent. She kept moving, the cry not ceasing as she pictured Bella sniffing the ground of this graveyard, pawing frenziedly at the soil. She had to find the girl; it felt vital in that moment.

In the farthest corner, she found a stone crypt, a low rail and a small gate around it. Her heart raced. It looked suitable for a local wealthy family. Steps led down to an ancient locked door, the keyhole thick with dust. *WEST*. Here it was. It didn't take long to scan the names of the occupants. There were no children. Nobody, in fact, buried since 1925: a Lord and Lady West who had both died in the same year, *Beloved Parents of Hamish*. Ava frowned. But where were the mother and child? Was the younger Lady West's suicide the reason they were not here? And where was this Hamish?

Next to the crypt an old, faded gravestone stood out for being so well tended: the grass was neatly clipped; the flowers, pinks and oranges clashing, upright in a proper vase – such love! *ANNIE HUGHES*. Ava started. This was the grave of Keven's mother. Did he bring his dad to this spot? Why had Mr Hughes been seen shouting at the lady of the house? She thought then of an old man somewhere in a care home in Dumbarton. Had a killer escaped justice for all these years? Was that why the house felt so unsettled? As if it was angry about something?

She left the graveyard and returned to her car. She pulled out her mobile – four missed calls from Fraser. Checking the time, she was shocked to see it was past five o'clock. His last voicemail message was simply a dropped call. She could picture the expression on his face as he was met with her answerphone message for the fourth time.

She called him back, her eyes falling on the bag on her passenger seat, the outline of the bone inside.

The lady of the manor didn't seem quite right.

He answered just as she was about to give up.

Help me.

'I'm sorry, sorry. I'm not sure where the time's gone . . .' She attempted to inject a lightness in her tone but knew the words were falling short.

'Are you back soon?' His voice was clipped.

She brushed her fringe out of her eyes. 'I . . .'

Help me.

What had happened to that girl? Why would she ask for somebody to help? Why were the letters facing out, away from the house? The bone still sat there. Ava's eyes rested on it – and then it dawned on her. 'I have to do one more thing.'

'You're joking?'

'Sorry, I really won't be long.'

'OK, Ava, you need to be back here by six, alright? Six thirty at the latest. Promise.'

She started the ignition. 'Promise,' she murmured, her hand reaching for the bag on the passenger seat, feeling the strange hard surface through the material, remembering the weight of it in her hand. 'Promise.'

Fraser had already hung up.

Before pulling away, she took one more look at the house, picturing that child's dusty room. It wouldn't take long, she convinced herself – a quick detour and home.

'Hey!' Pippa couldn't hide her surprise.

'Hey,' Ava said breathlessly. 'Sorry I didn't call. Well, I sent a message but I don't think you got it. It doesn't say you read it.' She was already inside the house. The living room door was open and Tommy was inside, running around in a Spider-Man outfit.

'Hey, Tommy.'

He didn't look up.

Pippa turned and went into the kitchen. 'Do you want a drink? I'm just re-heating something for Tommy for a late dinner.'

'No, I'm alright. I won't stay. I need to get back and make amends to Fraser. Is Liam around?'

Pippa took a plastic bowl with dinosaurs on it from a cupboard. 'He's away on a stag weekend. Tea?'

Ava slumped. 'Oh.'

'Did you want something?'

'Hmm?' Ava didn't want to reveal that she had only come around to see Liam. 'Just to check in. I didn't like the way we left things the other day.'

Pippa raised the kettle and an eyebrow.

'That would be great.' She couldn't help the glance over her shoulder at the clock.

She sipped at the tea as quickly as she could and made her excuses. Tommy wiggled in Pippa's arms as she carried him through for dinner. 'Cars!'

'Not now.' Pippa strapped him into his high chair, his feet now dangling below the bar they used to rest on. 'Auntie Ava's here.'

Ava ended up staying to watch Tommy eat, an agonisingly slow process that made her foot tap on the floor. Pippa soon warmed up and started chatting, lonely from a long day without help.

'Well, I'd better go,' Ava managed at last. Pippa wiped down Tommy, the chair and the floor around him. Ava felt her baby move, a reminder that she would be wiping things down herself within a few months. The thought surprised her, as ever. It was like being dragged back from somewhere else.

'I'm sorry, I'm sorry, I'm really sorry!' she stressed as she burst through their flat door. The words died on her lips as she took in an entirely silent flat, spotlessly clean, the smell of bleach and lemon hitting her. There was a brief note on the side from Fraser: *I waited till seven. Staying the night at Calum's.*

She felt her body sag and the note dropped from her hands. In the living room, half-moon marks on the carpet showed where Fraser had hoovered. He wouldn't have wanted her lugging the hoover around in her state. Christ – even angry, he couldn't help showing that he cared about her. Feeling heavy, Ava sank onto the sofa, picking up a cushion to shove behind her back. She frowned as two pink rose petals fluttered to the floor.

Chapter 34

MARION, 1939

He has stayed away. The worries about an encroaching war keep him in London. I try not to think of the chatter at the last ceilidh I went to. The rumours that my husband is a regular visitor to the nightclubs of Mayfair. More items are sent to Sotheby's: a small Monet and a silver teapot his grandmother was gifted by Queen Victoria.

I have found stubs from his cheque book, made out to The Astor, Murray's Club and other establishments. When home, he plays new, unfamiliar dance records on the gramophone and talks endlessly on the telephone. Whispers, laughter and plumes of smoke emerge from the cracks in the study door. Sometimes I believe he has forgotten I exist. As I wander the grounds, corridors and halls, I feel like a ghost.

The house sees me. The bridge guards my secrets. I feel them both, like solid arms around me, drawing me to them.

Hamish rents an apartment now in Mayfair but I do not travel down. I went back to London once for Father's funeral. The shock of the place – the grey, dirty, noisy streets, the crush of people, the jangle of bells and horns, the stench – made me shake. I pictured a mossy bank, silence bar the noise of running water. There was only Mother beside me at Father's funeral. The vicar had almost refused. It was 'ungodly' how he had died. I still picture a room with closed curtains, a knotted belt, my mother's scream.

Mother begged me to stay on for a few days, flinching at the feel of my jutting collarbone, the wisps of hair at my temple, but I insisted that the estate needed me – I was a vital cog. Mother understood. I didn't see Susan. She is companion to a rich widow in Pimlico, Mother tells me. She has a beau.

I have stopped bleeding now but I am not pregnant. Hamish has not visited me for months. I heard him once on the telephone – the word *divorce* stopping me as I passed – a thing more common now than when I was growing up. Still a shock to hear the term. How ungodly! He can't mean for us. We will be married ten years this summer.

I picture the girl I was when I first appeared here: plumper, livelier, excited. She is buried now, in little pieces beneath the bridge.

Perhaps he does mean us.

I try to be a good wife still. I wait for him under the bedclothes when he is home. I still want to be held, stroked, touched.

Today I saw a young couple meander across the bridge, not looking at the views, the birds in the sky soaring above them, the lush meadows bursting with wild flowers, the butterflies that dipped into view. They were immersed in each other, her face tilted to his, a peachy glow, a smile on her lips. He paused to hold her closer, lower his face to hers. I wished I could taste that kiss.

My palm left smears on the window that slowly disappeared as they moved out of sight.

Hamish has gone and I have stopped eating. I can't leave the house for my spot next to the river; the walk exhausts me, my muscles aching. I am so very tired.

Chapter 35

AVA

She didn't sleep. The flat was too hot and the weight on her stomach pinned her to the bed, making her feel nauseous until she rolled onto her side. Then she would see the empty space, remember the note he'd left.

Her dreams were twisted, grey-white skeletons and the oversized wheels of a wheelchair and a baby's urgent wail a soundtrack to it all. She woke sweaty, her body pulsing, her hair askew, one hand on her stomach until she caught her breath. She was OK. She was safe. The bone was in its bag on the bedside table, its vague outline just visible. Sleep returned and she tumbled straight back into the same dream.

He stayed away the whole weekend, told her he and Calum were going fishing. He was sure she would find some work to do. Term didn't start till Wednesday the following week so he was in no rush to come back. She had done this to them. Where had she been all summer? Why the hell hadn't she come straight home the other day? He rarely asked her for anything and she hadn't even given him that. She tried not to cry when she said, 'We have the scan.' Their twenty-week scan, their chance to discover if the baby was healthy, growing, a boy or a girl. His voice sounded choked as he told her he'd be there. The phone went dead after that.

She was exhausted when she woke early on the Tuesday morning after three nights of broken sleep. The dreams had been darker and more dreadful every time, as if the flat was possessed the moment night fell. She'd seen the towers and the bridge and the small diamond-paned window, its ivy choking the glass and the face inside, a little girl in a chair. She saw dogs leaping, a woman plunging, she saw them all dashing their heads on the rocks below and always the wail of an infant that made her sit bolt upright. Even with the bone now in the top drawer of the bedside table, she had brought Overtoun into their home. She could feel its reach wrapping itself around her even here.

Emerging from the flat, she was red-eyed and groggy, surprised at the daylight, the traffic meandering past, the gentle breeze, the smell of freshly mown grass. She started her car, lurched forward and realised there was something wrong. As she stepped onto the kerb, she stared at the nearside front tyre, which was completely flat. She swore. This was the last thing she needed. Reaching for her phone to call the local garage, she paused, a look darted over a shoulder, not sure why she felt such unease. The mechanic was kind, agreeing to come out and fix it while she was at work.

The train carriage was stuffy with the swell of people, the clash of body odours making her clutch the rail, her stomach churning. The sight of a man chewing opposite, croissant flakes on his jeans, forced her off a stop too soon, a hand covering her mouth, spitting bile on the platform, people watching her as they slid past. She could phone work; she could say she was ill.

She stepped up and out of the station on shaking legs. The short walk should have cleared her head, but she was so tired and unsettled that she was dizzy with the effort. There was a light sheen of sweat as she neared the office. She was late again. Her mouth was woolly, breath sour as she stepped through the space to the right of the car park barrier.

She tried to thrust her shoulders back and clear her face but she knew she must have looked a state. The clothes she had practically sleep-walked into needed an iron. Dark patches on her shirt would force her to keep her jacket on. She pulled out her small hand mirror and tried to clip her hair and wipe her eyes. The liner already smudged. Someone was watching her. She felt her eyes drawn towards the entrance to the building. A figure stood just inside the double doors and she strained to make out a face. Her eyes met Neil's for a second before he disappeared.

As she pushed through the revolving doors, she heard the clack of heels and a carrying voice. 'I've just finished the programme. Going to grab breakfast. I'm starving! Can you sneak off?'

Claudia stood in front of her, looking immaculate in a magenta-pink suit and with kohl-ringed eyes and a hair-sprayed chignon.

Ava shook her head. 'I'm already late.'

'Ah, but you are a senior reporter.' Claudia cackled. 'Surely you have the power!' She reached back to remove some hairpins from her chignon.

Ava's laugh was a little too high, a little too late.

One hand still in her hair, Claudia appraised Ava. 'You look like shit.'

'Thanks,' Ava said.

'Not what I mean. You look knackered.'

'I didn't get a lot of sleep.'

'All OK?' Claudia shoved hairpins into her handbag.

Ava chewed her lip. 'Yeah, yeah, just . . .' Where to start? Fraser? The bridge? The bone? She wanted to talk, but this wasn't the moment to share. Garry's face appeared in the small square door pane to her side and she winced. 'Sorry. I'm about to get told off.'

Claudia glanced at the door. 'Garry's cool, and he loves you.' She adjusted the strap on her handbag. 'Look . . . I'm about later, if you want to catch up.'

Ava nodded as Garry opened the door.

'Alright, Garry?' Claudia called as she moved away. 'Be gentle with our Ava, alright?'

Garry frowned as he approached. 'Hey, Ava, where've you been?' He tapped a clipboard with his biro over and over again. 'You missed the briefing. Again.' Garry was her friend, laid-back and jokey, but she'd been late a lot these last few weeks – and distracted when she did show up. 'Neil says you spent the bank holiday with him.' Garry waggled his eyebrows.

'That's not exactly true.' Ava forced a laugh. 'I'm sorry about the briefing.'

'It's OK. I covered for you.'

'Thanks, Garry.'

'We're friends, aren't we.' His face was serious for a moment.

'Of course.'

'I've got the info here. Shall I drive? We're off to see a woman who runs a funeral parlour.' He read from his clipboard. 'Jackie, fifty-seven.'

'Right,' Ava said, adjusting her handbag.

'Looters ransacked the place two nights ago. Stole jewellery with her mum's ashes inside.'

'Great!' Ava tried to inject some brightness into her voice. If she at least sounded breezy she might get through her day.

Garry gave her a strange look. 'You alr—'

'Hey!' Neil emerged from a side room as if he had only just arrived. Ava nodded at him awkwardly.

'Neil – hold on . . .' Garry put up a hand as if he was about to say more, but Ava didn't want to stick around.

'Well, I'm ready if you both are?' she interjected.

As she settled into the front passenger seat, Ava told Garry about her tyre.

'That's bad luck,' he said, and Ava nodded slowly.

Neil clambered behind her with all his equipment. As he leaned inside, she could feel his breath on her neck and a faint whiff of cigarettes. Garry started up the engine, and the radio came on – the sports news. She could feel him casting her small sideways glances as she rolled down the window, her eyes already drooping with tiredness before they even left the car park.

Jackie was waiting for them, her face peering out from behind thick, pale blue curtains as they parked outside the funeral parlour, the navy-blue facade peeling in places.

She emerged, face pudding-beige in the harsh daylight, powder collecting in the lines on either side of her mouth. She shook their hands. 'They disconnected the electricity,' she announced, as if they were already partway through their questions. 'I've had to call someone out.'

'I'm sorry. Talk us through what happened while Neil sets up.' Garry listened as they followed her inside. Ava knew he had most of this information already, collected over a phone interview, but it was obvious Jackie wanted to talk.

'We turn ashes to glass. Some is made into jewellery and they took a lot of that. And a laptop.'

'How dreadful!' Garry's head was tilted to one side, his voice low.

'They must have thought turning the electricity off would turn off an alarm. But I don't have an alarm. You don't think someone is going to steal from a funeral parlour.'

'You don't,' Garry agreed.

Normally, Ava would be the one to build a rapport, but today it was all she could do to sit there dumbly, removed from it all, her eyes twitching with tiredness. She needed to concentrate. But when she looked up all she could see were urns in every shape and colour, blurring. She was aware of Neil watching her as he fiddled with the hand mic. Her mind was still elsewhere, on urns, death, buried bones and a question just out of reach.

It took an age to get through it all. Garry asked Ava to go over it again as she fluffed her questions, repeated things Jackie had already told her. They filmed a segment outside in front of the parlour's signage. Jackie held up a pendant that was the product of turning ashes to glass. 'I could hear them moving around from the flat above.'

'And what could you hear?'

'Ava?' Garry said.

'Sorry.'

'I think they were looking for cash but we don't keep any on the premises,' Jackie said. 'I used to have a sign up saying that, but the tape peeled off and I threw it away.' She wrung her hands, clearly distressed. 'What kind of scumbags do this? Steal from a funeral parlour? The police told me they used gloves . . .'

'Was what they took worth a lot?' Ava tried to stay focused, aware of the time slipping away. She would be seeing Fraser soon. The thought threw her for the thousandth time. The woman in front of her bristled . . . Jackie . . . Jackie who ran the funeral parlour . . .

'Ava?'

'Sorry.' Ava shook her head and repeated the question. 'Was what they took worth much?'

Jackie still looked displeased. Two high pink spots emerged from beneath the powdery make-up. 'It wasn't so much the cost. One of the necklaces was made from my mother's ashes . . .'

'And how much was it worth?'

Garry gave her a sideways look.

'A couple of hundred pounds, perhaps. But the jewellery *meant* a lot. That's the *point!* It was a beautiful pendant. I don't have more of those ashes. That was my mum. They've *stolen* a bit of my mum!'

Ava blinked, the words circling in her mind. She lowered the microphone. 'I have to go. I'm sorry, I . . .' She couldn't miss this too. Fraser was already angry with her. This would be unforgiveable. And she needed him; today had shown her that. She didn't want to face everything on her own. She had prodded and pushed and dug up the past and she could feel the danger circling her.

Neil peeked out from behind the viewfinder at her. Garry stepped forward to put a hand on Jackie's shoulder.

They were all waiting for her to speak. But Ava turned and walked away.

Chapter 36

CONSTANCE

I can hear him howling somewhere in the house and I pound my fists on my bed. I think my heart is breaking, tearing in two, the pain in my chest taking my breath away. A yap, claws on tiles – or is it all in my head?

Mother won't talk to me when she visits, leaving and taking away trays, staring at congealed porridge, too-warm milk that coats the glass, soups with thick skins. She won't answer my questions. I plead, I beg, I scream, I shout. I want to run for the door, want to search the house but I'm frozen, not wanting to make her angrier. If I'm good she'll give him back. 'Please, Mama . . .' I cry again, tears that wet my cotton nightdress, stick it to my skin.

For a moment I think it is her, returning after breakfast, but then the door doesn't open. I tiptoe to the door and press my eye to the keyhole.

'Annie, Annie, please!' My voice cracks. 'My dog, please . . . ask Mother . . . please!'

'I . . .'

'I need him. Please, Annie, I need Crumpet. He'll be missing me. Please . . .'

She wrings her hands, turns back up the ramp then changes her mind as I softly start to cry.

'I'll ask, Miss. I'll ask . . .' Her footsteps are quick and fading. A door opens and closes.

I feel as if I have really lost a part of me. I dream of his drumming heart, his soft fur, the smell of him. I imagine waking to his tongue on my cheek. I pull at my hair. The ache in my chest is never gone now.

Then, after a few days, Mother visits me. We have an appointment with the doctor. She runs through what I have to say, if asked.

'But I will do the talking. You don't know the medical words.'

'I can't.' I shake my head.

'Of course you can. The doctor wants to make you better. Don't you want that?'

I just want Crumpet. I can't speak, curled into a ball on my bed. My arms are tight around my chest but I have nobody to hold. I can hardly remember how he felt, how he smelled. It is worse than before, when I had never known him.

'If you come and talk to the nice doctor you can have your dog back.'

I am still, as if I have imagined the words. 'Oh!' I am transformed. Struggling to sit up, I start to gush. 'I will, I will, I promise! My legs are weak. I can't walk at all now and I must always use my chair.'

'That's a good girl. See? Won't it be nice to see the doctor so that he can help get you well?'

'Yes. Yes, it will! Thank you.' I start to cry, my whole chest up and down, up and down. 'Thank you, Mama!'

The doctor greets me with a smile, his head tilted to his shoulder when Mother wheels me in. The baby angels on the ceiling watch, too. When I open my mouth to say hello, he stares at the gaps where my teeth were – another gone. It makes my smile slip away.

Mother tells him about my muscular atrophy, her worry about the strength in my left leg, and mentions some research from America. She knows such a lot and the doctor beams and tells her so. 'You are lucky.'

'Yes.' I nod. 'I am.' I think of Crumpet waiting back in my bedroom for me, his deep golden-brown body in my arms, his little heart next to mine, the tiny wags of his tail that mean he wants to play.

Mother doesn't sit. She watches by the mantelpiece, smoothing her hair when the doctor isn't looking.

He asks me to try to stand and wants to check my weight and I see Mother biting her lip and I know I need to do it *slowly* – show the doctor that my leg is very bad. Crumpet. The way he lies on his back demanding to be stroked, his lip curled if I refuse then wriggling when I always give in.

'Yes, Doctor.'

Clutching the chair, I stand slowly, making sure to wobble a little before I sink back into my chair with a big gasp and Mother looks across at the face of the doctor.

He is thoughtful, writing things on his notepad. I can't breathe as the silence stretches on. Then he closes the pad and asks Mother about the days where I am sick from my mouth. He gives her vitamins that might help my hair thicken and grow back. I touch it, imagining myself covered in thick fur like Crumpet. I just want to be with him and away from here.

'Is there an operation perhaps that might cure her?' Mother asks. 'I have read that some have to undergo amputation if they decline.'

I don't know what amputation is, but the doctor looks at me hunched in my chair. 'We will see,' he says. He thanks Mother for

184

another Dundee cake. 'Really excellent!' I am a lucky girl to have such a clever mother.

'I have heard about the real advances in prosthetics these days,' Mother says.

'We will see.'

I think Mother is pleased because she smiles. I think of Crumpet. Soon he will be snuggled in my arms and I can't help a wide smile back.

Chapter 37

AVA

The subway hummed beneath her, lulling her once more into a strange half-sleep, her limbs aching as she exited, queued and boarded a bus to the hospital. Why hadn't she ordered a taxi? She was hit by a smell of egg sandwiches and sweat as the bus hissed to a stop outside the enormous building.

A text message pinged on her mobile. *I'm here until 6 p.m.*

Will get to you just before. Pls wait if I'm late, she replied. She could head there after the appointment. She had the bone in her bag and she didn't want to take it back into their flat. She didn't want that thing by her bed another night. She trembled with the memory of her dreams, sweat beading at her hairline as she stepped off the bus.

Fraser was waiting just inside the entranceway. The sliding doors opened to a warning sign that someone had just wiped that part of the floor.

'You look . . .' Fraser clammed up as she stood practically swaying with tiredness in front of him.

'Like shit?' she supplied.

The response brought a half-smile to his face.

'Claudia already told me.'

'Nice of her.'

For a second, everything was alright. Then a shadow crossed his face. 'Shall we go up?'

It felt awkward to be side by side in the lift together and not touching, greasy fingerprints on the buttons, the faintest stench of vomit masked by bleach. Ava gulped the air as they emerged onto the second floor. They didn't really talk in the waiting room, rigid on their plastic seats. Both showed way too much interest in the posters, the signs, the others waiting. A cough, a rustle, a shout for a small child to 'sit still' all reminded them that if they spoke, everyone would hear them. And what could she say? She had screwed up.

So, she sat trying not to think about the hoovered floor and the rose petals. He had asked her to be back there for a certain time. What plans had she messed up? Sneaking a glance at Fraser's sad profile, she wanted to ask.

'Ava Brent!'

It was when Ava was instructed to get on the bed and roll down her skirt as before that it struck her: this was the twenty-week scan, the one in which they searched for any abnormalities. She had barely thought about her baby these last few weeks and that thought robbed her of speech.

Fraser stared at her for a while as she lay, her head resting back, following the instructions.

First came the reassuring beat of the heart. Ava clenched and unclenched her fists as the sonographer, a woman with a high top-knot and an Eastern European accent, stared at the screen, endlessly clicking, probing, clicking, reading out measurements Ava didn't understand.

'Is the baby doing well?' Fraser asked, his voice scratchy and self-conscious. Had he been waiting for her to ask the same thing?

'The baby looks very well.'

Fraser exhaled. 'Great, great.'

He had been thinking about the health of their baby. Why hadn't she?

'And Mum, you're looking after yourself? There's a note here from the nurse about your blood pressure . . .'

Ava could sense Fraser stiffening in his chair. She should have told him it was a little high.

'Do you want to discover the sex today?' asked the sonographer.

'I'm not—'

'I don't—'

It was something they hadn't resolved, something Fraser had asked, more than once, but she had never really answered. 'I . . . I don't think so?' It was tentative, a quick glance to confirm. Fraser, eyes turned down, nodded. This was a sad day; his figure drooped in the too-small chair as he leaned across, trying to make sense of the screen, trying to share in this moment. She had robbed them of a joyful scan. He shouldn't be staying with Calum or not finding out the sex of their child or not knowing what she wanted.

The gloomy atmosphere persisted as they left, despite clutching folders, a sheet of paper confirming all future appointments and the sonographer's cheery goodbye. The moment the double doors slid back and they were outside, Fraser turned to her. 'Shall we go somewhere to talk?' he suggested.

Ava was about to agree. Of course she wanted to talk. Nothing was more important right now. 'I do want to . . .' she began.

His face darkened.

'I just . . . there's something important I have to do. I need to see someone at work before they head home.'

Fraser frowned, not following, annoyance replacing the sadness. 'Who?'

'It's about a work thing. Important.' She tried to dance around the question.

'What's so important?'

'Don't get angry.' She tried appealing to him, palms up. 'We found a bone. At the house – well, the dog found it. That's where I was when I was late the other night. And I think it's important to check what we've found. I thought Liam could help – at the uni. He's a scientist after all and I thought they could test it, maybe. See where it had come from.'

'A bone,' Fraser repeated slowly.

'Yes. On Saturday . . . you know that . . . that bridge.' She gabbled, trying to make his glower lessen. 'The sniffer dog . . . well, she found something. That's why I was late back. It could be important, it could be . . .'

She knew from his face she shouldn't have told him where she was going. It had only made it worse. 'An animal bone? Some ancient dog or a bloody badger or something? You really think that's more important than this, Ava?' He indicated the space between them. 'Were you even going to bother to tell me about your blood pressure? What did the nurse mean?'

'It's nothing. It was a tiny bit high.'

'It's more important than a bloody bone!' Fraser said, his voice cracking.

How could she tell him what she suspected – what the bone might be? She had no proof, nothing tangible and yet something inside her felt sure that she had to do this. She had to get to the truth. 'I know, I know, it's just that I promised Liam and he leaves at six and . . .'

'Oh my God, so? It's *Liam*. Drop it round or see him later in the week. It's not exactly an emergency, is it?'

She thought of the bone in her bag. Could she make him understand why she thought they shouldn't take it back to their flat? That she didn't want it there? And it *was* important. She couldn't articulate what she felt when she thought of that bridge, that house, what had happened there. She knew Fraser wouldn't understand because she didn't understand herself.

'There's something about that place, Fraser. I see it. I dream about it. I feel something that I can't explain. When I'm standing there, it's like I'm . . . I'm part of something . . . the bone is important . . .'

Fraser rubbed his jaw, the frustration building as she tailed off. 'Go,' he said. 'We can't salvage anything much anyway. This has been a bittersweet week, Ava. Today was meant to save it.'

It was her turn to be lost.

'This was meant to be one happy day in among the shit ones. I'd planned to ask . . . You know September is hard, and the weekend . . . today . . . they were meant to be something good in all of that.'

What had he been planning that weekend? Rose petals, his insistence on her returning. Had he . . . She was distracted as she tried to order her thoughts. 'Why is it hard?'

The moment she said it she wanted to cram the words back in her mouth.

'Why?' Fraser's eyebrows shot up. 'Oh my God, Ava, can you not think of anything else apart from this fucking house? This supposed mystery?' The words oozed sarcasm, his palms waving. 'It's the month my mum died. Remember? Three years ago this month? Sitting by her bed? Holding her hand?'

'Of course,' Ava said. 'God, I'm sorry. Of course, Fraser. I'd forgotten. Lost track . . . I . . .'

A pounding started behind her eyes just as the sun shot out from behind the cloud, making her wince. It was as if a spotlight was being beamed on her utter inadequacy. 'I'm sorry . . . I . . . didn't get much sleep. I know about September, of course I do.'

She had loved his mum too. Her eyes filled with tears and her thoughts started to muddle.

'Really, Ava? Because you don't act like you do. You're my family now . . . you and our baby. Since Mum died . . .' His eyes filled as he looked at her. 'Just go. Go and see Liam and do what you need to do because I don't want to be with you right now anyway.' He gulped as if he was swallowing down the other things he wanted to say then straightened and headed to his car. He didn't offer her a lift and she didn't ask for one. She deserved this.

Chapter 38

AVA

He wasn't there. It was obvious from the feel of the place. The space that always felt like home was now like someone else's apartment. No familiar smell of cooking garlic, no sound of sizzling meat. She missed his bad dance anthems from the speakers in the kitchen and his call as he heard the door. Nothing. Quiet. Bare. Gone.

She wandered the four rooms of their small flat, noticing the changes: a single toothbrush propped in the mug; a missing framed photo from the wedding reception of one of his friends; the place in the hallway where he left his golf clubs, where she always moaned they took up too much space – she wished she was tripping over them now; the hooks exposed by the missing outdoor coats, anoraks and duffels – where other people bought shoes, Fraser bought jackets; the suitcase from the bottom of the wardrobe gone; his rail emptied.

A bowl and spoon had been washed up and dried. The surfaces were wiped down. There was a sheet of A4 paper on the side filled with his careful handwriting. She approached it slowly, knowing the contents of it were going to hurt her. Going to hurt them.

Calum had offered him a spare room. He would stay with him for a while. Ava felt bile rise in her throat, not noticing the buzzer to the flat until someone pressed it repeatedly.

For a strange moment, she imagined it was Fraser, who had changed his mind. He would stride in, seize the treacherous piece of paper and tear it into a hundred pieces. He would bring up his suitcases, return his golf clubs (that she'd never moan about again), the photo from the wedding, his toothbrush and he'd say it was all a silly mistake. She pushed her finger down on the entry button and poked her head out of the flat. 'Fraser I—'

It wasn't Fraser.

It was her mother, marching up the stairs towards the flat.

Ava was both crestfallen and dumbfounded. Her mother hadn't sent her a message or phoned her in days. She felt a mixture of relief and resentment.

She should invite her in, but there was the hurt of the last half an hour, the letter still there on the counter in the kitchen. And, although she wanted her mum – wanted a cuddle, wanted to be treated like a child for a short while, to be loved and listened to – she also was aware that she and her mum had drifted apart in recent weeks. Ava pulled the flat door towards her, blocking the view of the place.

Her mum looked uncomfortable, a tight fist around her handbag, her jaw tight. It was dinner time; right about now she should be in the kitchen wearing her apron and shouting at Dad to stop doing his jigsaw in the conservatory and help her lay the table, telling Gus to stop begging at her feet. 'Are you going to invite me in? Is Fraser here too?'

'He's out.'

Her mum stepped past her and entered without removing her coat or relinquishing her handbag. 'I was at Pippa's. I have Tommy on Tuesdays. Liam told me you and Fraser had a row.'

Ava bristled. 'Nice of him to have a good gossip about it. I suppose Pippa was there too, enjoying my fall from grace.'

'Don't be silly, Ava. She was concerned, if you must know.' Ava felt a flash of shame. 'And Liam wasn't gossiping. He thought I would want to know you were upset. Although when he told me . . .' The grip on her handbag tightened. 'Honestly, Ava. You had your scan and then you felt the need to traipse halfway across the city so you could ask poor Liam to risk his job finding out about some bone you fou—'

'It's hardly going to risk his job,' Ava said, flaring up.

'Well, I told him not to do it – not to indulge you in this . . . *obsession*. It's already caused poor Fraser so much pain.'

'You had no right to do that! And it hasn't.' *Poor* Fraser. Her mum had always adored him. And Ava had always loved that she fussed over and spoiled him. Now it just annoyed her.

'He came to see your father only a week ago,' her mum began. Why would Fraser go and see her dad? Ava could feel the dismay building. 'I made him stay for a good meal, poor boy. He said he'd barely seen you all summer.'

Ava crossed her arms. Now she really did feel like a child again – sullen at being told off.

'You're an obsessive, Ava. Always have been. That's why you went into journalism – always digging, digging – won't let anything go.'

'I thought you were proud of that. You always said you brought me up to be a strong woman!' She and her mum shared so many qualities: both outspoken, passionate while being private about their own emotions. 'Well, I'm sorry my job – the job I love, I should add – is suddenly so terrible!'

'It's not.' Her mum's face softened, her grip on the handbag loosening. 'But you've never before been such a pit bull, willing to sacrifice your own life, your own happiness, for it.'

Ava felt a throb at the front of her head around her eyes. Her overwhelming tiredness, the nightmares, the fight with Fraser . . . all of it had exhausted her.

'Where *is* Fraser?' Her mum looked as if she was seeing the flat for the first time, dropping her handbag on the hall table and moving into the living room.

Ava followed, massaging her temples. 'He's . . .' She could have lied but decided not to. 'He's staying at Calum's . . . just temporarily.'

Her mum turned with an open mouth. 'Ava, you need to fix this,' she said in a low voice.

The pointing out of the obvious only made Ava want to scream or break something. Had she been alone, she may well have done.

Her mum opened her mouth and then closed it again, her eyes troubled. What had she been about to say? 'I'm here for you, you know that.'

'Is that why I've seen so much of you these last few weeks?' Ava was on the verge of tears, her throat thickening. 'Is that why my phone hasn't stopped buzzing?'

'I . . . I'm sorry. I *have* been thinking about you. And about the baby. Whether you are doing too much, taking enough breaks. Pippa mentioned your blood pressure . . .' All the things her mother had obviously been carrying around with her, the little anxieties, tumbled out, and the barrage of it made Ava feel even more twitchy and on edge. How could she now admit she had barely thought about their baby these last few weeks, that her mind had been taken over by another baby, another child? Her mum was right: she *was* obsessive.

'I'm fine!' Ava snapped, moving to her flat door. 'I just want to be on my own.'

Her mum wavered, suddenly looking as forlorn as Ava felt. Ava straightened. *She* had been the one to come here, tell her off, make her feel bad. She didn't get to play the victim now.

Perhaps her mum understood, because she nodded once, picked up her handbag from the table and stepped through the open door. She turned on the mat, her lips beginning to part. Ava shut the door quickly so that whatever she was about to say was cut off once and for all.

Chapter 39

AVA

Ava drove in the dark. She didn't know where she was headed until she crossed Erskine Bridge, the River Clyde flowing black beneath her. She turned off down the familiar track, her headlights shaking, animals diving for safety in the verge. The sun had long set and the road was a ghostly blue as the car bumped and shook over the stones.

The small car park was deserted. As she swung her car into it, the headlights swept the line of pine trees. She pulled up and turned off the ignition. The clicking of the engine cooling was the only sound as she sat there, her eyes straining to see ahead in the dark, the crags hemming her in. She felt light-headed as she stepped outside. The ground seemed uneven. She was hungry, that was it.

You're obsessive, Ava.

The house stood even more imposing in the darkness, the towers lost to the night, the windows black holes. She stared at it for an age. Were all the rooms as tired as the grand drawing room with its ornate painted ceiling and flaking skirting boards? Had the house ever been full of light and life? She imagined parties crammed together, chatter, a thick cloud of smoke hovering above ladies in velvet, men in tuxedos, cocktail glasses tinkling, waiters standing nearby, round silver trays loaded with replenishments. The grand scenes dissolved as she stared at the forbidding blocks of stone.

She shouldn't be here. She had driven Fraser and her mum away, but the same fascination, something so strong she couldn't resist, called to her. The words on the windowsill, the discovery of the bone had only fuelled the feeling that this place harboured a dark secret and that somehow she was hurtling to the heart of it. She felt her baby turn, a strange flip-flop. What bone had they found? Anger flared that her mum had told Liam not to indulge her. He would do as he was told; he'd always been intimidated by her mum. She would call him, tell him to test it. She shivered in the cold, already moving towards the house like a sleepwalker.

Her footsteps crunched loud on the driveway, small stones skidding away from her as she passed beneath the high walls of the house, trembling as she pulled her jacket around herself. An oppressive silence as if the building was gobbling up the sound of her footsteps. Holding her breath as she moved beneath it, eyes ahead. The noise of churning water quiet at first, rising with every daunting step.

Stepping onto the bridge, her flesh was spotted with goose-bumps and the smell of damp filled her nostrils. Approaching the thick stone, her heart leaping, it seemed that she was the only person in the world. She pressed her stomach against the side, the cold seeping through her clothes. Her baby jerked, startling her, and she pictured the small foetus scrabbling at her insides.

She stepped onto the nearest parapet, the small step of stone. The wind whistled, bending the branches of the trees, whirling like soft voices around her. *One of the thin places.* The back of her neck prickled. What was it about this bridge, this place, that had affected her, seeped into every corner of her life? Why couldn't she get it out of her head? She wanted to stop thinking about it, wanted to fix the damage it had already wrought, and yet she felt a desperate need to be back here, to delve deeper. Why? The chasm was black beneath her, sucking its answers deeper under the water, further out of reach.

'Stop, please.' The voice was familiar, halting.

The shock of it made her wobble on the parapet, one hand quickly grasping the ledge. She sensed movement, a rush of footsteps. Arms clamped on either side of her as she was pulled back from the stone parapet onto the gravel of the bridge, her pulse beating in her ears. 'What the . . .'

Keven stepped back, both palms up, backing away. In the moonlight, his face seemed drained of colour, his eyes almost all white. 'I thought . . . You looked like . . .' His breathing was heavy.

Ava felt her insides settle. 'I . . . I'm sorry, I . . . I was . . .' What was she? How could she explain the strange impulse that summoned her here; that drove her to stay awake; that distracted her from her job, her relationship, her own baby; that triggered the things she heard when she was lying in the darkness?

'I saw you from the house. I thought . . .'

He didn't explain what he thought as Ava noticed a toothpaste mark on his lip and realised he was dressed in a dressing gown and slippers. He had obviously run down to save her. She stumbled out an apology. 'I didn't mean to scare you . . .'

He stepped towards her, glancing over her shoulder into the void. 'The lady . . . she jumped from this spot.' The quiet words almost lost by the noise of the water running below them. 'You look—'

'I wasn't going to jump.'

They both stood in silence for a moment. The bridge was like a living thing, breathing in and out, eavesdropping on them both. She didn't want to be standing on it any more.

'I saw it.'

A fox shrieked in the distance, making Ava's heart pound. 'Saw it?' Her voice was barely a whisper.

'I saw her jump. I was eight years old. I spoke at the inquest.'

'Oh God . . . I'm sorry.'

'When I saw you . . .' He dropped his head and Ava felt a desperate sadness for the poor man. Even sixty years later, it was obviously still a dreadful memory. What must he have thought seeing her on the bridge from the house? History repeating itself.

'I am truly sorry. I'll go now. I'm . . . I'm not sure why I came. I needed to . . .' She moved past him, her footsteps quick, away from the water, the bridge, the spot where so many terrible things had happened. She was swallowed up by the shadow of the house, heading back towards her car.

'Wait, hold on!' Keven followed her. She twisted back around. He was still breathing heavily. 'I'm glad you're here. I've wanted to apologise to you – about the other day . . .' She could barely make out his face as they stood beneath the stone tower.

'It's fine. I should have told you what we were doing.' Guilt about the stolen bone robbed her of any more words.

'I shouldn't have shouted. I've been stressed.' He raked a hand through already mussed-up hair. 'I've been wanting to attract visitors back here and I was worried that dredging up the dog suicides would stop people wanting to come.'

'I don't want to endanger that,' Ava blurted. 'But I suppose I've become . . . there's something . . . something here.' Her words were as jumbled as her thoughts. Keven waited as she tried to put them in order. How could she explain the feeling that overwhelmed her when she stood on that bridge, something unfinished, something she felt connected to? How did she tell him about the sounds she'd heard in the studio, the baby, her own body reacting as if they were communicating with her own child? The hands behind her on the crags? The words on the sill and the bone in the ground? The feeling

200

that something terrible had happened here? 'I find myself thinking about the place, the bridge . . .'

Keven pulled the cord more tightly around his dressing gown, his teeth chattering with cold.

'I'm sorry. I'll go.' She hadn't realised she was trembling, but as she drew her car keys from her pocket the metal tinkled and clashed.

'Ava, wait.' A hand on her shoulder. She froze. Keven took a breath, something clearly troubling him. 'I need to give you something . . . something I found in the house.'

Ava stood dumbly in the darkness, the moon slipping behind a bank of cloud.

'It was something I should have shown you before, perhaps. I think you need to see it.'

Chapter 40

MARION

The doctor has visited – a new doctor because the previous one has retired. This doctor is a great deal younger, with soft hands and a thin moustache disguising a lack of top lip and hair combed into the neatest side parting. His accent is English and that in itself is a comfort. He is from Hertfordshire but he moved to Dumbarton with his wife and young daughter because he had visited Loch Lomond as a child and fell in love with it.

'My first sight from the top of Conic Hill is one I will never forget,' he says.

I don't tell him I have never been. I crave for him to tell me more.

On his first visit I cannot do much but listen. Miss Kae had telephoned him. I have been fainting, struggling to climb the stairs to my bedroom, my bones ache, my skin is dry, Miss Kae tells me I am a skeleton, although I believe she exaggerates wildly. The doctor has prescribed bed rest and meals brought to me on a tray. He promises to return and see me.

The following week he is pleased. Miss Kae tells him I have eaten a little bread and soup every day and he takes my pulse, his fingers warm on the inside of my wrist. He smells of lemons and the outdoors and I want him to tell me about the views over Loch Lomond again, about the ache in his thighs as he climbed the last hillock, his breathlessness as he stared across the water and the fields. I want him to look at me earnestly, notice the infinitesimal changes, his moustache twitching with concern.

On the third visit, I am sitting up in bed and he has asked me more questions. My voice is scratchy and unused but I tell him about the babies I have lost. He reaches across and holds my hand and we sit there for an age. I could still feel his hand when he removed it, my own palm glowing from the contact. He told me I had extraordinary fortitude, that I must be very strong to have shouldered such hardship. He suggested that we pray together and I closed my eyes and allowed the words to wash over me and give me strength.

I look forward to his visits.

He rewards me with smiles and praise as I put weight back on, as I regain colour, as I move out of my bedroom again, as I am well enough to walk around the grounds once more.

Miss Kae pats me, relief in the tears that line her eyes. She's never married. She has a sister in the town and a young niece she visits, but mostly her life is this house and I. The doctor says I am a special woman, that others would not be so strong. He will visit me while I am recovering. I want him to stay always. I want to please.

I do get better. Gradually I find my strength. I garden, plant flowers for a new year, trying to brighten the grey facade of the house that seems to have absorbed the grief of the last few years: the stone duller; the stone walls cracked in places; a boarded-up window over broken glass; abandoned rooms, thick with cobwebs; the smell of festering damp that seeps into my clothes. I can see the house through the doctor's eyes: a glance at the bear; flinching at the clank of pipes; the whistling wind that can pass through a room without warning; the yellow stains on the ceiling of my bedroom like gnarled hands inching towards me in the bed, wanting to wrap me up.

When the war breaks out, I am relieved the doctor tells me he will not be called up. He will stay here and minister to his patients.

London is unsafe and so Hamish returns to Overtoun. I think he should fight, I tell him. That Hitler is a terrible man. We must all do our part. Hamish joins up.

The doctor says he doesn't need to visit me any more. I'm a perfect patient; he would that they were all like me.

The next month I get a dreadful migraine. I ask Miss Kae to summon the doctor back. He returns, kind face filled with concern, soft hands writing me a prescription. 'Does it hurt dreadfully?'

'Yes, Doctor.'

'Is this your first?'

'Oh, I have had them before, Doctor.'

'Does light make it worse?'

'Why, yes. It does, Doctor.'

The twitch of the moustache, the grey eyes darker as his brow furrows.

He promises to come back. He might do some tests. I feel a wonderful heat in my stomach. I watch him leave, his motorcar bobbing down the driveway to the road. He will be back.

Chapter 41

AVA

She drove home a few hours later. There were barely any cars about at this time. Street lights flashed past her and there were long stretches of dark road. The dusty item she'd been given lay on the passenger seat next to her. She shivered as she recalled what Keven had told her.

The block was quiet, the neighbours above and below her no doubt asleep. Once inside, she was stung by their perfectly made and empty bed. How long would he stay away? There was the blink of the microwave clock, the counters visible from the faint light of a street lamp, the note that began *Taking some time . . .* and signed with his name. She opened the fridge, light spilling out, the gentle hum of its motor. Lingering, she reached for the bottle of white wine and twisted off its cap. The acidic shock of it sharpened her senses. She picked up her newly acquired item from the counter.

Settling on her sofa, she clicked on the side lamp. The baby moved inside her, the feeling like bubbles. She'd put back the wine bottle and replaced it with water, one hand on her stomach by way of an apology. She fumbled to pick up the box, the items slipping inside it.

She had followed Keven inside the house, the heavy wide doors revealing a cavernous hallway, the bear lurking in the shadows, the temperature as cold as outside.

'It's in here.' Keven indicated the doorway to the right, down a few steps. She sucked in her breath as she followed him down to the locked door on the right, a wooden ramp, dusty and disused, propped on the wall next to it.

Keven twisted the key in the lock and Ava heard a click. She hesitated as he looked over his shoulder, imagining him bundling her inside for a mad second. *HELP ME* scratched into the window-sill. A prisoner? The door swung open and she felt a stuffy warmth drawing her closer to the entrance, a smell like warm oats. Beyond Keven she could make out the end of the single bed, the corner of a rug. Her eyes moved straight to the diamond panes of the window, the sill below.

'I kept it in a trunk,' he said, moving inside as Ava edged closer. There was a doll above her, its face lit with moonlight, sitting on a shelf thick with dust. Books slanted, their spines unreadable. 'I wasn't sure what to do with it. It didn't seem right to throw them away.'

He emerged clutching something to his chest. She got a last look at the room before he drew the door shut, pocketing the small metal key after he'd turned it. As she stepped out it was as if the house enveloped her back in its icy grip. She hugged her arms around herself, her back teeth shaking with cold. Keven walked up the steps and rested the item on the wooden pew that ran along one wall.

It was a shoebox, dusty smears on its lid. Keven watched her as she approached it, as she opened the lid to see yellowed notebooks and diaries.

'They found them when they tore up the floorboards of the master bedroom. From way back, the thirties . . . before she . . .'

Before she jumped.

Ava lowered herself onto the pew next to it, her eyes wide, her body tingling as she lifted the top diary from the box.

'Maybe reading her story will persuade you more than anything I say.' His expression was sad, mouth turned down as he looked at the box. 'It's a sad history, and that's why I haven't wanted it dredged up again.'

He had walked her and the box back towards the heavy front door. A clank of old pipes and an icy draught forced her head up. Keven shuffled beside her in slippered feet, his lined face exhausted, the bags prominent under his eyes. 'I think you'll understand when you read them.' She had left him there in that frozen corridor, his eyes following her as she made her way to her car.

Tucking her feet beneath her, she lifted off the lid of the box once more, unable to wait until it was light. She wouldn't be able to sleep knowing they were there in the flat, answers to questions, answers to things she hadn't thought to ask. The smell of aged paper, of damp, assaulted her. One or two of the books were watermarked and damaged. She sorted them into date order, hungry for information about the woman from the bridge. What had happened to her and how had it left its mark?

She took out her first volume, a small rectangular book with yellowed pages and a faded spine. The old leather cracked, dry and peeling, large sections already lost so the dried glue on the spine could be seen. On the inside cover in slanting blue ink was written *Marion Foot*.

She felt her baby roll and gurgle inside her as she reached to turn the first page, her mouth dry, a sip of water before she began to read.

The first entry was dated 1929. It made her smile. A tea dance in the Savoy. A man! She pictured beautiful people doing the Charleston, legs kicking, bright expressions, beaming smiles.

Marion wrote with a lovely innocent naivety. How would she end up so far away, jumping from a bridge in a remote estate in Scotland? Ava forced herself to slow down, not to skip ahead, to drink it all in. The first diary was full of hope and excitement, her courtship, the dances, her upcoming marriage.

She picked out the next, and the next, her smiles soon fading, all warmth slipping away, the writing increasingly messy and scrawled. She blinked at the appalling details, shivered at the memory of a baby's cry.

Ava's eyes ached with the effort of reading, dawn filtering into the room, the curtains never closed. She felt woozy and thick-headed, her mouth dry, the glass of water long gone.

The last diary was wrecked, loose pages that Ava carefully pieced together. So many losses. On the endpapers, a strange collection of disconnected words, some crossed out – *apples? plums?* – and a peculiar chart with dates and numbers. It didn't make any sense. But the last entry distracted her, and the words and chart fled her mind.

The final entry was written in a different style, capital letters on the page. No lengthy explanation but a short phrase:

I WANT TO BE WITH THEM.

So, this woman who had lost all her babies couldn't face a life without them.

Ava thought then of the room in the house: the books, the doll, a single child's bed – empty. A baby had lived. Ava was sure. What had happened to the child that had survived? Surely she would have been loved? Ava felt goosebumps on her skin as she thought of the words on the windowsill. Where in the diary did it tell about that child? Or did Marion never want anyone to know?

She pictured the bank on the edge of that burn, the dog's barks as he burrowed beneath the soil. Ava remembered the chill in that desolate spot. What had he sniffed out? What had she taken to Liam? If all the babies had been buried in the ground, was a sickly child buried there too? Was that what they had found? Depending on what bone it was, it could have been big enough.

She shut the last diary. She knew she would never forget what she had read, that she would never again wonder why the bridge was such a hopeless, desolate place. She sat still, hearing the cars moving past outside, people beginning their day. Her head and eyes throbbed with lack of sleep, staring at too-small writing and the things that filled the books.

Poor Marion. Poor Marion. Ava felt nausea build within her as she recalled the details of her losses, the terrible ordeal she'd been through on her own, the things that poor woman had endured. If she had lost a child too . . .

She felt the baby somersaulting inside her. Memories of the twenty-week scan returned to her: the moving image on the screen; the feel of the probe on her stomach, pressing and pushing to show Fraser and her all the healthy parts – heart, two legs, two arms, the brain, the fluid levels good, the measurements correct. Their healthy, growing baby. And she had barely thought about it, barely acknowledged how lucky they were.

She closed the lid of the box on the diaries. So much sadness contained inside. She felt tears line her eyes as she rested back on the sofa, as she hugged the box close to her chest and wept.

Chapter 42

AVA

She'd snatched an hour or so's sleep and woken with a sore back, a dry mouth, her breath stale. She had to leave early to get in on time.

Her head woolly, she decided to leave her car. She was in no fit state to drive it. She headed to the subway. Horns blared and early morning traffic was at a standstill. Almost there. Her eyes barely able to stay open, she thought for a moment she had imagined the figure moving in parallel with her on the other side of the road.

He was tall, a baseball cap pulled down low. She wouldn't have noticed him but for something about his movement; his occasional glances made her feel he was following her. Shielding her eyes, she turned to get a better look at him but a bus pulled up beside her with a sigh and obscured her view. The bus doors closed with a hiss and it set off once more. The figure had gone.

Perhaps it was the sleep deprivation, perhaps she had imagined it, but she recalled other times over the last few weeks: a feeling she couldn't quite pinpoint, that she was in someone's lens. She thought of the note. Maybe it was all related? She shivered at the connections. *You are being watched.*

The briefing in the too-bright conference room, its glass walls allowing the sunlight into the room, was a struggle. On the wall and under the harsh office light was a set of blown-up photos of her and her fellow reporters wearing their best toothpaste smiles. When had these been taken? She couldn't help but think of her red eyes, the bags beneath, the cracked lips.

Garry was late for the meeting, but when he did appear, he didn't glance her way. She offered to cover a story and spent the rest of the time doodling to stay awake. Afterwards, Garry talked to another reporter as Ava lingered, wanting to talk to him. A squeeze on her shoulder made her jump. 'For fu—'

Claudia stepped back and laughed. 'Sorry, I saw you through the glass. We need a catch-up. It's been ages.'

Ava was slow to respond. 'We do,' she agreed.

Claudia frowned. 'Are you alright? You look a bit . . . peaky.'

Ava touched her face self-consciously.

'Is it . . .' Claudia lifted both her eyebrows. 'Have you told work yet?'

Ava shook her head.

Claudia simply waited – a trick Ava had seen her use on guests in the studio.

'You know when people write in . . .' Ava blurted.

Claudia's eyes rounded. 'What do you mean? Viewers?'

'More like trolls. Have you ever had a letter?'

Claudia tilted her head to one side. 'Yeah . . . have you?'

Ava crossed her arms over her chest, nodding. 'I got a note. It was weird. Said I was *being watched.*'

Claudia grimaced. 'Gross. Any others?'

'Just the one.'

Claudia pressed her lips together, her pink gloss impeccably in place. 'Probably just a bit of a sad case. Keep it – or give it to HR.'

'OK.' Ava felt a small whoosh of relief that Claudia didn't seem worried.

'I've got one who sends them in purple ink that always makes my skin crawl.' Claudia's mouth screwed up in distaste.

Ava had received the odd email in the past, typically delivered as 'feedback': criticisms of her clothing or a new haircut. But never a physical note and nothing had ever felt so personal, so sinister.

'Look. Don't worry, alright? I've got to run, but promise me you'll get some sleep, OK? You don't exactly look blooming.'

'Charming.' Ava felt her mouth lift a fraction.

Claudia blew her a kiss as she rushed away. 'Love ya!'

Ava felt a tiny bit lighter as she turned back to Garry. The other reporter had left and Garry was shuffling papers on the desk. She stepped across to him.

'I wanted to apologise,' Ava blurted. 'About yesterday.'

'It's OK.' His voice was low. 'We got enough. I did the edit.'

'Thanks. I owe you, Garry. I really am sorry . . . it won't happen again.' Suddenly Garry's face was blurring in front of her.

'You alright, Ava?' His voice was full of concern and she knew he had forgiven her.

'I didn't sleep well. But . . . I'm ready to film. Can I drive with you, though?'

'Car still out of action?'

Ava nodded, not wanting to admit she hadn't felt in a fit state to drive. Was it just her imagination or did Garry seem suspicious?

Garry drew her into one of the empty editing suites, the room still musty despite the smell of furniture polish. 'Are you alright, Ava?' Concern etched his face. 'I've been worried. Recently you've been . . . different.'

'I know. It's been . . . complicated.'

He sat on the edge of the desk. 'You know you can talk to me. We're close, aren't we? Friends?'

'We are,' Ava said. They had started out in the newsroom around the same time, moved through the ranks together. Garry had often been an ally in briefings to the bosses. They ended up on a lot of jobs together and that suited her fine. They'd got into a good rhythm.

Garry and Fraser didn't have a lot in common, but Garry had met a girl called Katy and they had been on some double dates together. Katy was fun, a teacher at a secondary school in the city different from Fraser's. She and Fraser had bored them all endlessly with chat about pastoral care and Bloom's taxonomy while she and Garry would talk about story ideas and TV shows. For a time, she thought Katy and Garry would get engaged, but the relationship ended and, somehow since then, their out-of-office friendship had taken a back seat.

Now, sitting here with someone who actually knew her and Fraser as a couple, she found herself wanting to share all the worries she had been holding so close to her, that she hadn't told Fraser or even her best friend.

'Quick, duck!' Garry whispered as a man in a baseball cap walked past the glass square of the door. 'It's Neil. Don't want him finding us yet. Not exactly a man of many emotions, is he?'

'And you are?' Ava couldn't help but smile a little.

'I know you don't like your men too emotional. Said it made you nervous to see a man cry.'

Ava puffed out her breath. Had she said that? 'Not sure I've got a man any more,' she said in a small voice, her arms crossing her stomach.

Garry frowned, leaned forward so she could smell peppermint toothpaste on his breath. 'What do you mean? You've broken up?'

'No . . . well . . . God, I hope not. But . . . well . . . I'm pregnant. Twenty weeks. I'd decided not to tell anyone at work yet. We had the second scan yesterday. But Fraser . . . Well, we had a row and he . . . he sort of left.'

Garry didn't speak for a while. His eyebrows knitted together and his fist opened and closed on the desk. She couldn't read him at all as he cleared his throat, filling the small space as he stood up. 'I had no idea,' he said. 'Pregnant. And it's Fraser's?'

'Of course it's Fraser's!' Ava ejected a high laugh at the prospect of her baby being anyone else's.

Garry's face was still serious, his eyes dark and unreadable.

'But now he's left – I pushed him away!' She felt the despair rising as she pictured his face as she left him after the scan.

Garry pushed the hair back from his forehead. 'God, no wonder you've been distracted.' There was a glimpse of his usual cheery self beneath the intensity. 'I'm glad you told me.'

'I feel like I'm going a bit mad, to be honest. And what if Fraser doesn't come back? What if I have to bring up a baby on my own?' She wrung her hands as panic gripped her.

'Hey,' Garry soothed, reaching to put a hand on her arm. 'Hey, you won't be alone. Whatever happens.' He didn't speak for an age, chewing his lower lip. 'A baby . . . Well, whatever happens with Fraser you've got friends, Ava. Are you . . . are you going to keep it?'

'Yes, yes of course!' Ava's hand went straight to her stomach.

'You can survive anything. If you decide . . .'

'No. Garry.' Ava was appalled. Was he suggesting what she thought?

'You can heal after these things,' he said, his voice soft.

There was something in the words that suggested he had experienced just that.

'Garry? Did you and Katy . . . Did you have a baby?'

He gave her a faraway smile and then wafted a dismissive hand. 'Why don't you take the day off? Take some time to think. I can get someone else to do today.'

She nodded and whispered a thank you, everything too much.

'I'm glad you told me.' He stepped forward to give her a quick hug that caught her a little off guard. 'I'm always here for you.'

Chapter 43

CONSTANCE

I am good for months and months. We have a party in the green room when I become nine years old; I sit in my leather wheelchair with the red arms, Crumpet in my lap, and open presents. He plays with the string. The house feels strangely full up, egg-and-cress sandwiches on a tiered stand, scones with butter, smells and sounds too loud. The woman who cleans, who calls Annie 'hen', is there, and Annie and Mr Hughes and their boy, Keven. He looks different when he's inside. He doesn't talk to me, half-hiding behind Annie dressed in his stiff shorts and shirt. I wish he would.

Mother kisses the top of my head as she wheels me back to my room. 'Good girl.'

I go to the doctor in Glasgow more now. He showed me to one of the other doctors there – a surgeon. Mother's eyes glowed as they talked about me and my chair and my legs and how they don't work really since the polio I had.

Crumpet grows. Crumpet is my friend. My loving companion. Crumpet stops me being lonely. A lot of days I forget to remember about other children, about looking out of the window. I still move around the room, leave my chair, but never for long. I'm always scared that Mother will see, that she'll take Crumpet away from me again.

Then I see him on the bridge. The boy. Keven. He often comes, and today he is walking next to his father, Mr Hughes, the man with the hat and the big scissors. The boy is so much taller now with a pale, thin face, light red hair and a large laughing mouth. He is so alive he never seems to be able to be still – skipping, leaping, throwing stones from the bridge, whooping at the sky. He sometimes spots me in the window and, at first, I dipped out of sight, clutching Crumpet to me, burying my head in his fur.

This time, though, the day is dreary. The clouds are grey and fat when the boy bursts into view again, racing across the bridge. His shouts make me edge near the glass and peer out of the diamonds at him. I can't help smiling as he hops and jumps and runs about. How much fun it would be to be racing in the outdoors. If I could do that my legs would be strong again. I can feel them wanting to move, to wheel, to leap, to jump. I want to join him. I stand right up on my wheelchair, hands on the windowsill, watching.

The boy wears a long grey coat and boots and he has moved so close today, standing at the top of the stone steps leading down to the path that runs a little way from the window. He looks to his left and that is when he sees me.

I stare. I can't help it. I forget to dive away, to hide, and I find myself lifting a hand. I am waving at him, not realising how close I am to the window until my nose nudges the glass. The boy waves back and I feel like Crumpet when he leaps with delight. The boy grins and pokes his tongue out and I laugh in my small room and do the same, tapping on the glass with my fingers. How I want to play!

Suddenly the boy looks back over his shoulder, towards the bridge and I look too, wanting a glimpse of Mr Hughes, his kind

216

eyes crinkling as he watches his boy. I wonder if my father would have looked at me like that.

I wobble on the chair I have dragged to the window as I strain to see him. Mr Hughes comes into view. I'm still smiling when I realise he is walking with someone.

I am too late. I cannot get down in time. My mother looks across, her mouth still moving as she talks to Mr Hughes, a finger pointing towards the garden until she spots me, mouth falling open, arm dropping to her side like a stone. Even from here I can see the warning in her eyes. Mr Hughes looks at her, at me, frowns.

I slink off the chair, out of view, my hands slippery, my head pressed against the cold, whitewashed wall, wishing I could disappear through it and away. I stay listening for any sounds, not daring to look up out of the window and be caught again. Maybe it was in my head? Maybe she didn't see me at all.

I turn and face the room; every item in it accuses me. The walls seem to close in on me as I creep low, dust-coated feet quiet on the floorboards. Crumpet is still curled up asleep at the foot of my bed and I join him, curl my body tightly around him, squeeze my eyes tight, try to feel comforted.

She doesn't come. Time passes. Crumpet wakes and the sun drops out of the sky. I wrap my blanket around my shoulders, tummy empty and aching. I rub my thumb and forefinger together as I wait. I don't want to leave my bed. I don't want to leave Crumpet. I lick my lips and sit on the edge of my bed. My shoulders start to relax; maybe it will be fine.

I strain to hear the rattle of the tea tray. I reach out to ruffle Crumpet's fur. There are footsteps – I am sure of it. A key turns.

She appears. There is no tray and no bowl for Crumpet. She comes into the room and I stare at the floor, ready for the things I will say . . . that I must listen to her and the doctor . . . that I'll always stay in my chair . . . that I won't look out of the window. 'I am sorry, Mama.' She lets me talk and my voice gets bolder as I go on, my grip loosening.

She holds a blanket. She reaches across me and for a second I think she might be tucking it around me with a gentle word, that I need to keep warm, keep my strength. Instead, she grabs at Crumpet, folds him quickly into the blanket. There is a whimper and the material is jumping in her arms.

I watch in horror as she steps backwards.

'I trusted you,' she says.

I want to get up, to run, to beg, but I know if I get up it will make her angrier. 'Please, Mama.'

I can't bear it. Not to see him for days. My eyes don't leave the bundle in her arms.

'Go back to your window,' she says, and I freeze.

She locks the door clumsily and I do get up. I hear her walk up the ramp, across the hallway. The heavy front door to the outside bangs shut behind her. It is as if someone has turned up the sound, as if I can hear every step as she crosses in front of the house.

With my palms on the wall I trace her steps, back at the window, feel every muscle strain.

I see her walk past the top of the steps where the boy had stood. She turns and stares at me. My mouth is dry. I don't understand. I can't stop looking at the bundle in her arms.

I am right up against the glass, unable to tear my eyes away. What is she doing? Why is she taking Crumpet out onto the bridge? Why does she want me at the window?

And then I realise.

I watch every second.

I scream and scream and scream.

Chapter 44

AVA

The subway carriage rattled beneath her as she sagged in her seat. She would never have managed filming. Later, when she stepped out and climbed up into the street, she cannoned into passers-by who gave her filthy looks, her mumbled apologies coming too late. Her phone rang and she lifted it to her cheek, barely glancing at the name, just hoping to hear Fraser's voice.

Pippa was shrill as she greeted her. 'Mum said you kicked her out.'

'I didn't kick her out.' Ava was too tired for this. She was about to make her excuses, about to hang up, no time for sibling rivalry or tensions or another row. Then she realised Pippa was giggling.

'You poor thing! Forget about Mum – I was worried about you. Liam said you were really upset, that you and Fraser had rowed. And Mum told me he isn't in the flat with you any more?'

'It's true,' Ava gulped. She turned into her street and lowered herself onto the low wall outside their flat. 'Oh God, Pippa . . .' She cried then, a messy, snotty, blubbery mess – no words, just sniffs.

'Hey, hey, it's OK,' Pippa soothed. 'Ava, it's OK. It's going to be OK. Fraser loves you.'

Ava couldn't speak for a moment.

'Ava, stop it, come on. It's fixable. It's all going to be OK.'

Ava wiped her eyes with her shirt sleeve. 'I don't know, Pippa. He was right to leave. I've totally neglected him – and the baby.' She was wracked with sobs once more. A woman walking a dog on the other side of the road peered in her direction then sped up when she caught her eye.

'Well, you are having his baby at least, so that's one way to get him to see you.'

Ava couldn't help smiling in spite of herself.

'Look . . .' Ava pictured Pippa in her house, her head tilted to one side, phone tucked under her chin, a solemn expression on her face. 'You need to call him. Now. Today. And you need to say sorry. It doesn't even matter if you're not.'

'I am!'

'Well, that's even better! You need to say you're sorry, that you'll fix it, that you'll stop neglecting him, that you'll be . . . better.'

Better.

She wasn't used to Pippa taking control like this. Normally it was herself or her mum calling the shots. For a moment she considered what it was normally like for Pippa, caught between two competing alpha females. How exhausting that must be.

'Thank you,' Ava whispered. She was bent so low that her hair tickled her cheeks as it hung down.

'Hey, you're my big sister!' Pippa's jokey voice was back. 'I'm allowed to offer advice you'll ignore.'

'I won't ignore it. I'm going to do it.'

Pippa shifted gear, her words tumbling out in a hurry. 'Look, Ava, I haven't been a great sister recently. I'm sorry. I think, you being pregnant . . . it sparked something – a stupid thing. An old jealousy about you and Mum being closer . . . it's silly and embarrassing—'

Ava cut her off. 'I get it. It's fair enough. I know how Mum and I could be sometimes.'

'Well, I'm favourite now!' Pippa joked, and Ava wondered if the thick voice she could hear meant Pippa was crying too.

'She loves us both.'

'I know.' Pippa suddenly lightened. 'And Liam telling me about the scan? God, Ava, it woke me up, you know? You're pregnant! You are going to have a baby. I am going to be an aunt. And that is so bloody exciting!'

Pippa's words were like a shaft of sunlight and Ava was still smiling when they said goodbye. She knew what she had to do.

She woke from her nap feeling groggy initially but, after downing a pint of water, she felt as if she was transforming back into a functioning human being. Fraser had agreed to meet her in less than an hour and she wanted to be on time and looking fabulous.

Hair glossy, fringe straightened, teeth cleaned and make-up on, Ava felt more like herself than she had in weeks. Throwing a loose white cotton shirt over leggings, she headed out of the flat.

The streets of Glasgow were busy with mums dragging school-age children around, pencil cases, new shoes and uniform bursting out of bags. Ava's palms dampened as she rehearsed what she was going to say when she saw Fraser.

It was a cafe they hadn't been to before; Fraser was already sitting in an orange booth when she appeared in the door. He half stood up as she stepped inside before returning to his Coke bottle, his hand shaking as he raised it to his lips. Normally clean-shaven in term time, he now wore a thick layer of dark stubble; his eyes looked bruised, the bags prominent under the overhead strip lights. An approaching waiter melted away once she'd ordered a Diet Coke.

'Hey,' she said.

'Hey.'

Amid the banging of pans, the smell of frying onions, a bark of laughter from a group of teenagers in one of the only other occupied booths, Ava looked down, shame overwhelming her. All the things she'd planned to say dissolved. 'I . . .' She raised her head. 'I came to tell you how sorry I am. For everything. For ruining your summer. For being distracted. For . . . for forgetting about your mum. It was unforgivable.'

The wait was interminable as she looked back down at the floor, staring at Fraser's toes under the table, the faintest tan showing under a pair of flip-flops.

Finally came his voice, quiet in the hubbub. 'And I'm sorry – for walking out. I just didn't know what else to do. I couldn't keep nagging – you didn't seem to notice . . . anything . . . I had plans . . .' He swallowed. 'I had wanted to propose this summer. Make things official for . . .' He gestured at Ava's stomach.

She couldn't stop her mouth falling open, a gut-punch of regret and pleasure and sadness robbing her of words. She thought of the petals that had fluttered to the floor. *Oh God.* And she had been at Overtoun Bridge, lost in someone else's story, absent from her own.

'That's . . . that's . . .' For the second time that day she felt her eyes fill up, blinking as she tilted her head back, the bright light part-blinding her as she balled up her fists and stemmed the tears. The waiter with her Diet Coke on a tray had gone into reverse, lingering now by the counter.

Ava felt warmth and looked down at his hand over hers, realising how much she had craved his touch these past few days. 'I'm so sorry,' she said. 'I will make it up to you. That is . . . You are going to come back?' The breath was suspended in her chest as she waited for his reply.

Fraser smiled, the gap in the middle of his teeth on show. 'Of course I will.'

Ava didn't have the words to respond. She just gripped his hand, squeezing it as if she might never let it go again. *A lifetime.* He wanted them to spend a lifetime together.

She never had her Diet Coke. They left the cafe together, Fraser's arm around her as they moved down the street, Fraser telling her about his preparations for school, Calum's gross habits – 'Left his toenails in a tiny pile on the arm of the sofa, Ava.' She felt a surge of gratitude as she listened, as they headed back together to their flat. She was still smiling as she reached for her mobile, which buzzed with an incoming call.

'Is that Ms Ava Brent?'

It was a call to tell her the cost for her tyre being replaced. She thanked the mechanic and was about to hang up.

'It was slashed from the inner side,' he said gruffly. 'Deliberate, definitely. It's trickier to do than you might imagine. Thought you should know.'

She didn't remember saying goodbye. She felt almost out of her body as she lowered her phone and Fraser stopped and looked at her. Why would anyone slash her tyres? To stop her driving? Out of malice?

'Is everything alright?' Fraser asked.

'They fixed my puncture,' she said slowly. She didn't want to tarnish the hour with anything more. But something dark settled over her. *You are being watched.*

Chapter 45

AVA

She threw herself into feeling normal again, determined to keep her future on track. Although busy in his new role as head of sixth form, Fraser found time to erect flat-pack furniture, cart various things to the tip, remind her to take her vitamins, make her a packed lunch for work. He would stop, reach for her, one hand on her growing stomach, not saying anything.

She planned a week's holiday up on Skye for October half-term – called it a 'babymoon' – booked a two-bed cottage with views across the sea, windy walks. There was tea in flasks, books in front of the fire, the snap and crackle of apple logs, walking arm in arm for meals in a pub with low beams, the smell of spilled beer and the sound of murmured voices – and his low, gentle laughter.

And the baby was bigger now as autumn swept by, its limbs sticking out at strange angles, a ripple over her stomach, surprising her, winding her, pressing up against her so she couldn't forget even if she had wanted to. Which she didn't. The hard, rounded reminder gave her swollen ankles and back ache and searing pain that shot down her pelvis. She bounced on a birthing ball and toyed with names. They had decided to wait to discover the sex. A surprise. The future felt bright and golden.

Overtoun hadn't left her, still lurking in the background, a strange silhouette she couldn't expel. It returned sometimes in her dreams, that vertiginous feeling when peering over the edge into the swirl of water, black, bottomless and loud, the sound filling her up, waking her suddenly – a kick inside as if the baby had been disturbed too. She would turn to see Fraser's profile in the grey light and calm her breathing.

Guilt weighed on her when she thought of a wooden ramp, a windowsill, a bone. She had learned so much but knew she risked being sucked into the story, into the place, and it scared her. The diaries should have stopped her wanting to dig but instead she found she had more questions, not less. Something was just out of reach, teasing her from the shadows.

She didn't dare talk about it with Fraser. She didn't want to risk everything she had clawed back. She had so much to lose now. But there were days when she found her mind back there, wanting to get in her car and drive over the Erskine Bridge. She once made it as far as Milton without realising, a grey day at the start of November. The temptation to steer off the road, to bump up that driveway, to pull into that car park and head to the bridge had almost over-whelmed her. She swallowed it down, resisted the strange pull and headed home, not telling Fraser where she had been, the secret a hard stone in her chest.

At her last GP appointment, her blood pressure had still been a little high. 'We'll keep an eye,' the doctor had said. 'Is there any-thing causing you any emotional stress? Is work pushing you too hard?' Ava had shaken her head too forcefully, glad that Fraser hadn't been there. He'd only have worried.

The diaries sat on their bookshelf in front of a modest row of orderly books. They were cracked, peeling and discoloured but, having read the contents, she didn't feel she could just throw them away. Sometimes she found herself straying, taking one out, leafing through it, staring at the sad entries, pausing at the strange list of fruit, the chart with its numbers, as if Marion had been recording something, re-reading those last terrible words, their letters capitalised and shaky.

Why had Marion abandoned her diaries? Had she stopped writing them when she had finally given birth to a baby who survived? Perhaps happiness had meant she no longer needed to pour her grief into the pages? And yet she had kept them all her life, in happier times too, and her baby hadn't been healthy. Her baby had grown up to be a sickly child and that child had died. How? The curiosity tugged at her. She could return, she could find out—

Ava jumped as she realised she was in danger of becoming lost again, returning the diary to its place in the row. They all looked strange and out of place in their pristine flat with the boxes piled up neatly, flat-pack furniture complete, a pale blue wing-backed nursing chair, a white wooden mobile, a painting of the alphabet.

In the drawers of the changing table were impossibly small clothes. Pippa had gifted her bags of things: pristine white sleep-suits, thick sleeping bags, swaddling clothes, bibs in every colour, vests, blankets and more. Pippa was pregnant again, too – early days, her baby due in the summer. 'So I'll be on different seasons,' she insisted when Ava protested that she was too generous. 'I can always take it back.' She brought more. The thought that they would have children so close together made the whole thing more special. Ava hugged her tight. They shared much more than baby clothes these days; their messages sailed back and forth daily.

Colleagues had been kind. A few scattered congratulations cards were now propped up next to her computer, one from Garry that had made her eyes sting. He had been quieter since she'd told him; she tried to be sensitive to it, not mention the pregnancy despite a stomach so big it squeezed her lungs and made her catch her breath. Even a couple of viewers had written in, although one unsigned letter had made her blood freeze. It came with the job, she had convinced herself; there was always one nutter; almost all the broadcast journalists she knew joked about a 'stalker'. It didn't mean anything. And yet she couldn't get some of the sentences out of her head and they joined her midnight musings: angry words, reference to a 'betrayal'. She had handed that one to HR this time.

There was one person she had barely heard from as the trees were stripped of their leaves and the wind whipped them from the ground and the days grew dark in the late afternoon. She was at Tommy's party, his second birthday. All of them were crammed into Liam and Pippa's house, every radiator blazing but her dad still muttering about being cold. They'd sung 'Happy Birthday' and given presents. Tommy had missed most of it having a long lunchtime nap.

It seemed to Ava that her mum had melted away, always managing to find some task or other rather than talk to Ava. She once found herself standing in the living room, a hole opening up inside her as she watched her mum leave rather than be alone with her. Only a few months before, they had been sending each other daily messages, her mum delighting in FaceTime, which meant she could phone Ava from any hillock on a blustery walk to show her the deer in the distance or some view over a loch. She would sometimes meet her after work for a quick drink, just to catch up. She'd been so proud of her daughters, wanting to be involved in their lives.

'How long now?' Liam appeared by her side, startling her.

'I'm thirty-two weeks,' Ava said.

'Oh.'

Ava wished Fraser wasn't off helping her dad with the settings of his 'confounded iPhone'. She never quite knew what to talk about with Liam. 'Nice party.'

Tommy appeared, a cupcake in one hand and an apple in the other, cone birthday hat askew.

'Hey, Tommy!' Ava greeted him with maximum bonhomie.

'Liam!' Pippa called from the kitchen. 'Can you grab Tommy's apple? I need to cut it up otherwise he eats the whole thing.'

Liam bent down to Tommy. 'Did you hear that, little man? Mum says we have to cut up your apple.'

'Liam!'

'I'm doing it!' Liam called.

Tommy clutched the apple closer to his chest as Ava suppressed a smile.

'Please, Liam.' Pippa's face appeared, red-cheeked. 'I don't want him eating the seeds. It's dangerous.'

Liam looked up. 'If he digested them whole, it would take around a hundred seeds to have any kind of effect. If he crushed them, then perhaps—'

'Don't get all science-y about it, Liam, please. Tommy . . . pass Mummy the apple.'

Tommy held it even closer.

'Apple, please. Or I'll take away your cake.'

Tommy handed his apple over grudgingly and then ran out of the room to protect his cupcake.

Ava watched the exchange as if from afar. Despite knowing that she and Fraser would no doubt be involved in this kind of tussle before long, she still felt one step removed. The other thought came from nowhere, so forceful that she lowered herself onto Pippa's sofa. The sound of the party faded around her. Liam's mouth moved but she couldn't hear the words.

Was it possible?

She stood up, wobbling for a second as her centre of gravity readjusted. 'You know that bone I gave you?' she said, her voice low.

Liam glanced across the room and through the open door to the kitchen. 'Yeah . . .'

'Can you get it tested? Like you were going to.'

Liam shuffled on the spot, the familiar blush beginning at his collar. 'I'm not sure . . .'

Ava followed his furtive gaze into the kitchen, to where her mum spooned fruit salad into a bowl, her other hand gesticulating as Pippa looked on with Tommy wriggling in her arms. 'She doesn't have to know.'

Liam stayed silent.

'Liam, please. It's been months. I just need to know who it's come from.'

'What do you mean, *who?*'

'I mean where it's come from,' Ava said quickly.

'OK,' Liam said, almost a whisper.

Ava needed to leave; she needed to think. She could feel her pulse quicken, an insistent beat, beat, beat as Overtoun loomed large in her mind. She was there, back on that path, as Bella pawed that ground over and over again, urging them to look. What else would she have found if she had continued to dig? Who had the bone belonged to? Was it an animal at all? Her mum was heading towards them, angling her body towards Liam. 'Thank you,' Ava said. Liam was only able to nod once before bowls of fruit salad were thrust into their hands.

'With lychees,' her mum said, not holding Ava's gaze.

'Thanks, Frances.' Liam's response sounded too loud and enthusiastic. 'Yum!'

'I need to find Fraser,' Ava said, melting away. The urgency of what she needed to do overwhelmed her. Things gradually forming from murky thoughts.

Chapter 46

MARION

Hamish leaves for war, a weary look from a man who turned eighteen in 1919. He thought he would never see conflict. We all did. He clung to me in my bedroom the night before, my body pleasing to him again. When he departs, he reaches for me. I take his hand, feeling nothing but a coldness deep inside. He is frightened, that is all.

I imagine my father if he was alive, what he would think if he saw me watching my husband leave for war, khaki uniform, polished boots, a gas mask tied to his kit bag. History repeating itself – doomed always to repeat itself.

The house is as unkempt as its mistress these days. We don't use the dining room any more; the dust sheets are back over the long mahogany table and the other furniture that remains unsold. An inspector visits, but the house is not fit to be requisitioned, unlike some of the other large properties in the district designated to be given over in part for the war effort. I spend my days in the kitchen bundled into layers and layers of clothing that cover the downy hairs on my arms and disguise the weight I am losing once more.

Miss Kae has left; her sister has had a stroke and she must care for her. The doctor worries that I will be left alone. Miss Kae suggests that her niece, Annie, moves in. She is eighteen and engaged to be married to David Hughes, who is also away fighting in the war. She arrives with bright eyes and stocky legs and I feel even more insubstantial.

The thought of leaving the house makes me frightened now, when once I longed to roam, to travel, to chat with neighbours in a busy high street. It is as if my ankle is shackled by some invisible chain, looped around the grey stone, entwined in the ivy of my bedroom, lodged in the lines of the ceramic tiles of my bathroom, fastened to the head of the gargoyle on the bridge. Annie queues in the town for our rations, prepares sparse and plain meals, and I visit my babies, talk to them. I take in sewing that is needed for the war effort. I work long into the nights. The house watches me as I move soundlessly across its floors.

The doctor visits. The migraines are back and I have a pain in my chest. It comes and goes. I have fainted, yes. The chest pain is worse when he returns the following week. 'Yes, since yesterday, Doctor.' The thin moustache twitches and I meet his eyes, see something different there. Am I still brave? Special?

'Perhaps,' he says gently, 'these maladies are in your head.'

He doesn't visit for a month, even though I write to him. I tell him about a new symptom: a metallic taste in my mouth. I don't leave my bed for two days, I am so sick.

The war moves on and it seems hopeless. London takes a battering. Mother writes that Susan was killed – a bomb – walking back to her elderly companion from the post office. There is no body.

Hamish has leave and he doesn't stay in London. He returns to the estate, walks the gardens that Kemp designed, returns with his hair sopping, clothes stuck to him as he peels off his boots. He visits me one night. Afterwards, he cries in my arms. I can't even stroke his hair. I just lie there.

He leaves the next morning with a mournful glance back at me.

The doctor comes back when I write and tell him that I believe I am pregnant.

Chapter 47

AVA

She had taken her car despite Fraser telling her he'd sort a lift for her. He'd offered to go with her. She'd said no.

'Are you feeling alright?' Fraser's face had been full of concern when she told him she wanted to leave.

She could have said she was ill, had a headache – her hips were certainly aching – but she hadn't wanted to lie to him. 'No, I'm fine. But listen . . . and please don't get angry . . . I need to check something. For work.'

'It's something to do with that house, isn't it.' Fraser didn't look angry, his response weary and almost resigned, as if he'd been waiting these last few months for just this moment. He'd known it hadn't gone away.

She nodded.

Fraser sighed, furrows appearing on his forehead.

'Tommy won't even notice.' She gave him a half-smile.

'Your family will,' he muttered, barely moving his lips.

Her sister was hushing Liam and she sensed their mum watching them both as she bounced Tommy on her lap.

'I need to do this, Fraser.'

'I'm not stopping you. Just don't get . . .' Whatever he wanted to say died on his lips and he swallowed. 'Nothing. OK.' His smile was forced but she was grateful for it. 'I'll cadge a lift off someone.'

She knew what he was going to say: that he'd been worried about her, about the way she'd been affected before, that it might even have triggered her high blood pressure. She leaned forward to kiss him on the lips. 'Thank you. Will you make my excuses? I don't want a lecture.'

He agreed with a good-natured roll of the eyes.

As she left the party, she could hear Pippa asking him where she'd got to. 'Work,' he replied. Fraser could never lie either.

The sun was already setting as she left the city, though it was barely four o'clock. This November was colder than most and Ava fiddled with the heating in her car, her fingers numb without gloves. She was not absolutely sure what had prompted her, but resolutions to unanswered questions seemed to have inched closer.

She hadn't been there for almost three months and, over time, the house and bridge had shrunk in her mind, a summer sunshine softening its features. Although it returned to her in dreams she could dismiss the images as unreal. But as she bumped over the familiar driveway, avoiding the bigger puddles and potholes, the hairs on her arms stood on end. She cut the engine. The wind whipped around her, nudged her, as she stepped out of her car.

The house seemed to take up even more space; the turrets were taller, every corner more pointed, every stone darker. She shuddered as she stepped forward, pulling her coat around herself.

The covered portico smelled damp. Muddied wellington boots were the only sign that someone was around. There were no lights showing inside and the tiled hallway was almost dark in the fading light. She imagined the bear waiting around the corner just before she knocked loudly. Would he be surprised? She stamped her feet, her toes tingling, hands thrust into her pockets. Her bump was so big now that her winter coat didn't quite do up and her body was soon shivering. No one was going to let her in.

This now seemed like an insane move and yet she wasn't ready to turn back towards her car. Now she was here, she felt an irresistible urge to see it all, to see if anything had changed, if it still felt the same. The light had almost completely gone now and some stars were visible over the trees as she moved tentatively towards the bridge. She swallowed. There was still something inexplicable in the way the ground seemed less sure beneath her, in the line of the stones, crooked and shifting, when she looked up. It was as if she had never been away, as if months hadn't passed, as if the bridge had simply been waiting for her.

This wasn't why she had come, she reminded herself. As if in agreement, the baby inside her kicked and somersaulted against her, pressing back on her spine, urging her not to go forward one more step. Something moved across the sky, a shooting star – a blink and then gone.

Near her, the stone steps led down. Her gaze shifted to the window, almost entirely black, buried beneath its ivy cloak. An idea formed. The things she wanted would be in there and she had seen the sliver of a gap at the bottom of the casement window – a broken catch, perhaps? She swallowed once more, her mouth and throat dry. She walked down the stone steps, her feet sinking into the damp spongy patch that was more weeds than grass as she moved towards the window.

It was as if no time had passed. The words scratched into the surface were still visible. Darting a glance over her shoulder, she saw the bridge was still empty. Why then did she feel as if it had eyes that followed her every move, that the wind had claws wanting to grab at her, lift her hair? She clenched her teeth as she reached forward to push back the ivy. The crackle of the leaves and the feel of insects on her skin made her heart beat faster. The smell of damp and neglect overwhelmed her and she knew she should turn back, should not forge on.

And yet since that moment in the living room with Liam, the half-formed thoughts nudged at her, random words now took on new meaning. The answers were here in the house, in this room, under the bridge – in that place where she now knew babies were buried. There *had* been a child, and that child had slept and lived in this room. That child had written those letters on the windowsill, Ava was sure of it. She was dead, Ava knew that too, but she wasn't forgotten. She looked inside at shapes leaping out of the grey: the bed, the chair, the doll, the picture of the mountain, the trunk.

Years of damp and neglect meant the wood had swelled, putting pressure on the catch. There was the thinnest gap along the bottom of the window, which her nails now inched along. She lifted the catch, tiny, dry flakes of paint fluttering down as she pulled the window towards her. It opened. A cloud of fetid air reminding her of damp, day-old socks made her nose wrinkle.

With a huge effort, she lifted herself backwards onto the ledge on her bottom, her feet scrabbling against the stones of the house as her body protested. Bringing her legs up, her stomach pressed uncomfortably into her, squeezing her lungs. She twisted and hauled herself through the narrow space. Something caught as she tumbled inside. Fear coursed through her – what was she thinking? Her body smacked against the wooden floor, her breath expelled in one shocked huff.

It was impossibly dark and the floorboards were coated in dust that stuck to her cheek and clothes. As she got to her feet slowly, the outlines of furniture and things took shape. She saw the doll on the shelf, its glass eyes winking in the darkness as she took a step forward. Somewhere nearby, on the other side of the door, came a low gurgling sound – then silence. She was rooted to the spot, her breath suspended, her ears straining for more. The sticky warmth of the room seemed suffocating, so at odds with the temperature outside. Her skin was now sheened with sweat in her thick woollen coat. She resisted a craving to stick her head back through the window, to suck in the air. Another step . . .

What was it she was searching for? There was a chamber pot, a bed, books tilted on a shelf – children's stories, the Bible – she squinted, trying to read the titles in the darkness. The bed was still made and she rested on it a moment. As she gazed across to the other wall and the picture of the mountain, she was assailed by a sudden stench of vomit that made her cover her own mouth. There was another sound from the corridor – she was sure of it. Her hand dropped; her head snapped around. Though no light showed beneath the door, she imagined someone on the other side, breathing in and breathing out.

Her mobile rang, sudden, loud and insistent, making her gasp and convulse. She'd thought she'd put it on silent mode for Tommy's party. She pulled it from her coat pocket: a *no number given*. A work call on a weekend? She pressed to receive it, would make her excuses. Her whispered 'hello' was barely there. What if someone was in the house after all? She couldn't hear steps but she could feel something, something on the other side of that door, waiting . . .

'Hello?' she repeated.

There was no one on the other end.

Then, a sound that made her whole body freeze, the faintest squeal, a bark. She fumbled with the phone, its light cartwheeling as it slipped from her grasp, throwing up crazed shadows on the wall.

Bending, she snatched it up, her knees scraping the wooden floor, heart hammering. The weight of her stomach almost pinning her to her spot. She inched towards the trunk on her knees. There was no key in the trunk's lock. She put both her hands onto the catches and lifted. The lid began to open and there was a smell like old libraries and damp paper. But before she could push the lid fully open, it was as if someone had sat suddenly on it and her hands shot away as it slammed closed.

Ava jerked backwards, her breathing heavy now. It was darker as she fumbled again for the catch, the lightest wings fluttering on her cheek making her swipe at her face with her hands. It was a moth, she told herself, just a moth. She wanted to stay calm, could feel her body reacting. It wasn't just that she was breaking and entering or that someone could be still be there; it was as if the house was trying to stop her, too. Her chest tightened at the thought, palms clammy. There was a sudden pain in her abdomen as her baby dug into her insides with an elbow or a knee.

When she looked ahead, she could still make out the white snow on the mountain but it seemed for a second that there was a figure clinging to the rock face, dangling by their fingertips, seconds from oblivion. She blinked. It was just a mountain, nothing more. *Oh my God, Ava, why would you come here?* Help me. *Help me*, on the windowsill. *Think.*

She turned back to the trunk and prised up the lid, reached an arm inside, moving her palm across the bottom. The lid pressed heavily on her arm, then up, then down, buffeting gently. Her breath sounded loud in her ears as her fingers plucked at the things inside. Something skittered across her skin and she curled her hand into a fist. There seemed to be very little inside the trunk but, underneath its thick paper lining, she felt some loose sheets and drew them out, crumpling the pages, the lid snapping shut once more.

She stumbled up and backwards, wanting to leave, beads of sweat at her hairline, between her breasts, her bump sticky with it. The smell of vomit, curdled milk and a terrible stuffy warmth made her turn too quickly for the window. Dizziness overwhelmed her.

She stuck out a hand, grabbing at the windowsill. She noticed the wheelchair in the corner. She had to get out, or she felt the window would slam closed and keep her there forever.

She groped wildly, lifting herself carefully back out of the window, metal or wood pressing into her coat, painful even through the layers of clothing. Outside, the air was no longer still and rancid but whisking round her, faster and faster, the cold entering every pore, stinging her cheeks. Her feet sank into the spongy grass as her baby bucked in her stomach. She had only taken a few steps, the papers still scrunched in her hand, when the most unworldly roar lifted her hair, her whole body, pushed her away. It was as if the house was furious with her. The jabs from her baby made her eyes sting as she stumbled up the stone steps. She looked up and her blood ran cold when she saw her.

Chapter 48

CONSTANCE

Crumpet has been gone for more than a year now and Mother took all the furniture out of my room. My room looks like the rest of the house, with gaps where things used to be. Now all that is left is my bed, my shelf, my picture and a trunk with all my clothes and blankets. Most days I see the lost things as if they are still there after years and years of staring at the same shapes. My wheelchair is kept outside and Mother brings it in when I ring a bell. I can't see the edge of the bridge any more and I am glad of it. Every time I see the grey stone I am reminded of that day. That bridge is cursed.

I am always locked in my room now. I think the house likes it like that. It makes the corridor colder. A wind that sounds like whispering voices presses into the keyhole, makes my eyes dart to the door, makes me clutch at my bedclothes, makes goosebumps pop out on my skin. It likes me in here, as if it has Mother all to itself.

I sleep when it's light or dark and eat when I like, trays coming and going. Sometimes I walk back and forward, back and forward, imagining myself preparing to climb the mountain in the picture. I run on the spot and I don't care if someone sees me. Mr Hughes drew back the ivy and peered inside once, which made me gasp as he cupped his hands to the glass. I did a star jump with a defiant tilt of my chin as I met his gaze.

He stepped backwards, disappearing around the side of the house.

Another time, I heard Annie in the corridor, the shock of her voice so close.

'I thought I could go in and sit with her, Lady West. She might enjoy the company . . .'

'You cannot,' Mother said. 'Her health is so precarious. We must limit her contact.'

'I could read to her from outside the door, perhaps? Talk with her?'

'You have more than enough chores, Annie, and a family of your own to look after.'

'But . . .'

'I will hear no more of it.' Her words were final, cutting through to me in the room.

The tiniest sigh, footsteps, a line delivered from a distance.

'Lady West, my David's worried someone's been at the supplies again. He's missing a bottle of lead arsenate for the garden.'

A pause.

'What a bother.' Another pause, and then Mother's voice once more. 'I was stopped by Iris the other day. Asked me if I had a position for her. She's had a little girl, Mary. Needs the money. Work is so hard to find these days.' The words came slowly.

'It is, Lady West.'

'It is, Annie.'

More people drop in gifts and treats and Mother shows them to me. At Christmas she is sent homemade jams, chutneys, honey from a neighbour. Cards line the mantelpiece and she reads me the messages. '*Our prayers are with you* . . . *Bless you both* . . . *For two special ladies.* Isn't that nice?' Her face glows in the candlelight in the dusty mirror. Beside her I see myself, cheeks hollow, pale, my legs like yellow bones in my chair. Yet I feel the blood pumping to them.

I rarely eat what I am brought and Mother chews her lip and talks about seeing the doctor if I lose more weight.

We go to the hospital and I am admitted – very underweight.

'I can't get her to eat, Doctor.' Her eyes sparkle.

'There, there, we'll take care of her. You did the right thing to bring her to us.'

I stay for three weeks this time. Mother takes a room there and visits me much more than she does at home. 'We don't normally let people stay, duckie,' says one of the nurses, 'but your mother couldn't bear not to be by your side. Aren't you lucky?'

I am fed through a tube at first and I put on weight. My throat aches, lips cracked, agony the day they remove it. My voice is a whisper. I feel so bone-tired but sit, propped up on thin hospital pillows, the smell of disinfectant as they mop the ward floor. The food is simple and I nibble at it, listless, chewing long after I've swallowed it.

The doctor visits me at my bedside. Mother smooths her hair as he approaches.

'You look so tired,' he tells her.

'I just can't leave her.'

'You are so good. What a Christian lady!'

'Do you think, Doctor, she will be able to be healed? Perhaps if there was a way to be rid of the limbs that hold her back?'

'We can certainly observe muscle weakness.' He feels over my flesh and my leg jerks in response.

'I'm feeling a little better, Doctor,' I rasp.

241

But then at night, Mother cuts across. 'Oh, the pain she is in, Doctor. Perhaps you could give her a stronger dose of medicine? To help her sleep?'

'Yes, you might be right. We need you to keep your strength up, don't we, Constance?'

'And, Doctor . . . I did read more about amputation. Heaven knows it sounds an extreme measure, but if it will cause her to be in less difficulty . . .'

The doctor strokes his chin. 'Perhaps. I think we are right now to consider it.'

I watch them talk over my heads once more as I lie helpless in the grey, sterile room.

But I am getting older now.

I know what amputation is.

I know my legs can be strong.

I know my mother is bad.

I know I must escape.

Chapter 49

AVA

'Mum?' Ava gasped, squinting up at the figure standing at the top of the stone steps staring down at her.

Ava staggered forward, her breathing still ragged as she put distance between her and that room. 'Oh my God, you terrified me.' It was a half-laugh, half-sob. Shakily, she climbed the shallow stone steps towards the still figure of her mother. 'I thought . . . I thought you were the White . . .' The blood drummed in her ears as she reached the top. The bridge, her mother; everything blurred as her body swayed.

'Ava?' Her mother stepped forward as Ava lowered herself onto the top of the steps, the cold shocking as she sat and closed her eyes. 'Ava, are you alright?'

'I'm just a bit dizzy,' she mumbled, bile rising in her throat. She swallowed down the nausea. 'You scared me. I was . . .'

Her mother crouched down to look at her, one hand on her forehead as if she was a small child. 'You know you need to take it easy. Fraser told us about your blood pressure.'

Ava tried to push her hand away, slow her breathing. When she finally opened her eyes it seemed as if the air was throbbing, as if the earth was tilting, her body insubstantial, unable to orientate. The edge of the bridge was a few paces away, the noise of the water a perpetual reminder of what lay fifty feet below them.

The sounds seemed suddenly to crank up: the hurtling burn, the hoot of an owl, her mother's voice. Then the world calmed to a stop. She could see individual stars emerging in a dark blue mackerel sky, could make out her mum's pale hand now on her knee, her wedding band glinting. To her left, the house watched them both as she felt the nausea subside. 'Mum, what are you doing here?'

'Fraser told me you were coming here. This house.' Her mother had stood up, faced away from Ava, staring up at the nearest tower with its conical roof, her eyes tracking down, many of the features lost to the fading light.

'Yeah, it was for work, it was—'

'What were you doing down there?' Her mother pointed at the window.

Ava followed her finger to look, the ivy disturbed, the diamond glass panes grubby, blank.

'You've got ivy all over you.' Her mum plucked a piece from her hair.

Ava lifted a hand and brushed at it. She would have made marks inside the room, disturbed things. Would Keven guess it was her? Would he notice?

'I . . . there was no one in the house and I . . .' How could she explain? What she'd done would sound absurd. She had *broken in*, for God's sake. The urge to come, though, the gossamer thread she'd been tugging on had been so irresistible. 'I had to see. I needed to find out more.' She remembered the sheets she had stuffed in her coat pocket. What had she found?

She stood slowly, refusing her mum's help, moving away from the top of the stone steps in the direction of the bridge. Her mum stayed back, watching her.

'You went inside?' Her mother looked appalled.

Ava lowered herself onto the low stone wall next to the bridge, palms flat as she gripped the edges, barely feeling her numb hands.

'What were you thinking?' Her mum stood with arms folded. Ava only just noticed that she wasn't even wearing a coat. She was in the same grey-silver jumper and black trousers she'd been wearing for Tommy's party.

'Mum, why do you care? You've barely spoken a word to me in weeks so why have you chased me up here for a lecture?'

'You shouldn't be here, sneaking around in the dark. Chasing a fairy tale when you should be preparing to start your own family.'

'I had to come.' It was true. Overtoun had never left her. These last few months she'd been fooling herself that the bridge and house were forgotten. Sitting here on the low stone wall, she felt tied to them, something deep inside her needing to be here, to dig, to search. A patch of light flashed in one of the top windows, as if the house had blinked, reacted to her thoughts. She tipped her chin towards it, refusing to feel afraid even as her heart hammered from the memories of that room, of the roar when she had left it.

'You should be at home. You should be focused on your life, on your child.'

A shot of fury forced Ava to her feet. 'You can talk, Mum. How about you focus on your grandchild? I've hardly spoken to you in three months.' She gestured to her stomach. 'I'm about to give birth in the new year and it's been like . . . you don't even care.'

Her mum swallowed. 'I do care. Of course I care. It's not that.'

'So why the silence?'

'I haven't been silent.' She paced in front of Ava, the noise of the water accompanying her steps.

'But you've been . . . different. I thought we were close.'

At this her mum looked hurt, her head drooping. 'Oh, Ava, we are close. I'm sorry. I just didn't understand – *couldn't* understand – why you had latched on to this place . . .' Her eyes were unable to meet Ava's as they roved past her to the bridge, her body stilling as she stared at the huge stone structure. 'It's . . .'

'Unearthly,' Ava breathed, unable to keep the word inside.

'Nonsense!'

Ava felt a dull drop in her stomach. Was this crackle in the atmosphere, this feeling that she could disappear into some other place all in her head, the things she'd felt in that room been simply the inventions of her own frightened imagination? 'I don't know why. I can't explain it, not logically, but it's like something here responds to me being here, like . . . it knows.'

Her mum's face drained of colour, her pale skin stark in the darkness.

'I read the diaries of the woman who lived here,' Ava explained, her voice cracking.

'Diaries?' The word sounded lost to the water.

Ava nodded. 'They were so sad. She's the one they say haunts the place. People say they've seen her. On the bridge. They say it's why the dogs jump.'

Still her mum didn't speak. Ava felt desperate. Was this just any old house, any old bridge to other people?

'The poor woman went through so much.' Ava was desperate for someone else to understand.

Her mum looked up, an unreadable expression crossing her face.

A fox shrieked in the distance and Ava jumped at the sound. The sky was even darker now as the moon hid behind a sheet of pockmarked clouds.

Her mother turned to her. Over the years, Ava had grown familiar with her mum's every expression, but this was something new. 'You think the woman should be pitied?' she sneered. '*Pitied?*' The word was screeched, enough to set Ava's teeth on edge and send a panicked fluttering from some branches. Ava was made rigid by abject confusion. Then, without warning, her mum started to cry – great gulping sobs. Tears streaking her cheeks and her eyes were wild.

For a moment, Ava was too shocked to say anything. 'I don't . . .'

'She shouldn't be pitied. Not her. She was . . . she was . . .' Her words were lost in the tears. Then came another choked sob, a harsh, bitter laugh, then uncontrolled weeping.

What was going on? How had her mum any connection to Overtoun? To the woman and the diaries? 'I don't understand,' Ava said, finally. 'How do you—'

'My name,' her mum said suddenly. She tilted her chin as she looked at Ava. 'I changed my name when I left.'

Ava was silent, still. Her mum had changed her name?

'Frances means *free one*. Because that was how I felt.' She laughed again, that horrible, frightening laugh. 'I was free. I had escaped this place.' She glared at Ava, then past her, her face twisting as her voice dropped almost to a whisper. 'That woman . . .' Her body shivered in the fading light. 'That woman you pity so much? She was a *monster!*'

Then the hatred in her face dissolved as she stared across at Ava. 'She was my mother. My name was Constance.'

Chapter 50

AVA

There were only a couple of weeks left of work, she reminded herself, as she gripped the edge of the bath, the white walls still tilting as she steadied her breathing. Christmas had seemed an obvious stopping point; she would be at thirty-six weeks then. Right now, she wished she could stop work today.

'We are having *one* baby, aren't we?' Fraser had asked that weekend as he took another delivery.

'You were the one who said we *needed* a bath thermometer.'

'Safety first.' He'd stopped to rest a hand on her shoulder and kiss the side of her head.

'And the bath toys were ordered by . . . ?' She felt a glow where he'd touched her as he moved away, laughing to himself.

Moving around hurt, her stomach strained, most of her maternity clothes were already too tight.

She should tell him.

She hadn't spoken to her mum since that day at Overtoun and she hadn't returned any of her calls. When Ava had turned up to their house a few days later, her mum had been out on one of her big walks, Gus no doubt trotting dutifully at her side. She had left the box of diaries with her dad. 'Make sure she gets them,' she'd urged, pressing the heavy shoebox into his arms.

She hadn't included the scrawled pieces of paper from the trunk that she'd stuffed into her jacket. At first she had almost forgotten them, returning in a daze to the flat that night. Fraser had just passed out in front of a football match, a beer bottle empty on the floor beside the sofa. Switching on the lamp on her side of the bed, she had hunched over the sheets, smoothing them out, reading hungrily, desperate for any hint or clue.

There had been loose sheets written in Marion's hand that didn't make sense separately. There was a list of medical terms – question marks after many of them: *Polio? Tuberculosis? Chronic dyspepsia?* Had her mum had all of these things? Had she had polio? There were other notes too: an entry about a puppy, a Christmas at the house with almost forty cards from people living in Dumbarton! Another list for the garden, perhaps: *apple seeds* circled, making her heart beat faster. Ava scanned the disjointed information, snatched up the sheets as she heard Fraser call out and then appear, rubbing his face, berating her for letting him fall asleep in front of the football again.

She had barely slept, recalling her mum's face in the darkness, her features as grotesque as the gargoyles on the bridge nearby. Her mum didn't hate anyone; she didn't have time for that, too busy climbing a mountain or dragging Gus out on a walk, organising some petition about littering, raising money for the Crisis centre. Why had she been so angry? What had she escaped from?

Ava thought then of the bone she had found: not the child, but what? She felt a thin sheen of sweat on her top lip as fear seized her: she was Marion's granddaughter. Beneath her layers her chest rose and fell in rapid movements. She had a GP appointment the next day. The words in the diaries swam before her. Those babies. Marion hadn't been fine.

'You OK?' Fraser paused from doing up his tie, unable to hide the worry etched into his features.

'Just aching everywhere.' Guilt made her insides churn. But this wasn't her secret to share. How could she tell Fraser about her mum before she knew the truth?

And what is the truth? she asked herself for the hundredth time. She couldn't reconcile her mother with what she knew about the girl in the house: a sickly child in a wheelchair, a child who was apparently so sick she was thought to have died. Two words ran like tickertape beneath the pitiful image: *help me.* If her mum was that girl, what had her own mother done to her?

She wished she'd cancelled on Pippa. She didn't want to be tempted to unburden herself on her. She prayed the day's filming would be quick, that she wouldn't have to be on her feet too long. It was Mum's secret to tell. Ava knew she needed to stay silent.

She checked her mobile: still nothing. A rush of despair overwhelmed her again. This wasn't fair. Her mum needed to call her. She would have read the diaries by now. Why had they stopped before mentioning Mum? Her head was crammed too full; the task of a day's filming seemed insurmountable.

She almost missed the single sheet of paper as she left her flat, folded once and lying on the dirty brown mat, her name in capital letters: *AVA.* Inside the fold, four words: *You should stay away.* Ava turned it over in her hands and licked her dry lips. *What the . . .* The letters were bold and spaced out, impossible to tell the handwriting. Unease dripped slowly down her spine. Suddenly, all the tiny moments of the past few months fell into place. It had begun after her first visit to Overtoun and now she'd gone back. Someone didn't want her at that house, at that bridge.

The note disappeared into her handbag as she opened the door of their flat. Outside seemed full of dangers: the path was icy; figures in the distance seemed to look in her direction; a car passing slowly – watching her? She couldn't shake the mood, tense and alert to her surroundings, her body aching and stiff with the strain of it.

Town was busy. Christmas shoppers, with pink ears and running noses, clutched carrier bags as they pushed past. Ava stared at every single face, searching for someone familiar. She thought of the Dumbarton locals she'd interviewed. She must have given her card to twenty or so. They hadn't wanted her visiting the house. Would it have been so hard to find out where she worked? Where she lived?

'Ava!' Pippa waved, startling her as she pushed through the door of the cafe.

Pippa sat at the table in a bottle-green polo neck. Her skin smooth, her eyes bright in direct contrast to how Ava felt. She let out a bark of laughter when Ava removed her coat. 'Look at you!'

'Shut up.' Ava gave her sister a half-smile, her back aching as she lowered herself into the chair. She wore a black stretchy maternity dress; they were filming around the corner at the King's Theatre with a couple of the stars of the pantomime.

'You look fab.' Pippa's eyes softened and she reached across to give Ava's hand a squeeze. 'I just ordered you a decaf latte. How are you doing?'

How was she doing? The urge to share engulfed her. *Going quietly mad . . .* 'I'm good.' Ava took a breath; this wasn't the right time. And Pippa was already asking about the pregnancy. A waitress delivered a glass, sprinkled chocolate on frothy white milk, and Ava thanked her, composing her face. 'Well . . .' She looked up at Pippa. 'I'm good. And apprehensive. And terrified . . .'

Pippa started giggling and Ava felt a glow inside as she took a sip of the coffee. Why couldn't she just be thinking about her pregnancy? Why had she allowed herself to be pulled back to Overtoun? Recalling the note in her bag made her heart sink. The house was still reaching out for her, still linked with her own life.

'And everything's fine? The baby?'

251

It was a few seconds before Ava answered. She nodded quickly. 'I've got my thirty-four-week midwife appointment in a couple of days.'

'That's good,' Pippa said. 'I remember . . .'

Pippa's voice faded away as another shot of fear seized Ava's insides. Late miscarriages, blood loss, babies buried in a shady spot.

'. . . so Liam had to race back out and get it!'

Ava straightened in her chair, her head woozy again. She had barely eaten breakfast, though. It was the coffee.

'Ava?'

'You never told me much about Tommy's birth,' Ava said, a hand on her stomach. Had the baby kicked this morning? She felt a flutter of panic as she tried to recall the last time. Count the kicks.

Pippa repeated some of the facts and Ava tried to listen, tried to immerse herself in another person's life. 'And what about the first few weeks?' Ava asked, not able to contribute much, her stomach clenching. *Braxton Hicks*. She had Googled it, the strange sensation, as if someone was squeezing her insides. Just Braxton Hicks. She was fine.

'. . . was it tongue tie? Colic? A milk allergy? I used to look it all up at 4 a.m., convinced he had it all . . . I thought I was going mad . . . that it was just me.'

Ava sat taller in her chair and fired more questions at her, guilty that she had never asked this stuff before. Pippa had finished her cappuccino and tucked a strand of hair self-consciously behind her ear. 'It can be hard,' she said. 'And you might feel bad. You feel like you shouldn't complain. I so wanted a baby but it was so bloody hard and I was too embarrassed to admit I wasn't coping.'

'I had no idea.'

'Well . . .' Pippa bit her lip. 'I suppose we didn't talk about babies, stuff like that. Mum was great. She offered to help me. You know what she's like. She has more energy than both of us.'

Ava found herself shredding the paper napkin in front of her. 'She does.' Her neck muscles felt strained. She couldn't face talking about Mum, not today. Not before she knew more.

'She'll be great with you too. *Too* great. She'll be dropping in every second to check on you. I don't really remember those early days much but it's not the same for every mum.'

Would she be great? Ava felt her chest ache with the loss of her mum, alarmed that she could feel tears building at the back of her eyes.

Pippa pushed her cup and saucer aside gently and looked at Ava, a serious expression on her face. 'You will promise, won't you?' She reached across the table. 'You'll promise to tell me if you need help, or you're hating it all or anything.'

'I will.' Ava swallowed then smiled gratefully. 'I'm going to need you. Expect 4 a.m. phone calls.'

'Absolutely.'

Pippa had to go. Ava said she'd pay the bill. Shrugging on her knee-length black coat, Pippa pulled her hair free of her collar. The bob almost reached her shoulders now. 'Have you seen Mum recently? She's gone a bit quiet.'

'Not since Tommy's.' The lie slipped out easily, her voice a touch high but Pippa didn't seem to notice.

They kissed goodbye and Ava paid the bill and left. She checked her phone: no messages. She tapped out a text to her mum: *We need to talk, pls call me.* She almost careered into a woman walking past the cafe – a familiar face.

'Ava!' The woman pulled to a halt in front of her. 'Oh my God, hi! I've just had a coffee with Garry. He told me he was heading to a job. He didn't tell me it was with you. How are you?'

Ava dragged herself into the present, adjusted her features. Katy was standing in front of her, a gloved hand on her handbag.

'I'm well. We're filming at the theatre.' Ava remembered what Garry had hinted at when they'd been alone in the editing suite all those weeks ago. She should have called Katy afterwards. She had liked her. How had she let her life be so taken over?

'It's been ages. How's Fraser? Is he still at Fernhouse High?'

She hadn't seen Katy since a cosy dinner party in their apartment, Garry's arm round the back of her chair as they all played a drunken game of Pictionary. Ava pulled her scarf around herself. 'Still the same. He's about to finish his first term as head of sixth form, actually.'

'That's great. God, I wish he'd replace ours. She is the actual worst . . . And you're still doing the news? I see you sometimes. I saw you the other night – the piece on knife crime.'

A bicycle bell sounded and someone shouted. Ava's nerves felt frazzled as she tried to concentrate on what Katy was saying.

'We've got a careers event coming up, actually. It would be great to get you in to talk to some of our sixth formers.'

'Oh, I would but . . .' Ava trailed away, about to tell her that she'd be off work for a while on maternity leave. Her mouth opened and closed hopelessly. Should she tell her? Wasn't it obvious now, her bump pushing through her coat?

'And look!' Katy drew back both of her arms and inspected Ava. 'You're pregnant! How exciting! You and Fraser will make brilliant parents.' Ava felt her shoulders drop a fraction. 'When are you due?'

'Mid-January. I didn't know you and Garry were still together?'

'We're not. We're friends. Well . . . sometimes . . . Oh God!' She laughed, throwing up her hands. 'It's complicated. So, do you know if it's a boy or a girl?'

Ava was slow to respond. Garry hadn't mentioned Katy for months. 'We . . . um . . . we haven't found out.'

'A surprise, oh, that is lovely.'

'Katy . . .' Ava was unable to bear it any longer. 'I'm sorry I haven't called you. And especially since Garry told me, about you and him breaking up and the . . .' She trailed away. Why didn't she say 'baby'? She could hear the sound of a river, see a figure crouched in the dirt – another hole for another baby. She blinked and the smell of rotting leaves and wet soil faded, to be replaced by petrol fumes and onions from a nearby takeaway.

'About what?' Katy's smile was lopsided, a line forming between her eyebrows.

'I wish I'd known when it happened. I'd have wanted to have been there for you.' The cold bit at her face, stung her eyes. 'I just had no idea until Garry let it slip a few weeks ago.'

Katy's happy expression faltered, her voice dropping; a passing car almost smothered the words. 'What did Garry let slip?' The cold wind whipped around them both.

'That you were . . .' Ava took a breath. 'About the baby.'

'What baby?' Katy's eyes narrowed.

'Your baby. The one—' A bus hissed as it stopped nearby. Ava lowered her voice as passengers moved past. 'The one you lost. I'm desperately sorry.'

Katy's mouth parted. 'Ava, there was never any baby. I've never been pregnant.'

'I . . .'

'I need to go,' Katy said. 'That's my bus.' She moved away slowly, her brows knitted together. 'Good luck!' she said, almost as an afterthought.

Ava moved to catch up with Katy but her mobile phone interrupted. Maybe it was Garry with a meet place? What would she say to him? Had she imagined their conversation? With everything else going on she couldn't focus. What *had* he said? Had she somehow misunderstood?

Still lost in thought, she pressed the phone to her ear. Liam's voice was agitated when Ava finally tuned in.

'Ava! Ava, I'm glad I got you.' He was breathless, his voice rushed.

Ava tried to concentrate. Katy had now stepped onto the bus, lost among the Christmas shoppers. The doors hissed closed and it pulled away.

A car horn sounded. Garry waved and smiled from the other side of the road.

'I got the results from that bone back,' Liam said. 'Do you want me to tell you now?'

Chapter 51

AVA

The filming went quickly, the actors both keen to promote the pantomime, their stage make-up bright and preposterous in the winter sun. It would be a light-hearted piece for the news, which she edited from home. A text from Garry thanked her for it. *He's behind you!* She scrolled back up through a hundred or so messages from her colleague: light-hearted, professional, thoughtful. She must have been mistaken about their conversation about a baby. She didn't tell him she'd seen Katy.

Fraser had returned that evening, inching towards the end of term, forty reports still to write. He seemed distracted, making notes in between mouthfuls of food, Ava pushing mashed potato around her plate. She didn't say a great deal, listening to the scratch of his biro, relieved that Liam's call meant she didn't have to do anything more. The bone had been a dog bone. A reasonably large dog. Liam had known because of some hole that ran through a distal articulation. Ava had been too relieved to really listen to any more. She had known, of course, the bone could not have been a child but who knew what else could be buried at Overtoun?

'I bumped into Katy today.' Ava picked at her food. She wasn't very hungry. The baby pushed right up under her ribs, making her breathing shallow.

'Who?'

'Katy? Garry's ex?'

'Oh yes.' He looked up, ink on his cheek. 'How's she doing? Is she still at Downside?'

'She is.' She decided not to tell him any more. What was there to tell? And she didn't want to think about baby loss, couldn't help picking at her nails as the words of her grandmother's diary returned to her.

Fraser had finished; his knife and fork were together. She should tell him what she'd discovered about her mum. He'd make her feel better. He was discreet. He was her best friend.

'God, I'm going to be finished at 2 a.m. at this rate.'

Ava bit down the words and stood. 'I'll wash up. You crack on.'

Another day of work, another day checking her phone for news from her mum. Anger pooled inside her, bubbling beneath the sadness. It made her stomach feel heavier, her back ache more. She knew this couldn't go on forever; Christmas was around the corner, at least. Her mum would *have* to talk to her. They were going there for lunch, for God's sake. She still felt hurt as she left early for her thirty-four-week appointment with the midwife.

She'd told Fraser not to come, waved away his guilt. She knew he would need to arrange parents' meetings, end-of-term events, finish the reports. She knew he wanted to clear as much work as possible, anticipating having to take his paternity leave in late January during the next term. His shoulders dropped as she reassured him that she'd be fine to go alone this time.

It was fine: the usual blood tests; her blood pressure still not quite right, perhaps; the midwife bent over papers, horizontal lines deepening in her forehead as she made a note. Then came the urine test. There was a pause, the tiniest inhalation that made Ava's insides lurch. 'Your protein levels are high.' Her voice was slow as she tapped her computer. 'I'm going to book you an appointment with our specialist.'

Ava felt her mouth dry, unable to stop thinking about a woman hunched over soil, the same woman frightened in a bathroom streaked with red.

'The day after tomorrow . . . would that be alright?'

Ava nodded, allowed herself to be ushered out, barely asking a question. She wished Fraser was there, she wished . . . She lowered herself into a plastic bucket seat in the foyer and put her head in her hands. She wished her mum was there.

She was struggling in the bathroom on that morning, bending awkwardly, her stomach squashed uncomfortably as she reached to roll on her tights. Fraser was hastily adjusting his tie in the mirror. He'd returned late the evening before, wearily appearing after a sixth form parents' meeting, bloodshot eyes and grey skin. 'I need a holiday.' He'd smiled weakly. Ava didn't mention the new appointment, not wanting to add to his stress. If anything was wrong she'd tell him then.

Ava reached for her earrings, every move making her twinge. God, pregnancy was hard enough – lumbering around with this extra weight and still trying to function in the same way – without this extra anxiety. She had Googled various scenarios, frightening herself with online tales that had ended badly. Was she wrong to wait and tell Fraser afterwards? It would only freak him out and she'd hate for him to miss the end of term, the end of his first term as head of sixth form.

'Have you seen my other earring?' she asked, rootling on the top of the dressing table.

'Nope, sorry – and I've got to leg it if I'm not going to be late for my own breakfast meeting. Oh, by the way . . . I left a letter for you that got delivered to me at school.' He rushed across and gave her shoulder a squeeze.

'For me?'

He shrugged and flicked the one earring dangling. 'You are totally rocking the pirate look.'

'Ha ha,' she grunted. She twisted to watch him leave the room. 'See you later!'

'You mean "Harrrrrr haaarrrrrr"!' he called. 'Love you. Love you both.'

She caught her eye in the mirror and smiled, feeling marginally comforted. 'Idiot,' she muttered, removing the earring. Another twinge – a ripple through her stomach. God, only just over a week left of work and at least one of those a day of research – no need to be on her feet for too long.

She had almost forgotten about the letter but Fraser had left the envelope propped up against her handbag. She tore it open quickly, searching around for the boots she had kicked off the previous day, mentally preparing herself to squeeze into them. She drew out a white A4 sheet. Some Christmas-related junk mail? An invite to some Christmas party for her and Fraser? She unfolded it, confused immediately by the expanse of white nothing. *Look after your baby.* The words were written in a familiar black pen and she felt the hairs on her arms rise to attention, her breathing speeding up.

'What the . . .' Turning over the page, a cold stone lodged in her stomach. Someone had sent this to Fraser? For her? For a second the room tilted and she shut her eyes. Nausea nudged at her as she stared again at the words. Fraser and she didn't share a surname. How had they known to deliver it there? What did it mean? She checked the postmark: sent from the centre of Glasgow. That gave her nothing. She slid the letter back in the envelope and put it in her handbag. She needed to think about what she should do.

The newsroom was busy. Bright strip lights contrasted with the grey outside. The monitors all showed the morning programme: the lime-green sofa, Claudia in a lilac dress chatting to a rather earnest-looking guest. The red light was on, reminding everyone that recording was underway, and people spoke in low voices, huddling round desks, water coolers and doors to the editing suites.

Ava wished she wasn't on air, wished she could talk to someone. The note burned a hole in her handbag as she sat, barely present, in the morning briefing. She would show the note to Fraser. She would write down some of the other things that had happened over the last few months: the hand-delivered note at the flat; the letter at work; the slashed tyre; the feeling of being followed. But then she learned that Garry had already assigned her job that day.

'We're leaving for Overtoun in ten,' he said on the way past. 'I'll drive.'

'Overtoun?' Ava couldn't disguise the shock on her face. 'But why?'

'A dog jumped. Someone phoned.' He turned to talk to another reporter as Ava felt the blood drain from her face.

She shouldn't go.

She didn't want to give more attention to Overtoun, not now she knew about her mum's link to the place. She hadn't found out what had happened to her there. What she did know in her bones was that the bridge and house were central to the mystery, a menacing energy that recognised Ava, recognised her connection to the place. Marion had suffered so much loss, had jumped to her death. Someone had scratched those words in that room. What would she stir up if she returned there? She relived that moment outside the window when it had seemed the house had released a furious roar.

It didn't want her there. Fear dripped down her spine, a terrible foreboding. She should not go.

Look after your baby.

'Ava, come on!' Garry stood in the doorway of the newsroom, car keys dangling from his hand.

The weather had worsened as she made her way outside, brooding grey clouds overhead, trees that edged the car park slanting sideways in the wind. She felt freezing despite her layers. *Just under two weeks to go*, she reminded herself as she squeezed into the passenger seat and struggled to get the seat belt across her bump.

She sent a text message to her mum. *Another dog jumped. They're sending me back there. We have to talk. Call me!* What would make her mum get in touch?

Rain spattered the windows as they left the car park and drove out of the city. It was just them. 'Neil's going to meet us there.' Garry smiled brightly as he overtook another car. Ava gripping the handle overhead, one eye flicking to the speedometer. Did she imagine the stilted atmosphere in the car or was she simply paranoid?

The windscreen wipers swished frantically and the wind nudged the car as they sped north. The Clyde looked grim, its steel-grey surface choppy as they made their way over Erskine Bridge.

The Gothic facade of the house seemed perfectly suited to the wild weather as Garry parked. The rain fell like bullets onto the car's roof and glass. 'We could shelter in here for now,' Garry said. Ava suddenly didn't want to. She grabbed the cagoule she kept in her handbag and stepped out. The wind blew her hood off immediately and her face and hair were coated instantly with droplets. She wished they hadn't come. She wished she was at home now, making plans for Christmas, a happy cocoon with Fraser, terrible movies and all the food.

Her hips and back screamed in pain as they walked around the side of the house, sheltering for a moment under the portico, the howling gusts flattening the long grasses in the field in front of them. Puddles grew bigger as the rumble of distant thunder sounded.

'Shall we start on the bridge?' Garry called.

'Sure.'

Garry pulled out his phone. 'Neil's delayed. Accident on the A82.'

'Oh? Oh, right.' It must have happened just after they'd driven on it.

'Show me the way.' He smiled, shifting his rucksack to his other shoulder.

Huddled over herself, hood up, she stepped out from under their sheltered spot, turning the corner of the house. As she glanced down the stone steps, she couldn't stop her gaze resting on the window, the ivy broken in places where she had disturbed it. She thought then of the words scratched into the windowsill, her blood running cold. What had happened to her mum?

'Ava?' Garry had almost bumped into her as she'd stood rooted to the spot, the wind and rain still lashing them from every angle.

She shouldn't be here, the roar of the water merging with the howl of the wind, the rain in diagonal strips streaking down her cheeks, her neck, under her collar, into her clothes.

Help me.

'Are we mad?' Garry's voice in her ear make her jump.

Lightning flashed in the distance.

'We can't film in this. Let's get beneath the bridge – see if we can do something there.'

She descended the path, wondering now if everything she had felt about the place was because her own history was so caught up in it. Her maternal grandmother had killed herself right here.

The bank where they had found the bone looked barely disturbed, droplets clinging to the grass. There was some shelter from the rain underneath the canopy of dripping leaves.

'Here.' She pointed.

'Here?' Garry circled her, brushing her body as he moved past on the narrow path. She flinched. Another ache in her body winded her and she winced. 'So maybe we could start the piece standing here – the bridge in the background?'

Ava swallowed, her throat dry. The rain had eased but the noise of the swollen river seemed to fill her up. She started shivering. It was as if the house and bridge had realised she was back and were reaching their shadowy hands out to her, twisting around her limbs, suffocating her. It was so dark despite not even being midday. What had happened to her mother here? Being physically present suddenly made the questions more urgent.

Garry had taken out a notepad and pen, hunched over, trying to shield them from the wet. 'OK,' he said. He looked at the bank and then back to the bridge as he planned their piece.

Ava, however, was staring, staring at the writing on the page. The letters dragged her back to the present – to this moment. Something about the flourish on the 'A'. Her heart raced. Stepping backwards, she stumbled.

Garry frowned and moved forward. 'Ava?'

She couldn't speak. Her body was hurting, her hips and back grating. Pain shot through her as panic bloomed in her chest. Could it be?

A message on white paper . . . He knew where she lived. He knew where Fraser worked. He had lied to her about Katy. She was followed after work – followed home. Garry?

Why was she here with him? Oh my God, had a dog even jumped?

'Look, Ava . . .' Garry sighed. 'I know why you're being off. I spoke to Katy, OK? She told me what she told you . . . she was angry . . .'

'I . . .' The pain in Ava's side worsened, robbed her of her next breath. Her mind was cloudy, sluggish, as Garry's face swam in front of her, as his words swirled around her.

'I don't know why I said that stuff. It was . . . I wanted you to think I understood or . . . or something.'

She had shut her eyes, was breathing through the pain. It couldn't be what she thought it was. It was too early.

'Ava? Are you upset? Look . . . this is a bit embarrassing . . . but I suppose I sort of realised a few months ago that I . . . I liked you. And I thought you and Fraser might break up. I wanted you to know that I liked babies. I'm sorry . . . Ava?'

She felt real fear take hold, her baby kicking and moving as if sensing she was distressed.

'Ava, I really hope I haven't screwed up our friendship. It means a lot and it was just a mad moment. It's why I've kept my distance a bit these last few weeks. I'm totally over you now . . .' He laughed and the noise made her squirm. The words of the note flashing across her mind.

'Ava . . .' He gripped her arm and she let out a small cry. 'Ava, what's wrong?'

'I've got to . . . I think . . .' The panic was overwhelming her, her stomach squeezing, making her gasp and double over. The air seemed to shift, the bridge quivering in her eyeline. Time slowed then sped up again. *A thin place.* The pain in her body, her mind too full. She thrust her hands to the sides of her head. She didn't know what to think. *Oh my God!* Her brain was swimming. What was happening to her? Could she make it back to the house? If she did, would anyone be in? She didn't have her own car. Was Neil even on his way?

'Ava?' Garry's hands shot to right her before she fell on the path, concern filling his eyes as she sucked in her breath. 'Ava, are you alright?'

A fresh wave of pain threatened to wind her and she gasped and bent over herself. She couldn't respond, just shook her head from side to side. 'I'm getting . . .' She was only thirty-four weeks – it couldn't be, it *couldn't*. Her breathing got faster as her fear exploded inside. 'I think I'm . . . I need help!' She looked back up the path, the climb suddenly insurmountable, the bridge itself looming over them, casting a shadow. Rain stuck her eyelashes together, ran into her mouth, flattened her hair. The smell of soaked foliage and thick mud filled her nostrils.

If she could just get back onto the top of the bridge . . . Another shot of pain fired through her and this time she lost her balance, one knee sinking onto the path. She wailed.

Garry's face peered at her. 'Is it the baby?'

She nodded, clutching her stomach, barely able to speak. 'Please. Oh my God.' Fear almost choked her; they were in the middle of nowhere, the estate miles from a hospital. This wasn't Braxton Hicks. The baby would need help. Above the bank to her right she could just make out the diamond panes of the ivy-covered window. The dusty room behind.

Help me.

Chapter 52

MARION

I am ready for the blow. I will telephone the doctor when it happens. He has been attentive throughout, knowing my history. But it doesn't come. This time my stomach grows, protrudes, making my clothes uncomfortable. Annie takes them out, delighting in my state. Did Miss Kae tell her niece of my losses? Lord West will be thrilled. She sends a telegram. I am not sure he receives it.

Hamish is missing, presumed dead. I can't find the tears for him. Miss Kae visits and cries for us both. A poor soul, a poor lost soul. I imagine, in a grand house forty miles from here, there is a blonde weeping buckets, her elderly husband no comfort as he sits wrinkled in a chair.

I drink the milk Annie brings from a neighbouring farmer's cow and place a hand on my stomach. It is spring and the estate stirs into life. The thought of war feels as remote as ever; the bombing raids nearby were more than two years ago. The sun peeks shyly through cotton wool clouds and sheep bleat as lambs roam around their ankles. Leaves bloom on the trees, rich and full. Flowers grow, buds opening to reveal a riot of merry colours.

The pregnancy progresses and I take gentle walks around the garden. I make sure I am eating well and not listening to music at loud volumes to harm the baby. I am astounded to hear the heartbeat from the doctor's stethoscope, feel the hard, round head beneath my skin.

'You have a good colour in your cheeks,' he says. He is rapt, concerned that I am taking care. 'After the losses before, we must be careful.' I assure him I am following his advice. He beams. His perfect patient. He'll be back to check on me soon. It is my turn to smile.

The baby is born at home in my bedroom, the ivy blurring as I clench the sheets into a fist. The walls of the room contract and expand as if they too are experiencing this moment. It is painful, shockingly so. A white and wide-eyed Annie brings towels, not yet twenty and horrified by the scene. I scream into the pillow, which is soaked with sweat and tears. I feel like I am being turned inside out, torn in two. I need it to stop, I am begging for it to stop and finally, impossibly, as the sky turns a midnight blue and I realise I have lost the day to this agony, I feel an enormous pressure. The doctor has come and it is he who removes the fragile being, who cuts her from the strange sinewy rope. She bawls and I collapse backwards, the foreign sound reminding me of nothing else.

She is tiny, her eyes squeezed tightly shut, her legs tucked up to her chest. I feel my world tilt. What I had dreamed of over a decade ago now lies asleep and peaceful in my arms. It is so late that the doctor stays in my husband's room. Annie has been still dusting and readying it in case the vanished master of the house returns.

The next morning, I have put her to the breast where she rootles pointlessly. Tongue clamped between my teeth, I try everything I can do to help her. Dawn has broken and the sunlight shows up the mess of the room and myself, both exhausted, the tang of blood heavy in the air.

The doctor appears, breakfast eaten quickly from a tray. Baby Constance has barely slept. He checks her, comments that she is on the small side. 'We should take her to the hospital,' I suggest, feeling my eyes widen.

'Perhaps best,' he recommends.

I am weak – very weak – so an ambulance takes me there. A kind nurse helps my sore bruised body into a wheelchair. The driver cranes his neck as we draw away from the house, the stone seeming to shimmer with my nerves. Everybody turns as I am wheeled through the corridor. Sympathetic looks as they realise that I am holding something so small, so new. Good news these days is seldom found. I sit up straighter as they roll me along.

'She is on the small side,' I explain in a solemn voice.

They peer at the shut-eyed pink face, lines meeting in the middle of her brows. 'We'll get her right. And you.'

We stay in hospital for a couple of days and the nurses fuss over us, cooing around the curtain as they go about their rounds. The doctor visits too, pleased that she is doing better: sleeping, feeding well and putting on weight, opening her unfocused eyes, unfurling her legs.

'There'll be no need for you to stay,' he says, 'you can return home.' He watches me hold her.

'Could you check her chest again, Doctor? She does get a nasty cough at night and it doesn't sound quite right to me.'

'Does she bring up her milk?'

'Yes, Doctor, she does.'

'Well, we must keep an eye on that.'

'Thank you, Doctor.'

Chapter 53

AVA

She couldn't move, was rooted to the ground under the bridge, the path impossibly steep.

'I'll get help.' Garry's eyes were rounded, his face draining of colour.

'Can you?' She hadn't realised she had collapsed onto her side in the dirt.

'I'll go to the house. Ava, it's going to be OK!' he called, already halfway up the path. 'Wait there! I'll be back!'

She watched him go as she crawled off the path, palms slick with mud, realising she was lying in the patch where Bella had found the bone. As she was wracked with pain, she was certain she could hear the sound of the baby again. How many were buried under her? And what had her mum to do with any of it? From this angle she could just make out the top of the bridge, imagining her own grandmother appearing there, a face twisted with pain before she hurled herself onto the rocks below. She squeezed her eyes against another crippling contraction, her vision blurring as she saw a figure moving down the path towards her.

Arms dragged her upwards as a man's voice called her name. 'Ava, come on, love.' Keven. It was Keven. His distinctive accent coaxing. She wanted to weep with the relief of it.

'Garry, he might be . . . he . . . and . . . my mum . . . the baby . . .' She knew she wasn't making any sense, jabbering, her body trembling with the cold. A rumble of thunder and the relentless noise of the water sounded furiously in her ears.

'We can shelter under the bridge!' Keven called, supporting her weight as she staggered, slipping in muddy trenches towards the archway that might provide some protection from the weather. They should go back up to the house. This wasn't a good idea. She needed an ambulance. Had Garry called one? Where was he?

'Garry, he . . .'

'I've got you, love,' Keven said. 'You're alright. This way.'

The archway loomed in front of her; her neck craned. She could barely make out the top of the bridge from this angle and she had a horrible image of a dog leaping over to its death, into a river of bones, muscle and fur still clinging to their surfaces. She shut her eyes, cried out once more. 'Oh my God! Oh my God!'

'It's OK, Ava. I'm here. I've got you . . . one more step.' He lowered her onto the dry ground, curling leaves and pebbles digging into her hands.

She could see Keven more clearly now, wiping the rain from her face. A smear of mud on his cheek, his trousers damp, no coat at all, hair soaking. She moaned as her stomach contracted.

Keven scooted behind her. 'You're alright, you're alright,' he said. Her body went rigid as he clamped his arms around her, his legs trapping her too.

The shock stopped any more sound, the stones digging into her flesh, the surging pain that seized her stomach and made her lose her breath. Keven was muttering, his breath tickling her ear.

'Keven . . .' She tried to keep her voice light. 'I need an ambulance . . . the baby . . .' She took a breath, her muscles squeezing so hard she thought she'd cry out again. 'Garry was getting one,' she said with more confidence than she felt. She didn't understand. Why was Keven clinging to her like this?

'He didn't get one.'

Icy cold filled her chest. 'But he . . .'

'I took his phone. I locked him in the room. He can't help you.'

She was rigid with fear, then she started to wail. 'Keven, please. Let me go . . .' She struggled, but his grip was tight and she soon gave in.

'No, no, no, no . . .' It was almost as if he was talking to himself, his head shaking behind her.

'Please. I need to get to a hospital . . .'

'No, not yet. You can't. You can't keep looking. The body . . . if people keep coming . . .'

Ava couldn't follow his ramblings.

'They always said it was my dad but I saw it all. I *saw* her jump. But there was never a body and I was his son. They thought I'd lied . . .'

Ava could barely breathe, damp inside and out of her clothing. Oh God, she needed a hospital. She was going to lose the baby.

'And you kept coming here. Even after the notes . . . the warnings I sent . . . back for me . . . dredging it all up again, even now . . . and with Dad still alive . . .'

Look after your baby.

'That was you?' she whispered. *Oh my God.* Her head pounded as she strained against Keven's arms. Maybe somebody would hear if she called out? She let out a scream that was stifled almost immediately, his hand clamped over her mouth.

'Stop it.' He shook her. 'Stop it now . . . you just need to promise. You . . . you need to leave it alone.'

The bank farther up was a graveyard for the babies. The water was a graveyard for the dogs. What body was Keven talking about?

'You have to promise, Ava. Promise you'll drop this – that you'll stop looking. I know you came here. I know you got into that room.' Ava slumped backwards. 'I don't want anyone searching around here. They were good people, my parents. Both good people and she was evil. I know what she did to her child. I kept the diary. If he *did* push her, she would have . . . she would have deserved it.'

The edges of her vision were narrowing; her lips felt numb. He'd kept back one of the diaries. It made sense now. That strange last entry. Short, capital letters, not in the same style at all. He'd ended her story where he'd wanted her to end it, tried to convince Ava she'd jumped. 'She didn't jump?' She hadn't meant to say it out loud.

'I saw her!' he roared, the words echoing against the walls of the bridge.

She was crying again. 'Please,' she whispered. 'Please . . . we'll stop . . . we'll leave.' So had Keven's dad pushed her? Was it not a suicide after all? Was that why the bridge did what it did to dogs? To punish people for not discovering the truth?

There was barking – furious barking. Through her tears, her blurred vision, she made out a shape on the path in front of her.

Keven got up, went to shoo the dog away, looked up. Ava watched him lurch backwards, his face pale, all the whites of his eyes showing. 'No!' he shouted as he stared transfixed at whatever was on the top of the bridge.

Ava crawled to where he was standing, stared up at what he was seeing, tried to focus.

There was a woman – a woman peering right down at them from the top of the bridge. The White Lady.

'It can't be . . .' Keven had lost all concentration as he walked, unseeing, past her, one hand up on the stones of the bridge for support. He too was crying now, his body shaking. 'I saw her! I saw her . . .'

Ava got up and crawled forwards. The dog was closer, still barking – returning to her. 'Gus! Oh my God!' Her muddied hands groped for him, her hand in his wet fur. Was she hallucinating? She thought of the bridge, the dogs that had all jumped before. The thin place. She felt her world tilt, things that were real and unreal, everything spinning out of her control.

Her mum stood in front of her now, horrified as she looked down at her lying in the path, dripping hair flattened to her scalp, one hand on her stomach.

'Mum . . .' Her voice was feeble, her body convulsing with pain. 'Mum . . .'

But her mum wasn't looking at her; she was looking over her shoulder, at Keven under the archway.

'Mum!' Ava cried, as she drifted towards her, as if she really was the White Lady. 'I need an ambulance. MUM!'

It was as if her mum couldn't hear her, as if she was somewhere else.

Gus was still barking, water roaring as her mum moved past her unseeing. Ava watched as she spoke to Keven, then embraced him. They were locked tightly together. Ava cried out. Her mum didn't seem to hear. Ava's vision swept in and out of focus – and there was someone else. Someone else gripping her arm, saying her name. Someone gentle, a voice filled with kindness.

'Ava! Are you OK?' Neil looked both perplexed and worried as she stared up at him.

She moved with him, hunched, still wracked with pain, one shoe pulled off, mud coating her clothes, streaking her skin. 'The baby . . . I think . . .' She could hardly speak, could only gesture, frightened sounds. 'It's coming!'

Gus was circling, making a high, keening noise, his whole body tense. He yapped at Keven, at her mum, at the water as if he was possessed. Her mum was still there, still looking at Keven, their mouths moving, their words drowned out by the torrent under the bridge, their faces wet from rain or tears – Ava couldn't tell.

'Ava, I . . .' Her mum turned towards her then, concern on her face.

'Well done, Ava. Just up here . . .' Neil was guiding her, meeting her eye for the first time in forever. 'You'll be alright. Well done.' His words were sweet in the air – strong. 'The car's just by the house. Not far. Well done. Almost there.'

'Keven . . . Mum . . .'

'You're OK.'

Miraculously, they made it to the top of the bridge. She could see Neil's car parked just beneath one of the grey walls of the house. Her eyes glanced to the window at the bottom of the stone steps, the window where her mother had once looked out.

'Mum . . .' she croaked. Her mum hadn't followed. She was still under the bridge with Gus and Keven.

She prayed she was safe from the bridge that had brought so much death.

'Mum!'

Chapter 54

CONSTANCE

I wait until I know she is upstairs – listen for the tell-tale creak – or until the front door has opened and shut – the slight change in the air – and I sit up slowly, move my bare feet out of bed and begin my exercises, slowly at first.

I eat a little more and I am less sick. Mother talks about my upcoming operation as if it is another birthday. I turned ten a few weeks ago and I look down at my ten toes. I want to keep them all. I lift my leg, hold it, lift it again. I run on the spot, gently and then harder, always sure to listen, listen, listen. I get back into bed twice when I think I hear her nearby.

It is Annie. She whistles in the corridor. She talks to the bear. I can't make out the words but she always sounds a little afraid. I think of the feeling I get when I am out of my room and shiver. Mother calls out from the green room. She never leaves to run her errands now when Annie cleans.

I get out of bed and start again, pleased I can do more than yesterday. If I can walk then I can run and if I can run then I can run away.

Maybe it is because I'm thinking about this that I don't see him until he is right up against the glass. I let out a sound and glue my feet to the spot. The boy's face is right there, staring right at me standing frozen on one leg. I sweat from my star jumps and from the fear that seems to turn my insides to stone.

But then his face changes, his mouth wide, his straight teeth on show as he gives me a small wave. I hear his delighted laugh through the glass and something in me opens up. A friend. I know he is a few years younger than me but we look the same age. I find myself waving back, smiling hard, my mouth tightly shut so he won't see my missing teeth and run away and be frightened.

He disappears, and without thinking I dart to the window, not ready to lose him. I can feel the blood running through my body, my legs holding my weight as I tiptoe up, now tall enough to see right outside. Mr Hughes is there. The boy tugs his hand, talking and pointing, and Mr Hughes is rubbing his chin.

The boy waves again and I can't help but wave back. There's something about them both – open and friendly. I wish I could climb out of these windows and tell them to take me away. The footsteps in the corridor are loud and quick. Rushing to the bed, I am barely under the sheets before Mother is inside. Will she notice my quick breaths, the sheen on my skin, my guilty look?

'The doctor just telephoned,' she announces. Her face seems to be glowing, the corridor behind her seeming to pulse with her mood. 'He's agreed that you are a priority. He thinks you and I have been terribly patient, but a spot has come up next week, so we can go. It will be a long hospital stay, of course – visits from their new physiotherapist, fittings with the prosthetics department. They can do wonders, so he tells me.' She isn't talking to me any more – just listing things I don't understand, long words that aren't in my books, long words I'm afraid of. My hands clutch the sheets so tightly my knuckles turn white.

All I can do is nod as she sweeps around the room, lifting the lid of the trunk, talking about clothing, making things more comfortable for afterwards. I can smell my own stench as I breathe, the rot inside my mouth, in my stomach and it is too late for the bowl as it bursts out of me, everything familiar and raw, and she is there, circling my back.

'You must build up your strength or they will refuse to operate,' she says. 'Let me fetch a cloth and some bread. First, I must go upstairs and find my carpetbag. I didn't ask about sleeping arrangements, but I am sure they will let me join you in the hospital for such a serious operation. I am sure.' She is already out of the room, her words fading with her steps.

I sink back into my pillow, my lips coated, some pieces still sticking to my chin.

On my shelf, I see the book about Dick Whittington. I think of all the other orphans I read about and the stories aren't too bad. I feel my body solid beneath the sheets. Swinging my legs over, I run back to the windowsill. They are gone. There is just the grey stone of the bridge and the bank that drops out of view and the clouds that sit along the treetops.

I remove my hairpin and stare down at the windowsill and scratch the letters in case the boy comes back, in case he and Mr Hughes plan to rescue me.

HELP ME.

Chapter 55

AVA

'Hello, Ava. I'm Dr Patel and I'm your anaesthetist today. I hear you've had a bit of a shock so you just try to help us help you.' She wanted to stay fixed on Dr Patel's eyes, wanted to have faith in that calm voice, that direct look over the mask.

Her body had started to shake in Neil's car and was still seizing her now, so they struggled to get a spinal block into her. Every time she tried to breathe, she imagined herself back under the bridge, arms clamped around her. She pictured her mum walking blindly past her in the mud.

'Alright, Ava . . . stay as still as you can.'

It seemed an impossible thing to ask: after the events of the morning, her body trembled so much that the nurse attaching pads to her skin had to still her as best she could. Dr Patel poised on a stool behind her, exchanging words with other people in the room. She sensed movement, hushed voices, urgency crackling in the exchanges.

'Please . . .' Ava spoke no one in particular and in a pleading squawk that didn't even sound like her own voice. 'Please, help the baby.'

'We are going to take excellent care of you, Ava,' Dr Patel soothed. 'Try to relax. Try to breathe. We're going to get something to stop that shaking.'

Ava couldn't speak. There was another agonising clench as her stomach went rigid. She cried out. There were other bodies appearing in the room. She had pads on her stomach. A monitor showed a heart rate in a way that Ava didn't understand. There were white walls, blue outfits, looks, whispers, long words she couldn't make out.

Two nurses stood at her side, holding her still as Dr Patel continued to talk to her. 'So, a nice, slow breath . . . That's good.'

Ava felt a sharp pain in her lower back followed by the sensation of ice dripping into her veins. It moved down and around her limbs as she was lowered slowly onto her back.

'That's great, Ava,' said Dr Patel. 'Well done. You're doing brilliantly.' She called to another person dressed in blue and the double doors were opened. Fraser appeared dressed in scrubs, eyes red rimmed and scared above a blue mask.

'There you go, Ava. He's been straining to get in here.'

He looked so out of place. Fraser, who was normally dressed in jeans and scruffy T-shirts, was suddenly a cast member in a hospital soap. For a crazy moment, Ava felt a bubble of laughter rise unbidden. It morphed into a sob as he gripped her hand, squeezed it so that she gasped from the pain, her eyes filling with tears.

'I'm sorry . . . Neil told me. Oh my God . . .'

'The baby, Fraser . . . What if the baby isn't OK?'

A screen had been erected over her so that now she was unable to see her legs or stomach. Dr Patel's head appeared. 'Can you feel that? I'm tapping there?'

Ava answered, aware that every second mattered.

Fraser kneeled by her head, stroking her hair back from her face. His hand was warm; he smelled of pine needles and aftershave.

A small part of her relaxed, relieved she wasn't alone. 'It's going to be OK,' he whispered as she told Dr Patel she hadn't felt the last tap.

Everyone looked grave and spoke quietly. She took more glances at the monitor that made sounds she didn't understand. There was a heartbeat, though, that she could cling to. But would the baby survive? Thirty-four weeks . . . surely it would be too small?

The pain had been excruciating as Neil had raced her away from the house, tyres skidding on the pebbles. They had both been gabbling, the adrenaline rushing through her as they'd sped away.

'Thank God I walked down there. I couldn't understand it. Garry's car was still there.'

Garry. She'd remembered then that Garry was locked inside the house. 'He's still there!' she breathed, and tried to explain.

'It's OK, don't talk,' Neil had said. 'It's OK. Let's get you to a hospital.'

'My mum, she . . . her mum . . . suicide at the bridge . . . where the dogs jump . . .'

'What?' He almost swerved, the car juddering before he gripped the wheel and straightened up, his voice strong. 'Sorry.'

'Oh God, it's so early. It's *too* early. I'm not due for six weeks.'

'Don't worry . . . the doctors are great. My mum had cancer treatment there.'

It was a different Neil who swung onto the A82 back towards Glasgow with a screech and a smell of burned rubber, gabbling about a disastrous band rehearsal the previous day – a drummer who'd got so drunk he fell off his stool in the middle of it. She'd tried to focus on the story, knew he was trying to distract her from the situation, punctuating his tales with encouraging words.

'Almost there,' he said. He swerved past other vehicles and ignored any speed limits.

He had taken her phone, asked for the code and told her he was ringing Fraser as they wheeled her away through double doors and people calling out instructions. She could see him mouthing into her phone, pale faced and with mud all over his clothes, which she realised was from her.

The surgeon arrived and Dr Patel melted away. An older man with narrow shoulders and crinkled eyes loomed over her. Strands of white-grey hair peeked from under his blue hat. 'Hello, Ava. I hear you've had quite a morning. I'm Mr Bain and I'm going to be delivering your baby. You try to relax.'

There were so many people in the room now, bustling about with their own set tasks.

'In a normal procedure, we'd introduce everyone, Ava, but we haven't got time for that.' She could tell from the somewhat strained expression above his mask, the way he checked the timing of the spinal block, that seconds mattered. A machine beeped and whirred and people were telling him numbers she didn't understand.

The spinal block meant she couldn't move her legs or wiggle her toes and her arms were numb right up to her shoulders. Nausea swirled and it wasn't long before she felt the strangest sensation, a huge pressure on her ribs as if someone was pressing down on her, tugging inside her. The screen hid everything from view. She tried to keep calm, to listen to Fraser, to not think too much about the tiny baby coming too soon or the fact they seemed to be heaving out her organs to reach it.

'Look. Can you look?'

Fraser peeked over the screen, his face tinged green either by it or the sickness he felt seeing her insides. 'They've cut you,' he said. But nothing more.

'Is the baby OK?'

Fraser looked back and she stared hungrily at his expression, unable to understand what was happening below her ribs. She was desperate for information, her tears running, her head shaking, goosebumps – that she *could* feel – prickling the skin on her arms. 'Fraser?'

'It's a girl,' he whispered. His eyes had filled with tears.

She would be placed on her chest, she'd read about it online – in the books.

She had imagined this moment, the feel of the baby on her bare skin, their hearts beating next to each other but she knew something was wrong, knew from the way the baby was whisked away, from the frantic energy in the room, from the dreadful silence.

Fraser had frozen too, his hand reaching for hers, his eyes following the tiny bundle that they were transferring to a table on one side.

'What's happening?' Ava could lift her neck but little else. There should be noise, there should be something. 'Oh my God, Fraser, is she OK?'

Someone was on the phone calling for blood, for her or the baby, she wasn't sure. The bustle and energy increased; no one had time to answer any questions. Fraser was shunted to one side too, both of his hands on his cheeks.

'Oh my God.' Ava started crying, her head pounding with more tears, dripping down by her ears and onto the paper beneath her. 'Fraser . . . oh my God . . . our daughter!'

A shady spot, tiny holes. It couldn't happen to her. She had felt the menace of the bridge pervading her body. Had it got inside her? Was it doing its damage?

His voice was choked too as he kneeled at her side, tried to whisper. 'She's with the doctors . . . she's with the doctors.'

'What did she look like? Fraser, is she going to be OK?'

He couldn't speak. She knew she was asking the impossible but she felt so inert, incapable of getting up, swinging her legs over the side, racing around that screen to find out more. Her arms were useless at her sides. She felt nausea explode within her, vomiting while on her back, feeling pieces almost choking her as Fraser tried to help.

A nurse helped wash it off, soothing words that Fraser couldn't say over the stench of vomit. Then she thought she heard the sound of a baby crying. Her head snapped up as far as it could. Fraser leaped to his feet.

'Oh my God.'

It was definitely a cry. Not in her head this time, but in the room with her. A cry.

Ava didn't want to interrupt the doctors but the wait felt like the longest minutes of her life. Please, God, could they not tell her what they were doing?

Fraser was back at her head. Their eyes met and it was all they could do to drink each other in. He lowered his forehead to hers and they stayed that way for a few seconds.

'I love you, Ava, whatever happens . . .'

She sobbed. Had she caused this? Had Overtoun done this?

'We have to stitch you up . . .'

She lay there, feeling the small tugs as they worked on her, picturing the tiny figure on the other side of the room. Her daughter. It was a girl. Her whole body felt hollowed out, a large piece of her missing. She had to be OK. She had to be . . .

Oh God.

Chapter 56

MARION

She is such a sickly baby. Those early days lured us into a false sense of security.

She continues to bring up the milk I feed her, losing weight and having to return to the hospital. My own supply has dried up, the baby too weak to take it from me. The nurses suggest we try a bottle and she is fed milk from a wet nurse. They adore seeing her, brave little Constance, whose father, it has been confirmed, died fighting the Nazis. They praise my strength and bravery. It must be terribly difficult. All alone and she is so sick, too. God will be kind.

She is bonny for a while, lying on a rug in late summer, delighting in her own hands, fingers waving in the air as she tries to roll from her back to her front, straining, head tilted. I worry she is not moving correctly. The doctor comes.

Months pass. She has had lots of the symptoms. I know of other cases in other children – polio, I am sure.

'I'm not sure, Lady West,' the doctor says. 'I have seen other children with polio.'

'Can you see? Where the muscles are weak? And she struggles to swallow sometimes, Doctor.'

'I can't see anything that concerns me. She's a bonny wee lass, doing nicely.'

A firmer voice. 'Are there some tests you can do, Doctor? She really isn't right. A mother's instinct. I'm so grateful to you. My little girl needs the best care.'

He leaves moments later, past the brown bear. For a second I imagine the beast stepping off his plinth and chasing him out of the door, his claws tearing at his clothes as he slips on stripy tiles to get outside. As the front door closes behind him, I wait, fists curled, my breathing so loud I think the noise is filling up the corridor.

Constance gets thinner as the weeks pass and I am desperate with worry, pacing the nursery, holding her to my chest. Annie has summoned the doctor again, who appears with a wary look in his eye. 'But she is definitely ill, Doctor.' I show him where she has regurgitated her dinner. He weighs her and agrees that she needs hospitalisation.

'Annie tells me you prepare all her weaning meals.'

'I do.' My voice sounds a little shrill, but I am frightened. My baby is unwell.

Another ambulance is called. There are grave faces as we wait for her to have blood taken from her. Her bony arm is thrust out, her cry piercing as the tube fills red. 'There, there. You are a good mother, so caring.'

The next year it seems her walking is delayed a little, perhaps. I worry about the slight limp in her left leg. The doctor doesn't believe she limps. He doesn't come back when she still suffers with sleeping problems or when she struggles to breathe. She might need an iron lung, I insist. He could check the squint in her right eye – it comes and it goes. She can't see things in the distance, I am sure of it.

We visit another doctor in Glasgow, a specialist who takes my concerns seriously. A battery of tests is undergone when he hears of her various ailments. I tell him she had polio as a child. He is very concerned.

'You poor woman! What a great deal you have been through – and a war widow, too! We will take care of her as best we can, you can be sure of that. Would you like a sweet tea while you wait? The nurses here think she is just adorable. What a poppet!'

Now I think, going forward, we should perhaps try a stick to help her walk.

Chapter 57

AVA

Today was the day.

Fraser had returned to work reluctantly and it was one of their first days on their own together. She had arranged to meet her in town, in a cafe neither of them had been to before. Anonymous. Neutral. Ava hadn't allowed herself to think too much about it and her hand shook as she applied lip salve and a dash of mascara.

She lifted her daughter, Leonora, into the pram. Her eyes already closing, fists curled, arms thrown over her head. She had weighed 3lb 15oz when she was born, the smallest scrap of a baby, her legs so thin they seemed all bone, her body covered in fair hair. She was whisked away on that first day for checks, Fraser and Ava clasping each other's hands as they waited for news. But, apart from her size, she was perfectly healthy. The days after were a strange blur of aching, blood, terrible daydreams, red eyes, pills, slow walks to the communal toilet, injections in her stomach, resting her head in her hands, crying.

Leonora stayed in an incubator. She and Fraser were allowed to touch her through holes in the side. She spent hours under a UV light and being fed with a tube through her nose, making Ava's heart break every time she looked at her.

Her mum was desperate to talk, to explain, but Ava wasn't ready yet to talk about that day. She was too full up with her own daughter, their future.

Ava was moved to a ward, intermittent coughs and the never-quite dark of the place, a constant reminder that she wasn't at home. The early days she had envisaged of the winged armchair, the mobile turning, the night feeds were a distant dream, the pristine nursery still waiting for them.

The nurses were kind and efficient, giving her pills, cups of sweet tea, later showing her how to give Leonora bottles, encouraging her to pump her breast milk and save it to give to her daughter later. Ava healed slowly, the scar livid and raised, the area devoid of feeling. Her stomach sagged unpleasantly around the mark, the skin dimpled.

Cards arrived, along with soft toys and messages from friends and colleagues. Claudia sent her a letter full of work gossip: Neil's band had played at the office Christmas party and he had sung; Daniel, the cameraman she'd been sleeping with, had got a new job in London; the man who wrote letters to her in purple ink had finally been arrested. She'd kept another card from Garry, a short, sad note apologising again for getting it so wrong, hoping he could come by in the new year and meet her baby. Her bed was decorated with cards. She stared at one for an age.

She became used to the routine of the day on the ward, the nurses' rota, the checklist for meals, the gossip around the desk outside. She watched them put up tinsel and decorations and then take them down again. In the snatches of downtime, they told her about their own families, their own dramas. In visiting hours, Fraser would appear armed with fruit and news and reassuring smiles that soothed her strained face.

She thought this strange new reality would never end, but gradually Leonora was allowed to rest in her arms, the feeding tube was removed, she would drink from a bottle, the matchstick legs slowly uncurled from their permanently tucked-up state. Ava put her in impossibly small nappies, watching carefully for the yellow line to turn blue, indicating a need for a change. She whispered to her, took photos on her mobile that she stared at when Leonora slept beside her.

She thought then of the diaries, the pain Marion had gone through. And yet she had gone on to have a healthy child, to have Mum. What had happened? How had it all gone so wrong? Now that she was emerging from the shock of the birth, these questions had engulfed her once more.

Then suddenly the car seat was brought in, a folder was signed, appointments with a visiting midwife were made, a dozen leaflets and adverts for baby things and she was walking outside the hospital to the car, her senses reeling after so long inside. The January wind nipped at her face before she slid into the passenger seat of the car, almost to the day when she had been due to have her daughter in the first place.

The cafe had steamed-up windows and plenty of empty tables. The air smelled of cinnamon and caffeine as Ava pushed inside, the pram sticking on the thin rubber threshold so that her stomach pressed into the handlebar. She was still numb where they had cut her all those weeks ago.

Her mum sat at a table right at the back near sliding double doors that overlooked a concrete square of courtyard outside; tables and chairs meant for the summer were pushed back into the corners. The space outside was a bleak eyesore: cracks in the stone, withered weeds poking out of them. In a small pile on the table sat the diaries and Ava was jolted to see them there. Her mum stood up, knocked over the small cactus in the centre of the table and spilled tea into her saucer.

'You look well,' she said as Ava removed her outer layers. 'And look!' Her mum gazed down into the carrycot, her fingers twitching with the desire to pick her up.

Leonora stirred and Ava bent over her, unzipping the pram suit and lifting the tiny figure out.

'Do you want to hold her?' she asked in a soft voice.

Her mum's eyes filled with tears as Ava gently passed Leonora over. Ava left them both while she ordered a coffee. From the counter, she watched her mum gaze at her granddaughter in adoration. She was glad she'd come.

Taking her coffee back, she couldn't help her eyes straying towards the diaries, remembering the words within them. Her grandmother had lost so many babies. She had sounded so loving, so desperate for a child. And she had gone on to have a healthy baby. So, what had gone so wrong?

She watched her mum smoothing the feathery hair on Leonora's head, too soon to really tell what colour it would go, the fine strands golden.

'I read the diaries,' her mum said softly. 'It was . . . difficult. To try to reconcile the woman in them with the woman I knew.'

'What was she like?' Ava clutched her mug in both hands.

'She was . . . evil.'

Ava stilled, shocked by the simple term. 'What did she do to you?'

Her mum's face was drawn, lines etched deep into the sides of her mouth. 'She . . .'

Ava had to lean forward to hear her.

'She made me ill.' Her mother held Leonora to her, drawing comfort.

'Ill?' Ava didn't understand.

Her mum nodded. 'She told me I couldn't walk. That my legs were weak. That I needed to use sticks, a wheelchair or they would break. Later, she told me I would . . .' Her mum gazed out over the courtyard, not meeting Ava's eyes as she swallowed. 'That I would lose them.'

Ava set her coffee down and the noise of the cafe melted away as she stared at her mother. 'That's . . .'

That feeling at Tommy's party. The words on the endpapers.

'She made me sick. Most days. She told me I had digestive problems. I had an operation on my stomach. I had so many tests, I felt like a porcupine. I had days when I could barely get out of bed.'

The strange disconnected lists. Apple seeds. Pesticides. Numbers. Quantities. Some words and figures circled.

'But she was doing it?' Ava was horrified, her eyes landing on the smooth skin of her own daughter. To think anyone could do that to a child, to *their* child. She felt her stomach swirl.

'We went to different doctors. She would speak for me. Tell them new things. That I had polio as a child, that I had a wasting disease. She made me go in a wheelchair when I knew I could walk. I knew . . .'

Ava covered her mouth as it all spilled out, her mum's tears falling onto Leonora's oblivious head. She had seen those medical terms, had never imagined this scenario.

'The gardener, Mr Hughes, suspected. He saw me some days, in my room, leaping from bed to rug, making stepping stones with my books, anything to alleviate the terrible boredom. Waiting for hours, watching that bridge.'

Ava thought back to the small bedroom, the single bed, the dusty shelf of books, the scratched words on the sill.

'He was married to the housekeeper.'

'Keven's parents,' Ava said slowly.

'Yes,' her mum whispered. 'They were so kind to me. After my mother . . . after she jumped, they helped me leave. They had a friend in Glasgow who agreed to take me in, promised to hide my whereabouts. They gave me a small amount of money. I changed my name.'

'But surely Keven knew, then?'

Her mum shook her head. 'They told him – they told everyone – that I had died. Everyone had heard that I was in a wheelchair and that I was sick.'

Ava's mind was reeling. 'And the family that took you in?'

'Carol. She was a woman in her fifties, whose son had emigrated. She was kind. She died when I was seventeen.'

'So, whose funeral was the one I remember?'

'It was Annie's funeral. 1987. I can't believe you remembered that. You were so young.' She looked up then, gave Ava a watery smile.

'Here . . .' She passed Leonora back, cradling her head as she reached down for her handbag and pulled out a packet of tissues.

Ava felt her body melt into her daughter's as she felt her tiny heartbeat thrumming its rhythm. *Sleep on, my lovely girl.*

'I'd kept in touch with Annie over the years. I told her when I got married, when I had you and Pippa. I wanted her to know she had done a good thing.' Her mum dabbed at her face and took a slow breath. 'I didn't want to cause any trouble. There had been . . .' She pressed two hands to her eyes as her voice wobbled once more. 'Rumours . . . rumours that Mr Hughes had pushed my mother, even though Keven was there and saw nothing of the sort. He said so at the inquest but the locals thought he was covering for his father.'

'And was he?'

'I asked him myself. That day under the bridge. He thought he'd seen a ghost. He thought I was her returned. He told me he saw her jump. That she killed herself.'

Ava felt her skin break into goosebumps, not ready yet to return to the mud and the fear of Overtoun Bridge or the image of a lady tumbling to the rocks below.

Her mum was crying softly. 'I knew I couldn't go to Annie's funeral but I wanted to be there that day. But Keven might have recognised me, blamed me for the rumours, and I couldn't risk him telling anyone I was alive, telling them who I was. No one knew.' She looked up and met Ava's eye. 'Until now.'

'What about Dad?'

Her mum's head drooped onto her chest. 'I never told him. I never told anyone what she did to me, never told him about Overtoun. I fabricated a story: an abusive drunk, a belt, a story told a hundred times before. He accepted it. I think he knew on some level I was hiding something but he trusted me.'

That was Dad. He loved her mum so much. She thought of his anger on the phone that day on the crags, the hurt in his voice. He had known something wasn't right.

'I'm going to tell him everything,' she added.

'I think he'd like that.'

Her mum wiped at her eyes. Leonora stirred and Ava dropped a kiss on her head. Mum reached across to tap the top diary with one finger. 'I tortured myself for years with why she did it, why she made me ill. I always thought it was because she resented me or hated me or was just plain evil but these . . .' She lifted the top one from the pile and turned it over in her hands. 'They've made me think she couldn't help it. That her losses twisted her.'

Ava shivered despite the tropical temperature of the cafe. Her mum was finally breaking down. 'If you hadn't gone there, if you hadn't given them to me, I might never have understood.'

The noise was pitiful as her mum's face crumpled. Ava darted to put Leonora back in her pram so she could scoot round and draw her mum to her. Though people were looking over, nothing mattered as Ava hugged her mother to her. 'It's OK. I understand now. I do. I'm sorry.'

'Keven said you found a bone.' She sniffed. 'That you're going to keep filming there . . . that others might look into the story, bring up the inquest all over again.'

'We won't . . . we won't . . .'

'He said he always wondered if his dad *had* done it. They'd both known what she was doing to me. But I knew he hadn't. I'd seen his dad in the garden. He couldn't have done it. But if you do keep filming, maybe others will bring it all up. Maybe he *will* be hounded.'

'Mum, I promise, it's over.' Ava rocked her. 'Of course we won't. I'll tell Garry there's no story. He owes me anyway. I'll tell him we'll stay away. I'll sort it.'

Her mum pulled a handkerchief from her handbag and blew her nose loudly. Leonora jerked in her sleep in response. 'Thank you,' she whispered, her hand over Ava's. 'Thank you.'

Chapter 58

CONSTANCE

I am standing on my bed, dressed in my white cotton nightdress, stained from the day. No clothes today. No leaving my room. Mother is still busy preparing.

My feet are bare, my mouth open, the scream long and loud. I repeat it. I repeat it until I hear footsteps rushing to my door. Murmured words.

'I am here! Wait! I am here!'

I scream some more.

There's a key in the lock.

I am pointing now, pointing at the diamonds on the window. A longer scream, high, tearing through her as she explodes into the room, almost tripping over my lunch tray, the crusts rejected.

'What is it? What is it? Where does it hurt?'

She stops. I am not meant to be standing. My legs can't hold me and I collapse down quickly, not wanting her to see through the fabric, wonder about what I'm wearing beneath my nightdress. I don't let her speak, I just scream and point until she pulls me towards her on the bed, cradles me in her lap as if I am a small child again, stroking my hair as she asks, 'What is it? What is it?'

I keep screaming. She lifts me back to sitting, rattles me like a doll; my eyes roll back, my jaw is jolted.

'You're scaring me. What is it, Constance?'

'The bridge! I saw something jump! It jumped – I saw it.'

'What? What jumped?'

I make big, tearful sounds. 'Please! Please check it's alright! Mama, please!' I grip her sweater, begging her, begging.

'I will, of course I will.' She leaves the room quickly, my screams and sobs following her along the corridor. I hear the big front door shut.

I move quickly, grabbing the bag, the shoes, the coat, my screams so loud she had forgotten to lock the door behind her. I run from my room and follow her. Her house slippers are abandoned on their sides by the door as I pull it with all my strength. For a moment it is as if hands are stopping me, pulling me back inside the house, as if it won't let me leave. The handle freezes in my grip – cold, as if I am already outside. I cry out, real tears now springing to my eyes. She will return. I need to leave. I won't stay. I won't. The door swings open.

I wobble for a moment – dizzy. I mustn't fall. *Come on!* I'm out into the weather, the fields a mushroom-grey in the late afternoon, rain spattering my face as I turn and stumble, try to run, stones digging into the soles of my feet, muddy water wetting my nightdress, my flesh dotted with cold as I move as quickly as I can towards the bridge. I could run down the road. I could run to Mr Hughes and Annie in Dumbarton.

But I see her. She is on the nearest ledge to me, the parapet closest to the house. She is leaning over the thick stone, shielding her eyes as she searches. For a second I'm frozen, remembering another time when she was on the bridge, Crumpet bundled in her arms.

I step onto the bridge, aware suddenly of a movement in the ravine below. An animal? Or is it a face I see?

I speed up, staring at her wellingtons, the thin strip of pale skin above them. I approach softly. The rain is so heavy, bouncing off the surface of the bridge, puddles merging with each other. I can't see anything at all over the height of the wall.

A clap of lightning makes me jump. For a second, all the windows of the house seem to flash a furious blue as it watches me, a rumble of thunder like a warning as I tiptoe right up to her, crouching low.

She is still looking, her body bent right over.

I move quickly, grab the strips of pale skin in my hands and throw my weight upwards and over. It is surprisingly easy.

The shortest scream, the splash lost to a host of other sounds: of the river and rain and the rumble of thunder. She is gone.

See, Mother, I think as I turn and race back to the house, back to my room, unpack the small running-away bag, take off the clothes beneath my nightdress, hop into bed to be found sleeping peacefully in the morning by Annie, *my arms and legs* are *strong*.

Epilogue

PRESENT DAY

The dog was a collie – Sandy, perky, curious, rushing on ahead of her owner, a woman visiting the area for the first time, a smile on her face as she thought of their long walk up from the nearby town of Dumbarton. Spring was around the corner, the trees along the driveway filled with tiny buds.

She only noticed the sign at the last moment, as she set foot on the bridge, the water a roar far below her. Sandy was still trotting up ahead. She felt the lead sticking out of the pocket of her Barbour and was about to call for her. It didn't look like a dangerous place; in fact, for a second, when the sun shone, it seemed as if the stone of the bridge became translucent, shimmering in the weak sunshine. Her hand dropped to her side. Sandy spun joyfully to check she was following.

She took a few steps forward, a sudden gust of wind blowing the hair back from her face as the light flickered and faded, the sun gone. Up ahead, the Gothic grey house loomed, towers pointing to the heavens, blank windows staring down at her, poised. The roar of water filled her head, the smell of damp all around her. Her smile slipped, her skin prickling. Over the noise of the water, the sudden wail of a baby made her twist her head to the side.

'Sandy!' She reached into her pocket to take out the lead.

It happened so quickly that in the moments afterwards she thought she had imagined it.

Her lovely dog, her faithful companion who had been by her side throughout her long illness, witnessed her children leaving the nest, who had walked the hills by her side, suddenly stuck up her head, nose twitching. And with a few simple leaps she bounded straight for the wall, leaping onto the parapet without a pause, only to sail straight over the thick stone, suspended for a second in her mind's eye before plunging out of view, a strange, startled howl before a splash and then silence.

The house seemed to breathe in and out as the woman raced over to the edge of the bridge, watching her as she peered below, her mouth open, screaming over and over into the void.

HISTORICAL NOTE

Creepy goings-on have always fascinated me and the mystery surrounding Overtoun Bridge is no exception.

It is believed that since the 1950s, more than fifty, if not upwards of five hundred, dogs have leaped to their deaths from this bridge.

Why Do the Dogs Jump?

A Thin Place

There is a Celtic belief that the house and bridge form one of the 'thin places' – where heaven and earth are only separated by a thread.

Certainly, Overtoun fits the bill for such a place, with reports of fairy sightings in the grounds in the late nineteenth century and plenty of witnesses to the supposed ghost that haunts the estate – the White Lady. There is even a photograph of her in an upstairs window of the house, looking out as if staring at the bridge.

A Tragic Place

There have certainly been plenty of tragedies to befall Overtoun. In 1994, a man was committed after throwing his young baby over the bridge to his death and then attempting to leap in after him. Bodies have been found in and around the estate, miles from where they are meant to be, with spent guns lying next to them. Some locals fear that the bridge does exert a strange pull on people and is to be avoided.

Scents or Sounds

Some point to the introduction of mink in and around the 1950s. Supposedly the scent of mink proves so powerful to dogs that they leap, unknowing, towards it and plunge to their deaths. The stone wall is thick and high enough that the dogs cannot see. This heightens their other senses, notably the sense of smell, so they are driven to distraction by it.

Others have theorised that a nearby nuclear base emits a terrifying frequency that only dogs can hear, driving them wild enough to leap.

Some dogs have been known to jump from the bridge, survive the fall, get back to the top of the bridge and jump from the same spot again.

A warning sign was commissioned to warn dog walkers to keep their animals on their lead as they cross the bridge.

If you would like a more detailed look at the mystery, a book by Paul Owens titled *The Baron of Rainbow Bridge* proved helpful during my research.

Overtoun House and Bridge

You can walk around the estate today, which is currently a Christian centre. There is a charming tearoom where visitors can take a look inside the house. Although looters did clear the house of many valuables, you can still see the incredibly ornate painted ceilings, plasterwork and even the wonderful silver bannisters on the staircase.

For the purposes of my story, I did ignore certain historical facts. Overtoun House was in fact used as a convalescent home during WWII, for instance, and the family who owned it was not the Wests, but the Whites. The truth about the mystery of the dogs, however, remains as I have written it, the first recorded incident occurring in the 1950s.

Munchausen by Proxy

I became fascinated by the tragic story of Gypsy Rose and her mother Dee Dee Blanchard in the US. When Dee Dee, the mother of a terminally ill girl, was found murdered in her bed in 2015, the whole country was shocked. Worse still, her daughter, who could only get about in her wheelchair, was missing. A hunt was launched and Gypsy Rose was found. Soon a very different picture emerged.

Dee Dee Blanchard had in fact been abusing her daughter from birth. Suffering from Munchausen by proxy, a condition in which a person will fabricate or induce illness in another person to gain attention, she had been making her only daughter extremely ill. Gypsy Rose underwent countless operations as an infant, was told that she had sleeping problems, muscular atrophy and cancer. She had a feeding tube, she moved around in a wheelchair and her head was shaved.

As Gypsy Rose grew up, she secretly discovered the online world and met a man who went on to help her kill her abuser. She is currently serving a lengthy prison sentence for her part in her mother's murder.

It is rare to speak to people who suffer from this illness because they do not want to admit that they have it and often switch medical practitioners if it is suspected. I wanted to explore how somebody might develop a desire to gain attention from a kindly doctor and look at the lasting damage it could cause.

ACKNOWLEDGMENTS

As ever I have plenty of people to thank.

I am indebted to both my editors – Jack Butler and Jane Snelgrove – who were enormously understanding, patient and good humoured through early drafts of this book. Their insightful editorial feedback at every stage really transformed this novel and I am so grateful to them for their efforts. Thanks also to Edward Handyside and Becca Allen for their thorough line and copy edits and to The Brewster Project for the cover. A big thank you to Nicole Wagner and the entire Amazon team for their support.

Thank you to my agent, Clare Wallace, and the entire Darley Anderson team for finding ways to keep working through this mad time in the book world. To Mary and Kristina in the rights department, and Georgia for such encouraging early feedback. To Sheila for all her work in the film and television department.

Thank you to Lisa Howells for shouting about *The Other Girl* and alerting me to the Dr Phil podcast, thus triggering the acorn of an idea for part of *The Thin Place*. An enormous thank you to Emily Kerr and Claire McGlasson, who spent a large amount of time answering my questions about broadcast journalism. Any errors are down to me and my dated knowledge of a regional newsroom!

Thank you to the dog lovers in my Book Camp crew for their varied stories of being owners. To Michael Jenkins for information about detection dogs, to Ginny Skinner for local walks and keeping me sane during lockdown. To my sister, Naomi, and my parents, David and Basia, for reading early drafts of the book. Another thank you to the Lady Novelists for their advice on a whole range of writing-related things.

Thank you to my family, who needed to be extra patient as I wrote drafts of this book during a global pandemic. To Ben for never complaining when I was in the shed. Barnaby for spending an inordinate amount of time drawing pumpkins so I could write. The twins, Lexi and Ness, for lifting all our spirits and to Dena for looking after them so well.

Lastly, the biggest thank you must go to the many authors, bloggers, readers and reviewers who supported *The Other Girl* with sales, reviews and shout-outs. It was wonderful to feel so welcome in the crime and thriller world. I hope you take *The Thin Place* to your hearts too.

ABOUT THE AUTHOR

C D Major is the pen name of Cesca Major. Cesca has always been fascinated by extraordinary stories from the recent past. Her last book, *The Other Girl*, set in an asylum in 1940s New Zealand and inspired by the strange phenomenon of children with past life memories, hit number one in the Amazon charts.

Cesca has presented shows for ITV West and Sky channels in the past. She often films vlogs about the writing process on her YouTube channel. She runs writing retreats twice a year in the West Country and teaches creative writing courses for the Henley School of Art. She writes other books under the pseudonym Rosie Blake. Cesca lives in Berkshire with her husband, son and twin girls.

She loves to hear from readers so please feel free to send her a message over at Twitter or Instagram or visit her website, www.cdmajor.com.